BITE ME

BITE ME

A LOVE STORY

CHRISTOPHER MOORE

WM

WILLIAM MORROW

An Imprint of HarperCollinsPublishers

BITE ME. Copyright © 2010 by Christopher Moore. All rights reserved. Printed in the United States of America. No part of this book may be used or reproduced in any manner whatsoever without written permission except in the case of brief quotations embodied in critical articles and reviews. For information address HarperCollins Publishers, 10 East 53rd Street, New York, NY 10022.

ISBN 978-0-06-177972-5

BITE ME

Hello Kitty

BEING THE JOURNAL OF ABIGAIL VON NORMAL,
Emergency Backup Mistress of the Greater Bay Area Night

The City of San Francisco is being stalked by a huge, shaved vampyre cat named Chet, and only I, Abby Normal, emergency backup mistress of the Greater Bay Area night, and my manga-haired love monkey, Foo Dog, stand between the ravenous monster and a bloody massacre of the general public. Which isn't, like, as bad as it sounds, because the general public kind of sucks ass.

Still, I think that this battle of dark powers; the maintenance of my steamy, forbidden romance; the torturous break-in of a new pair of red vinyl, thigh-high Skankenstein® platform boots; as well as the daily application of complex eye makeup and whatnot, totally justify my flunking Biology 102. (Introduction to Mutilation of Preserved Marmot Cadavers, with Mr. Snavely, who totally has his way with the marmots when no one is around, I have it on good authority.) But try to tell that to the mother unit, who deserves this despair and disappointment for cursing me with her tainted and small-boobed DNA.

Allow me to catch you up, *s'il vous plaît*. Pay attention, bitches, there will be a test.

Three lifetimes ago, or maybe it was like last semester, because like the song says, "time is like a river of slippery excretions when you're in love"—anyway—during winter break, Jared and I were in Walgreens looking for hypo-allergenic eye makeup when we encountered the beauti-ful, redheaded Countess Jody and her consort of blood, my Dark Lord, the vampyre Flood, who was totally disguised in jeans and flannel as a loser.

And I was all, "Nosferatu." Whispered to Jared like a night wind through dead trees.

And Jared was all, "No way, you sad, deluded little slut."

And I was all, "Shut your fetid penis port, you spunk-breathed poseur." Which he took as a compliment, so that's how I meant it, because while Jared is deeply gay, he's never really gayed anyone up, except maybe his pet rat, Lucifer. Strictly speaking, I think Jared would be considered a ro-dentsexual, if not for the difficult geometry of the relation-ship. (See, size does matter!)

Note to self: I should totally set Jared up with Mr. Snavely and they can talk about squirrel-shagging and whatnot and maybe I won't have to repeat Bio 102.

Anyway, Jared is a fitting support player in the trag-edy that is my life, as he dresses dismal chic and excels at brooding, self-loathing, and allergies to beauty products. I've tried to talk him into going pro.

'Kayso, the vampyre Flood had me meet him at a club, where I offered up myself to his dark desires, which he totally rejected because of his eternal love of the Countess. So he bought me a cappuccino instead and appointed me to be their official minion. It is the duty of the minion to rent apartments, do laundry, and bring the masters a sack with a tasty kid in it, although I never did that last part because the masters don't like kids.

'Kayso, the vampyre Flood gave me money and I rented a *très* cool loft in the SOMA (which is widely accepted to be the best 'hood for vampyres because there's mostly new buildings and no one would suspect ancient creatures of purest evil to hang out there). But it turns out, it was like half a block from the *très* cool loft in the SOMA that they already lived in. 'Kayso, when I take the key to them, hoping they will bestow the dark gift of immortality upon me, this limo full of wasted college-age guys and a painted blue ho with ginormous fake boobs pulls up. And they're all, "Where is Flood? We need to talk to Flood. And let us in," and other demanding shit. And I'm all, "No way, step off Smurfett. There's no one named Flood here."

I know! I was all, Oh-my-fucking-zombie-jebus-on-a-pogo-stick! She was blue!

And I'm not racist, so shut up. She clearly had self-esteem issues that she compensated for with giant fake boobs, slutty blue body-paint, and doing a carload full of stoners for money. I'm not judging her by the color of her skin. Everyone copes. When I got braces I went through a Hello Kitty phase that lasted well into my fifteens, and Jared maintains that I am still perky at heart, which is not true. I am simply complex. But more about the blue hooker later, because right then the Asian guy looks at his watch and says, "Too late, it's sunset." And they drove off. Which is when I opened the door into the stairwell to the loft and was confronted by Chet, the huge shaved vampyre cat. (Except, at the time, I didn't know his name, and he was wearing a red sweater, so I didn't know he was shaved, and he wasn't a vampyre yet. But huge.)

So I'm all, "Hey, kitty, go away." And he did, leaving only William, the huge shaved cat homeless guy, lying on the steps. I thought he was dead, because of the smell, but it turns out he was only passed out from alcohol and partially drained of blood and stuff. But I'm pretty sure he's dead now because, later, Foo and I found his stank-ass clothes on the steps of the loft, full of the gray dust that people turn to when a vampyre drains them.

So upstairs I'm all, "There's a dead guy and a huge kitty in a sweater on your steps." And the Countess and Flood are all, "Whatever."

And I'm all, "And there was a limo full of stoners here who were totally hunting you."

And they were all, "Whoa." And they seemed more freaked out than you'd think, for ancient creatures of dark forbidden romance and whatnot. And it turns out they weren't—I mean, aren't. I mean, sure, their love is eternal, and they are creatures of unspeakable evil and stuff, but they are not ancient at all. It turns out that the vampyre Flood is only like nineteen, and he's only known the Countess for like two months. And she's only like twenty-six, which, while a little crusty, is not that ancient. And despite her advanced age, the Countess is beautiful, with long, totally natch red hair and milky skin, green eyes like emerald fire, and a smoking body that could turn a girl totally lesbo if she wasn't already a slave to the mad, man-ninja sex-fu of the delicious Foo Dog. (Foo keeps insisting that he can't be a ninja because he's Chinese and ninjas are Japanese, but he's just being stubborn and goes all *Angry, Angry Asian* on me whenever I bring it up.)

'Kayso, in the master's loft I see these two bronze statues, one of this crusty businessman-looking guy, and the other looks like the Countess, except it's totally naked, or in a leotard, and bronze. And I'm all, "Exhibitionist, much, Countess? Did it come with a pole?"

And she's all, "Help Tommy move furniture, Wednesday." Like that makes any sense at all. (Turns out that Wednesday is a Gothish character from some crusty movie.)

'Kayso, later, by virtue of my extensive research and sneaking around and whatnot, I find out that the statues aren't statues at all. That the Countess used to be inside the statue of her, and that inside the crusty businessman statue is the real ancient creature of unspeakable evil, the nosferatu that turned the Countess. And the vampyre Flood, who wasn't a vampyre at all at the time, had bronzed the two of them when they were sleeping the deep sleep of the day-time dead, which is like the deepest sleep you can get. (You should know right now, that there's no yawning, gentle drift into sleepytime for vampyres. When the sun breaks the horizon, they drop rag-doll dead on the spot, and you can pose them, paint them, put their hands on their junk and post the pics on the Web, and they won't know a thing until sundown when they come on like a light and they're wondering why their naughty bits are green and their in-box is full of propositions from elfin_love.com.)

I know. Whoa!

It turns out that Flood, who was known as Tommy, was chosen by the Countess as her day-minion, blood lunch, and love monkey, because he worked nights at the Safeway. Then, the old vampyre, who had turned the Countess only like a week before, started fucking with them—saying he was going to kill Tommy and generally harsh Jody's reality. 'Kayso, Flood and his stoner Safeway night crew (called the Animals) hunted down the alpha vampyre, who was sleep-ing in a big yacht in the Bay, and they stole like jillions in art from the yacht and blew it up with the vampyre in it, which seriously put habaneras in his 'tude lube, but when he came out of the water, they fucked him up a good long time with spear guns and whatnot.

I know! Oh-my-fucking-god-ponies-in-the-barbecue! I know! It just goes to show you, like Lord Byron says in the poem: "Given enough weed and explosives, even a creature

of most sophisticated and ancient dark power can be un-
done by a few stoners."

I'm paraphrasing. It may have been Shelley.

'Kayso, the Countess saves the old vampyre from being
toasted, but she promises the cops (there were these two
cops) to take him away and never come back to the City,
but when they go to sleep, Flood, who couldn't bear to lose
Jody, took them downstairs to the biker-sculptors and had
them bronzed. But when he was trying to explain to the
Countess about why he did it, he drilled holes in the bronze
by her ears, and she turned into mist, streamed into the
room, and turned him into a vampyre. Which totally surprised him, because he didn't even know she knew how to
do either of those things. (Misting and turning, I mean.)

So then they're like, both vampyres, eternal in their love,
but somewhat lame in their night skills. Because Jody had
been feeding off of Tommy, she hadn't thought through
what they would eat after Tommy turned vampyre. So, first
they went to this homeless guy we'll call William the Huge
Cat Guy (because that's what people call him) because he
used to sit on Market Street with Chet and a sign that said,
I AM POOR AND MY CAT IS HUGE. And they ended up renting
the huge cat, Chet, to be their shared blood lunch. But it
turned out that a large part of Chet's kitty hugeness was fur,
so in order to facilitate the biting process, they shaved him.
I'm just glad that I wasn't their minion yet, because I think
we all know who would have ended up shaving the kitty.

But no! It didn't work. I'm not sure why. But William

got totally, date-rape-level hammered on the liquor he bought with the huge cat rent money, and they ended up feeding on him. Which is where I, the new princess-elect of darkness, was brought into the fold. (Into the "fold" means, like, the gang, as in gang of sheep, not fold like in what you do to T-shirts if you're a casual cotton slave at Old Navy.)

It was I, who turned Tommy onto the needle exchange program, where he was able to use his pale thinness to convince them he was a junkie and get syringes so they could take William's blood and put it in the fridge for the Countess to have in her coffee. Turns out that the only way the vampyre can tolerate real food or drink is if it has a little human blood in it. (The Countess likes blood on her fries, which is at once *très* cool and deeply fucked-up.)

So, as soon as the Countess and Flood figured out the deal with blood and food, William the Huge Cat Guy wandered off and the Countess had to go find him, since she has more experience at hunting the night, while Flood and I moved stuff from one loft to the other. But I had to get lice shampoo for my useless little sister, Ronnie, who was plagued by vermin, and Flood sent me home early to spare me the wrath of the mother unit because he didn't want his minion on restriction. (So noble. I think that's when I fell in love with him.) Then he took the bronzed old vampyre down to the water to dump him in the Bay before the Countess got back. It was clear to me that Tommy had jealousy issues with the old vampyre, and wanted to get rid of him. Except he ran out of dark before he got to the Bay and had to leave the old vampyre sitting by the Ferry Building on the Embarcadero and run from the sun for his life. At the last minute, the Animals drive by in their limo with their stupid blue ho and scoop the vampyre Flood off the street just before he was incinerated by the sun.

I know. WTF?

(FYI, when I type WTF, you are supposed to read it *What the Fuck*? Same with OMG, and OMFG, which are *Oh My God* and *Oh My Fucking God*. Only a completely lame Disney Channel nimnode pronounces the letters. Even BMLWA, or *Bite My Lily White Ass* should only be spoken as letters if you are hanging out with nuns or other people who are embarrassed about being told to bite asses.)

'Kayso, the Animals go back to work at the Safeway, but not before they tie Flood to a bed frame, where the blue hooker tortured him to get him to turn her into a vampyre, because now she had like all the money that the Animals had gotten for the old vampyre's art, which was like six hundred thousand dollars, and she wanted to take her time spending it, so she wanted to be immortal. But Flood was like a complete vamp noob. He'd never even killed anyone and turned them to dust or anything, so he didn't know how to change someone. The Countess didn't tell him that the chosen had to drink the vampyre's blood to receive the dark gift. So the blue ho tortures the shit out of him.

I know, what a bitch.

Meanwhile, the Countess found the huge cat guy, and I found the lice shampoo, but we don't know where Tommy is. But the Countess was burned from going out on some hot water pipes, so she fed on me, right there in the loft, and I was all, "Oh shit, I'm going to get the dark gift and I'm, like, wearing my lime-green Chuck Taylors, which are totally not the kicks for becoming a creature of unspeakable power in." But no, the Countess just partook of my sanguine nectar so she could heal. That's probably where I fell in love with her. Anyway, she goes asking around about Tommy, and this completely crazy homeless guy who thinks he is the Emperor of San Francisco (you see him and his two dogs in the north end of the City all the time) says that one of the Animals was asking around about Flood.

So I'm all, "Uh-oh."

And the Countess is all, "Yep."

Next thing you know, we are at the Marina Safeway and the Countess—wearing her black jeans and red leather jacket, but no lipstick—underhands a steel reinforced trash can like as big as a lesbian gym teacher through the big front window, and she just walks right through the falling glass, badass as shit, into the store and starts kicking stoner ass. It was glorious. But she didn't kill anyone, which turned out to be a mistake, as was, in my humble opinion, not wearing any lipstick. For while it was a heroic ass-kicking as has ever been delivered in real life, it would have been that much cooler if she had some black lipstick on, or maybe something in a dark maroon. But they told her that Tommy was tied up at Lash's, the black guy's, apartment.

And their shit was all busted up, and I was like, "You bitches have been powned!"

And the Countess was like, "That's cute. Let's go get Tommy."

She can be kind of a bitch sometimes. Anyway, we go to the apartment where Tommy is being held, but when we get there, he's still tied to the bed frame, but stood up against a wall, all naked and covered in blood, even his junk. And the blue ho is dead on the floor.

And I'm all, "Uh-oh."

And the Countess is all, "Yep."

And she says something about how the blue ho must have broken her neck or something, because if Tommy had drained her, she would have turned to dust and there would have been no body. Anyway, the cab ride back to the loft was *très* awkward, you know, with Flood naked and covered with blood and the two of them all, "Oh I love you" and, "Oh I love you, too." And I was being kind of a mopey little emo queen because I was jealous of both of them because they had their dark and eternal love for each other and I had like my lime-green Chucks and Jared the gay-bait rat-shagger.

So that was good. The rescue and whatnot. Because we found the old vampyre art money that the Animals had paid to the blue ho, which was like a half a million dollars. But then we found out that the blue ho was not dead, but somehow had accidentally drunk some of Tommy's blood when she kissed him during his torture and now she was nosferatu. And she turned all the Animals. Which, you know, was bad. And not in the good way.

And the old vampyre had somehow escaped his bronze shell, and he was coming after Tommy and Jody, and even me? He even shook the living shit out of William the Huge Cat Guy while Jared and I watched from an alley across the street.

I know! We were all, "Whoa?"

So it's like, Christmas night, and Jared and I are watching the midnight show of *The Nightmare Before Christmas* at the Metreon. And we're all traumatized and whatnot from watching the vampyre pound the huge cat guy, and the Countess calls us. And she and my Dark Lord Flood meet us for coffee at this Chinese diner, which is like the only thing open because the Chinese totally blow off Christmas because there are no dragons or firecrackers in the story.

Note to self: Write narrative poem exploring Christmas if the three wise men had given baby Jesus firecrackers, a dragon, and mu-shu pork instead of that other crap.

So, after all night drinking coffee laced with Jared's blood and getting the story on the old vampyre from the Countess and Flood, we go back to the loft and there, in the stairway, is the old vampyre, naked. And he's all, "I had to do some laundry. That guy peed on my tracksuit." (He was wearing a total gangsta yellow tracksuit when we saw him shaking the huge cat guy.)

So we like ran, and we had to hide my masters in some rafters under the Bay Bridge when they went out at dawn.

No yawning or anything—they just became dead. Well, undead.

So we wrapped them in trash bags and duct tape and moved them to Jared's basement lair in Noe Valley. (His basement lair is sacrosanct—his father and stepmother are afraid that they might walk in on him wanking to gay porn—so it was safe for the masters.) Meanwhile, I went back to the loft to feed Chet the huge shaved cat and decapitate the old vampyre with Jared's dagger so I could get extra-credit points with the masters, but it turned out that I had not calculated sundown quite right. Since when does the sun go down at like five o'clock? That's just fucking juvenile.

Anyway, when I'm on the steps I hear the old vampyre moving around upstairs. And I'm all, "Awkward." Then I hear a car pull up and I run out, right into the arms of this blond ho, who it turns out is the blue ho, who is now nosferatu, along with three of her vampyre minions who used to be the Animals. I know, "Uh-oh."

So she grabs me and is just about to tear my throat out, when the old vampyre grabs her by the neck and puts her face print in the hood of a Mercedes. He's all, "You're breaking the rules, ho. You can't just go turning people willy-nilly."

So I was doing a minor booty-dance of ownage at the blond ho, when they all turned on me. So I pull out Jared's dagger, but just the same I know they are going to have a huge group suck on my pale frame, when this totally fly, race-pimped Honda comes tearing out of the alley, and everything goes white light around the car. And my manga-haired love monkey, Foo, is totally in hero shades, and he's all, "Get in."

'Kayso, he swept me away in his magic nerd-chariot, which he had rigged with ultraviolet floodlights that totally toasted the vamps with simulated sunlight. I know! I'd have done him right there in the car if I was not trying to maintain my detached aura of aristocratic chill. So instead I kissed him within an inch of his life, then slapped him so he didn't think I was his personal slut, which I totally was. Would be.

It turns out that Steve, which is Foo Dog's day-slave name, had totally been staking out the Countess Jody's apartment for like a month, since he figured out that she was a vampyre when some blood from one of the old vamp's victims turned up in his hemo-lab at Berkeley. Foo is like some kind of biotech über-genius, in addition to having mad ninja-driving skills.

Then Foo dropped me off at Tulley's on Market, where I met Jared and Jody, who sneaked by Jared's parents by pretending to be lovers, which is disgusting in so many ways I kind of gagged a little when I typed it. (Jared is my emergency backup BFF, but he *is* a pervy little rat-shagger, as the Countess affectionately refers to him.)

So the Countess is all, "I'm going back to the loft to get the money."

And I'm all, "No, the old vampyre."

And she is all, "He is not the boss of me." (Or something like that. I'm paraphrasing.)

And I'm all, "Whatever, make sure you feed Chet."

So we go back to Jared's, and when we get there, the vampyre Flood is all fucked up from trying to climb face-down a building in the Castro after a delicious drag queen, like Dracula does in the book (only in the book it's not in the Castro and Dracula isn't after a drag queen).

Note to self: When I am finally made nosferatu, do not try to climb face-down a wall.

So then my sweet love ninja Foo shows up. And he's all, "I couldn't leave you out here, unprotected." And secretly I was all, "You rock my stripy socks, Foo," but publically I just kissed him and tastefully dry humped his leg a little. So we all got in his fly Honda and went back to the loft.

When we got there, the second-floor windows were open, and Flood could hear that the old vampyre was up there with Jody.

And Foo was all, "Let me go." And out of the hatch-back, he pulls this long duster that's covered with little glass warts. And Foo is all, "UV LEDs. Like sunlight."

The street-level fire door was locked, so Flood was all, "I'll go."

But Foo was all, "No, it will burn you."

But they covered Flood all over, gloves, hat, and a gas-mask that Foo keeps around in case of emergency biology and whatnot, then he put on the duster. Foo gave him a rubber tarp and a baseball bat, and Flood starts working the street like a half-pipe, running up a building on one side, then up the other, until he goes feetfirst through the upstairs window. Personally, I think the Countess could have just jumped up there, but she's been a vampyre longer than Flood and has better skills.

'Kayso, there's this blinding white light from the windows, and next thing we know, the old vampyre comes crashing through the window like a flaming comet and hits the street right by us. And he gets up all blackened and snarly and whatnot, and Foo holds up his UV floodlight and he's all, "Step off, vampyre scum." And the old vampyre ran off.

Then Flood comes out the door carrying the Countess, who is looking way more dead than usual, and we took them to a motel to hide them until we could figure out what to do. Foo stole some donor blood from the lab at his college and gave it to Flood and the Countess so they could heal. And Foo's all, "You know, I've been working on the blood I found on the victims, and I think I can reverse the process. I can turn you human again."

Which is totally why he had been stalking the Countess when I met him. So Tommy and Jody were all, "We'll think about it."

'Kayso, Flood is holding Jody on the bed, and they're talking softly, but I can hear them, because I'm just by the door and the room's not that big. And it is clear that their love is eternal and will last for eons, but Flood doesn't like being a vampyre because the hours suck and whatnot, and Jody likes being a vampyre because of the power she feels after feeling like a little wuss-girl for many years, and they more or less say that they are going to split up just as the sun rises and they go out.

And I was all, "Oh, hell no."

So I had them bronzed.

I'm looking at them now. We posed them like Rodin's *The Kiss* and they shall be together unto the end of time, or at least until we figure out how to let them out and not have them tear out our throats and whatnot. Foo says it's cruel, but the Countess told me that they could go to mist, and when they are mist time passes like a dream and it's all good.

But Foo did figure out his serum thingy. We lured the Animals to our love nest and while I was wearing the fly leather jacket that Foo made me, complete with the UV LED warts, which is very cool and cyber, I drugged them and Foo changed them back to human. And the crazy old Emperor guy said he saw three young vampyres take the old vampyre and the formerly blue ho away on a ginormous yacht, so we don't have to worry about them anymore.

Foo wants to cut Flood and Jody out of the bronze statue during the day, while they are sleeping, and turn them back to human. But the Countess doesn't want that. So I think we should just wait. We have this *très* cool apartment, and all of the money, and Foo almost has his master's in bio-nerdism or whatever, and I only have to go home like twice a week so the mother unit still thinks I am living there. (The key was to condition her from age twelve that sleepovers are normal. Lily, my former sleepover BFF, calls it slowly boiling the frog, which I don't know what it means, but it sounds darkly mysterious.)

So, we are secure in our love nest and as soon as Foo gets home I am going to reward him with the slow booty dance of forbidden love. But something is screeching outside. BRB.

Fucksocks! It's Chet the huge shaved vampyre cat, down on the street. He looks bigger, and I think he ate a meter maid. Her little cart is running and there's an empty uniform on the curb.

Bad kitty! GTG L8erz.

Test

1. The Countess Abigail Von Normal is:

    A. *Emergency Backup Mistress of the Bay Area Dark.*

    B. *A Gothic hottie consumed by the banal hopelessness of existence.*

    C. *Not perky, but dark, complex, and très mysterious.*

    D. *All the above, and possibly more.*

2. The vampire Flood and his nosferatu maker, the Countess Jody, were imprisoned in a bronze shell in the pose from Rodin's *The Kiss* because:

    A. *Their love is eternal and their mingled souls will live on in romantic embrace to the end of time.*

    B. *Foo and I were pretty sure that the Countess would go FOAKES (Freak Out and Kill Everything in Sight) when she found out our plan to turn the Animals back to human.*

    C. *We just like to look at our friends, naked and bronzed, because it gets us all hot.*

D. *I can't believe you picked "c." You should get a big "L" tattooed on your forehead to save people time in figuring out what a ginormous loser you are! You wish that Foo and I needed pervy preludes to stimulate our orgasmic, toe-curling soul-sex. Trust me, the sun weeps that it cannot achieve the blistering hotness of our nookie.*

3. Despite myths perpetrated by jealous day dwellers, the nosferatu are only vulnerable to the effects of:

A. *Garlic. (Right, because pizza and the breath of vegans will quell their ancient power.)*

B. *Crosses and holy water. (Oh right, because creatures of darkest evil are total bitches of the baby Jebus.)*

C. *Silver. (Uh-huh, and aluminum, because that makes sense.)*

D. *Sunlight.*

4. My and Foo's greatest challenge as minions is to protect our dark masters, the Countess and Lord Flood, from:

A. *Cops, specifically Inspector Rivera and his clueless Gay Bear partner Cavuto.*

B. *The most crusty old vampire and his mysterious fashion-vamp posse.*

C. *The Animals, slacker wastee night crew from the Marina Safeway.*

D. *All of the above and whatnot.*

5. Our best chance of defeating Chet, the huge shaved vampire cat, is:

A. *Mouse ninjas.*

B. *A big hug while wearing my most fly UV-LED leather*

*jacket, fashioned for my protection by my aforementioned
muffin master, Foo.*
C. *A saucer of tuna blood laced with sedatives and kitty-butt
flavor. (I observed in his former mortal form, that Chet loves
kitty-butt flavor.)*
D. *Make a vampire Rottweiler to rock Chet's worldview.*
E. *Either "a" or "c," but definitely not "d"; wouldn't "a" be*
très *cool? Mouse ninjas!*

Answers:

1: D, 2: B, 3: D, 4: D, 5: E
Give yourself one point for every right answer.

Score:

5. *You rock my stripy socks.*
4. *Loser!*
3. Très *Loser!*
2. *Such a Loser that Losers pity you.*
0–1. *Spare us your contagious loserness. Next bridge you
pass? Over you go.*

The Samurai of Jackson Street

TOMMY

When he first arrived in San Francisco, Tommy Flood had shared a closet-size room with five Chinese men named Wong, all of whom had wanted to marry him.

"It's horrible—like being packed into a take-out box of Kung Pao chicken," Tommy had said, and although it wasn't like that at all, and Tommy was just trying to use colorful language which he felt was his duty as a writer, it *was* very crowded and smelled strongly of garlic and sweaty Chinese guys.

"I think they want to pack my fudge," Tommy had said. "I'm from Indiana, we don't go for that kind of stuff."

As it turned out, the Chinese guys didn't go for that kind of stuff either, but were, in fact, very much interested in getting green cards.

Fortunately, only a week later, in the parking lot of the Marina Safeway where he worked nights, Tommy met a gorgeous redhead named Jody Stroud, who rescued him from his confinement with the Chinese guys, by giving him her love, a nice loft apartment, and immortality. Unfortunately, little more than a month after that, their minion, Abby, had them bronzed while they slept, and Tommy awoke one night to find that despite his great vampire strength, he couldn't move a muscle.

"I'd rather be trapped in a take-out box of Kung Pao chicken," Tommy would have said if he could have said anything, which he couldn't.

Meanwhile, right next to him, sharing the same bronze shell, his beloved Jody drifted in a dream-state, a side effect of being able to turn herself to mist, a trick she had learned from Elijah Ben Sapir, her vampire sire. Between the dead sleep of daylight, and the floating in a dream-world, she could endure decades inside the statue. Tommy, however, had never learned how to turn to mist. There had never been time to teach him. So come sundown, his vampire senses came on like neon, and he experienced every second of his confinement with an electric intensity that nearly had him vibrating in his shell—an alpha predator pacing the cage of his mind and shredding his reason. Of course, he did the only thing he could do: he went barking at the moon mad.

CHET

He'd have to lick about a mile of kitty-butt to get the taste of meter maid out of his mouth, but Chet was up for it. He raked a couple of hind-leg kicks through the dust that was the meter maid's remains, and headed across the street and into the alley, where he curled up in the dark and set about blunting the human taste.

It was only a little over a month since the old vampire had turned Chet, but already he was losing all sense of his former self. Time was, that he spent his days on Market Street, napping next to William, the homeless man who made his living with a paper cup and a sign that said, I AM HOMELESS AND MY CAT IS HUGE. Chet was indeed very large, and while much of his volume had been fur, he had achieved a weight of thirty-five pounds on a diet of semi-used hamburgers and French fries donated by passersby outside of McDonald's.

Now Chet hunted the night, taking down nearly any warm-blooded creature he encountered: rats, birds, squirrels, cats, dogs, and even the occasional human. At first it had only been drunks and other homeless, and the first time he had drained one, his old friend William, who turned to dust in front of him, Chet yowled, ran, and hid under a Dumpster for the rest of the night and all of the next day. There was no regret, simply hunger and elation of the blood rush. It was beyond the satisfaction of the kill, it was positively sexual, something Chet had never known as a normal cat, as he'd been neutered by the animal shelter when still a kitten. But along with speed, strength, and senses far more sensitive than even a human-based vampire, Chet, like his human counterparts, found that he was physically restored to perfection. In other words, his junk was working.

He found that soon after the kill he desperately needed to hump something, and the more squirmy and wailing, the better. Above the smells of bus fumes, cooking food, and urine-bathed curbs that pervaded the City, he caught the scent of a female in heat. She might be a mile away, but given his newly heightened senses, he'd find her.

A wave of excitement undulated under the fur of his spine, fur that had mostly grown back since the humans had shaved him, mated in front of him, and drank his blood, which served to traumatize his little kitty consciousness before he was turned vampire, and motivated a whole new feeling he'd grown into as a vampire cat: vengeance. For since his metamorphosis, it wasn't just his senses that had expanded. His brain, which before had run a loop of "eat-nap-crap, repeat," was now growing into a whole new awareness, getting bigger, even as Chet grew. He was a good sixty pounds now, and roughly as smart as a dog, where before he'd only been a little brighter than a brick. Dog. The hated. There was dog on the air. Coming closer. He could smell it—them—two of them. And now he could hear them. He arose from his butt bath and screeched like an electrified lynx. In response, the neighborhood echoed with a chorus of yowls from a dozen other vampire cats.

THE EMPEROR

"Steady, fellows," said the Emperor. He laid his hand across the neck of the golden retriever and scratched under the chin of the Boston terrier, who squirmed in the great pocket of the Emperor's overcoat, looking like a frantic, black-and-white, bug-eyed kangaroo mutant.

"Cat! Cat! Cat! Cat! Cat!" barked Bummer, with a spray of doggie slobber across the Emperor's palm. "Cat! Murder, pain, fire, evil, cat! Can't you smell them? Everywhere! Must chase, chase, chase, bite, bite, bite, let me go you insane, oblivious old man, I'm trying to save you, for the love of God, CAT! CAT! CAT!"

Unfortunately, Bummer only spoke dog, and while the Emperor could tell that the Boston terrier was upset, he had no idea why. (Anyone who translates dog knows that only about a third of what Bummer said actually meant anything. The rest was just noise he needed to make. Human speech is about the same.) Lazarus, the golden retriever, having battled vampires on and off for the last two months, and being steady by nature, was much calmer about the whole thing, but despite Bummer's tendency to overreact, he had to admit, the smell of cat was tall in the air, and what was more disturbing, it wasn't just cat, it was dead cat. Dead cat walking. Wait, what was that? Not cat—cats. Oh, this was not good.

"He's right about the cat," Lazarus ruffed, nudging the Emperor's leg. "We should get out of this neighborhood, maybe go over to North Beach and see if anyone dropped a beef jerky or something. I could sure use a beef jerky. Or we can stay and die. Whatever. I'm good with it."

"Easy, men," said the Emperor, alert now that something was amiss. He knelt down, his knees creaking like rusted hinges, and as he looked around, kneaded the spot between Bummer's ears as if he were readying to make doggy-brain biscuits. He was a great, woolly, thunderstorm of a man—broad shouldered and gray bearded, fine witted and fiercely loyal to the people of his city. He had lived on the streets of San Francisco as long as anyone could remember, and while tourists saw him as a raggedy, homeless wretch, the locals viewed him as a fixture, a rolling landmark, a spirit, and a conscience, and for the most part, treated him with the deference they might pay royalty, despite the fact that he was a raving loon.

The street was deserted, but a half a block away the Emperor saw the three-wheeled cart of an S.F.P.D. parking enforcement officer, stopped behind an illegally parked Audi. The cart's rotating yellow caution lights chased themselves around the surrounding buildings like drunken, jaundiced Tinkerbells, but there was no officer in sight.

"Strange. It's long past time when a meter maid should be working. Perhaps we should investigate, gents."

But before he could stand, Bummer leapt out of the Emperor's pocket and made a beeline for the cart, trumpeting himself into the charge with a staccato barking fit. Lazarus took off after the black-and-white fur-rocket, and the old man ambled along behind, as fast as his great, arthritic legs would carry him.

They found Bummer on the far side of the Audi, snorting and snuffling inside an empty police uniform, and covered with a fine gray powder. The Emperor's eyes went wide. He backed across the sidewalk and stood against the fire door of one of the industrial lofts that lined the street. He had seen this before. He knew the signs. But when he had seen the old vampire and his companions board an enormous yacht in the Bay over a month ago, he thought his city rid of the bloodsucking fiends. What now?

There was a crackling static noise from the police cart: a radio. *Call it in.* Alert his people to the danger. He rolled to the cart, fumbled with the door catch, and reached for the microphone.

"Hello," he said into the microphone. "This is the Emperor of San Francisco, Emperor of San Francisco, protector of Alcatraz, Sausalito, and Treasure Island, and I'd like to report a vampire." The radio continued to crackle and distant voices ghosted through the ether, uninterrupted.

Lazarus padded to the old man's side and barked furiously, "You have to push the button. You have to push the button." Unfortunately, while the noble retriever understood English, he only spoke dog, and the Emperor did not get the instruction.

"Button! Button! Button! Button!" Bummer barked, springing up and down in front of the police cart. He scurried around to the door and jumped in on the Emperor's lap to show him.

"Yeah, that helps," growled Lazarus sarcastically. Golden retrievers are not a very sarcastic breed, and he felt a little ashamed and, well, catlike, using that tone of voice. "Okay. Button! Button! Button! Uh-oh."

"Button! Button! Button! Uh-oh, what?" barked Bummer. A short ruff from the retriever: "Cat."

Lazarus boiled out a low growl and laid his ears back against his head.

The Emperor saw two of them: cats, coming down the sidewalk toward them. But they didn't look quite natural. The light from the police cart was reflecting back from the cats' eyes like red coals.

A screech, there were two more coming across the street. Lazarus turned to face them, snarling now. A chorus of hisses from behind. The Emperor looked in the rearview mirror to see three more cats stalking from behind.

"Quick, Lazarus, in the cart. Up, boy, in the cart."

Lazarus was spinning now, trying to watch all of the cats at once, warning them off with bared teeth and bristled hair. But the cats came on, baring their own teeth.

"Come now," said the Emperor into the microphone.

Something landed hard on the roof of the cart and Bummer yelped. Another thump and the Emperor looked back to see a large cat in the bed of the cart, coming up on two legs and trying to claw around the back window. The old man pulled the door shut. "Run, Lazarus, run!"

Lazarus caught the first cat in his jaws and was shaking it furiously when the rest fell upon him.

STEVE

"There's nefarious shit afoot, Foo," said Abby. "Bring portable sun and fry these nosferatu kitties before they nom everyone in the 'hood."

Steven "Foo Dog" Wong had no idea what his girlfriend, Abby, was talking about, and it wasn't the first time. In fact, much of the time he had no idea what she was talking about, but he had learned if he was patient, and listened, and more important, agreed with her, she would mercilessly sex him up, which he liked quite a bit, and occasionally he got the message. He used the same strategy with his maternal grandmother (without the sexing-up part), who spoke an obscure, country dialect of Cantonese, that sounded to the uninitiated like someone beating a chicken to death with a banjo. Just wait, and all would become clear. This time, however, Abby, whose tone ran from tragically romantic to passionately dismissive, was sounding much more urgent, and the patience gambit wasn't going to work. Her voice in his Bluetooth headset was like having a malevolent fairy bite his ear.

"I'm in the middle of something, Abby. I'll be home as soon as I finish up here."

"Now, Foo. There's a herd, or flock, or a—what do you call a bunch of kitties?"

"A box?" Foo offered.

"Fucktard!"

"A fucktard of kitties? Okay, sure, that could be it. A pride of lions, a murder of crows . . ."

"No. You fucktard! There's a bunch of vampire kitties about to eat that crazy Emperor guy and his dogs right outside on the street. You need to come save them."

"A bunch?" Steve was having a hard time getting his head around the idea. He'd only recently gotten his head around the idea of one vampire cat, but a bunch, well, that was more. He was just a couple of months away from having his master's in biochem at age twenty-one—he wasn't a fucktard. "Define a bunch," he said.

"Many. I can't count them because they're stalking the golden retriever."

"And how do you know they're vampire kitties?"

"Oh, because I drew blood samples from them, ran it in that centrifuge thingy of yours, prepared some slides, and looked at the blood cell structure under a microscope, duh?"

"No, really," he said. She was flunking high school biology, there's no way she prepared blood slides. And besides—

"Of course not, you douche nozzle, I know they're vampires because they're stalking a golden retriever and a homeless fuck who's hiding in the vaporized meter maid's cart. That's not standard kitty behavior."

"Vaporized meter maid?"

"The one Chet ate—sucked her to dust. Come now, Foo,

turn your sunbeam full-on and get your luscious ninja ass over here." Steve had rigged the hatchback of his tricked-out Honda Civic with high intensity UV floodlights, which he'd used to flash fry a number of vampires, thus saving Abby and, for the first time in his life, having a girlfriend and someone who thought he was cool.

"I can't come right away, Abby. The sun lights aren't in the car."

"Oh my fucking God, there's some little old guy with a cane coming out of the alley. Well, he's toast. Fuck!"

"What?"

"Fuck!"

"What?"

"Oh fuck!"

"What? What? What?"

"Oh-my-fucking-god-ponies-on-a-stick!"

"Abby, you need to be more specific."

"It's not a cane, Foo, it's a sword."

"What?"

"Come now, Foo. Bring the sun."

"I can't, Abby. My car is full of rats."

THE EMPEROR

The Emperor watched in horror as the cats leapt onto the back of his noble captain, Lazarus. The golden retriever shook himself violently, dislodging two of the fiends, but they were replaced by two more, and three more leapt on top of them, nearly bringing Lazarus to the ground. But they weren't pack hunters, and as each maneuvered for the throat, another attacker was pushed off, his claws shredding both predator and prey as he fell.

Blood splattered the windscreen of the police cart. Bummer bounced around inside the tiny cabin, barking and snorting, and throwing himself against the glass, covering everything with angry dog slobber.

"Run, Lazarus, run!" The Emperor pounded on the glass, then pushed his forehead against it as he tried to squint back tears of anguish and frustration.

"No!" He would not do it. He would not watch his companion slaughtered. Outrage filled the ancient, boiler-tank of a man and condensed to courage. He was fighting the door latch when half a cat hit the side window and slid down trailing gore.

The door handle snapped off in his hand and he threw it to the floor of the cart. Bummer immediately attacked it and broke a tooth on the metal. Through the haze of blood spray, the Emperor could see another figure in the street. A boy—no, a man, but a small man, Asian—wearing a fluorescent orange porkpie hat and socks, tight plaid trousers that looked as if they'd been teleported out of the 1960s, and a gray cardigan sweater. The little man was brandishing a samurai sword, bringing it down again and again on Lazarus in quick snapping motions, but before he could cry out, the Emperor saw that the sword wasn't even grazing the retriever's coat. With each stroke one of the cats fell away, beheaded or cut in half, both halves squirming on the pavement.

There was no spinning, no wind-up or flourish to the swordsman's movements, just grim efficiency, like a chef chopping vegetables. As his targets moved, he pivoted and stepped just enough to deliver the cut, then snapped the blade back and sent it to its next destination.

The weight and fury removed from his back, Lazarus looked around and whimpered, which translated to: "Whaaa—?"

The swordsman was relentless, step, cut, step, cut. Two cats came at him from under a Volvo and he quickly re-treated and swung the sword in a quick, low arc that ap-proximated a golf stroke and sent their heads back over the car to bounce off a metal garage door.

"Behind!" the Emperor warned.

But it was too late. The low attack had thrown the swordsman off—a heavy-bodied Siamese cat launched itself from the roof of a van across the street and landed on the little man's back. The long sword was useless at such close range. The swordsman arched in pain, even as the Siamese clawed its way up his back. He spun, then threw his feet out before him and fell hard on his back, but the Siamese took the impact and dug its fangs into the swordsman's shoulder. A half-dozen vampire cats came scurrying out from under cars toward the struggling swordsman.

Lazarus, his fur matted with blood, caught one of the cats by the haunch and bit to the bone. The cat screamed and squirmed in the retriever's jaws, trying to claw his eyes. The others fell on the swordsman with fang and claw.

The Emperor threw his shoulder against the Plexiglas door of the police cart, but there was no room to move, to gain momentum, and while the entire cart rocked and went up on two wheels under his weight, the door latch would not give. He watched in horror as the swordsman writhed under his attackers.

The Emperor heard a steel fire door hitting brick and light spilled across the sidewalk and into the street. Out of the doorway ran a thin, impossibly pale girl with lavender pigtails wearing pink motocross boots, pink fishnet stockings, a green plastic skirt, wraparound sunglasses, and a black leather jacket that looked studded with glass. Before he could warn her, the girl ran into the street and shouted, "You motherfucking kitties need to step the fuck off!"

The vampire cats attacking the swordsman looked up and hissed, which translated from vampire cat, meant: "Whaaa—?"

She ran right at the swordsman, waving her arms as if shooing birds or trying to dry some particularly stubborn nail polish and screaming like a madwoman. The cats turned their attention to her, and were crouching, readying to leap, when her jacket lit up like the sun. There was a collective screech of agony from the vampire cats as all around the street, cats and cat parts smoked, then ignited. Burning cats made for the alley across the street or tried to hide under cars, but the thin girl ran after them, darting here and there, until each ignited, then burned and reduced itself first to a bubbling puddle of fur and goo, and finally, a pile of fine ash.

In less than a minute, the street was quiet again. The lights on the girl's jacket went dark. The swordsman climbed to his feet and fitted his orange porkpie hat back on his head. He was bleeding from spots on his back and arms, and there was blood on his plaid pants and orange socks, but whether it was his or the cats' was impossible to tell. He stood before the thin girl and bowed deeply.

"*Domo arigato,*" he said, keeping his eyes at her feet.

"*Dozo,*" said the girl. "Your kitty-slaying skills are, if I may say so, the shit."

The swordsman bowed again, short and shallow, then turned and trotted across the street, down the alley, and out of sight.

Lazarus was digging at the Plexiglas door of the police cart with the pads of his paws, as if he might polish his way through to release his master. Abby scratched his nose, nearly the only part of him not covered in blood, and opened the door.

"Hey," she said.

"Hey," said the Emperor.

He stepped out of the cart and looked around. The street was painted with blood for half a block, punctuated by piles of ash and the occasional charred flea collar. Parked cars were sprayed in red mist, even the security lights above several fire doors were speckled with gore. Acrid smoke from burning cats hung low in the air, and on the sidewalk greasy gray ash spilled out of the sleeves and collar of the parking officer's uniform.

"Well, you don't see that every day," said the Emperor, as a police cruiser rounded the corner, the red and blue lights raking the building.

The cruiser stopped and doors flew open. The driver stood behind his door, his hand on his gun.

"What's going on here?" he said, trying to keep his eyes on the Emperor and not look at the carnage that surrounded them.

"Nothing," Abby said.

Good-bye Love Lair

BEING THE JOURNAL OF ABBY NORMAL,
Triumphant Destroyer of Vampyre Kitties

I weep, I brood, I grieve—I have sniffed the bitter pink Sharpie of despair and mascara tears stripe my cheeks like a mouthful of chewed-up black Gummi bears has been loogied in my eyes. Life is a dark abyss of pain and I am alone, separated from my darling delicious Foo.

But check it—I totally kicked ass against a gang of vampyre kitties. That's right, kitties, meaning many. No longer does the huge shaved vampyre cat Chet stalk the City alone; he has been joined by many smaller and un-shaved vampyre cats, many of which I turned to kitty toast with my most fly sunlight jacket. Right outside our loft, they were attacking that crazy Emperor guy and his dogs and I saved them by running out into the street and hitting the lights.

It was pure techo-carnage, blood everywhere, and a

little Japanese guy with a samurai sword doing the serious Ginsu on the kitties as they attacked.

I know what you are thinking.

Ninja, please . . .

I know, OMFGZORRO! A samurai in Sucker-Free City!

I didn't even try to convince the cops when they came.

They were all, "What up?"

And I was all, "Nothing."

And they were all, "What's all this?" Pointing to the blood and steaming kitty ashes and whatnot.

And I was all, "Don't know. Ask him. I just heard some noise so I came out to check it out."

So they asked the Emperor and he tried to tell them the whole story, which was a mistake—but he's kind of insane, so you have to give him a break. But they put him in the car anyway and took him and his dogs away, even though it was totally obvious that they knew who he was and were just being dicks about the whole thing. Everyone knows the Emperor. That's why they call him the Emperor.

'Kayso, Foo finally came home and I jumped into his arms and sort of rode him to the ground with a massive tongue kiss so deep that I could taste the burned cinnamon toast of his soul, but then I slapped him, so he didn't think I was a slut. (Shut up, he had wood.)

And he was all, "Stop doing that, I don't think you're a slut!"

And I was all, "Yeah, well then how did you know that's why I slapped you, and where the fuck have you been, my mad, manga-haired love monkey?" Sometimes it's best to turn the tables and start asking questions when your argument sucks ass. I learned that in Introduction to Mass Media class.

And Foo's all, "Busy."

And I'm like, "Well you missed my heroic warrior-babe assault." And I, like, told him the whole thing and then I said, "So, now there's a lot of vampyre cats. What's up with that, nerdslice?" Which is a pet name I have for Foo when referring to his mad science skills.

And he's all, "Well, we know that there has to be an exchange of blood from the vampyre to its victim before the victim dies, otherwise it just goes to dust."

And I'm like, "So Chet's smart enough to know that?"

And Foo's all, "No, but if a cat's bitten, what's the natural thing for it to do?"

And I'm all, "Hey, I'm asking the questions here. I am the boss of you, you know?"

And Foo totally ignores me, and he's all, "They bite back. I think Chet is changing the other cats by accident."

"But he drained that parking cop and she didn't turn."

"She didn't bite him back."

And I'm all, "I knew that."

And Foo's like, "There could be hundreds of them."

And I'm all, "And Chet led them here. To us."

And Foo's all, "He marked this as his territory before the old vampyre turned him. He sees this as his place. The stairway still smells like cat pee."

And I'm like, "That's not all."

And Foo's all, "What? What?"

And I totally slip into my dark mistress voice and I'm all, "Chet has changed. He's bigger."

And Foo's all, "Maybe his coat has just grown back."

And I'm all ominous like, "No, Foo, he's still shaved, but he's a lot bigger, and I think—" I paused. It was very dramatic.

And Foo's like, "Tell me!"

I sort of fainted all emo into his arms. And he totally caught me like the dark hero of the moors that he is, but then he harshed the romantic drama of it all by tickling me and going, "Tell me, tell me, tell me."

So I did, because I was close to peeing myself, and I'm totally not into that kind of thing. "I think we have to worry about the little samurai guy turning, which would not be good, as he is full badass, despite his deeply stupid hat and socks."

And Foo was all, "Did he bite them?"

And I was all, "He was full-on covered in vampyre kitty blood. Maybe some drops got in his mouth. Lord Flood said he accidentally turned that blue ho from one kiss on the bloody lips."

And Foo's like, "Well we need to find him, then. Abby, we may not be able to handle this. We need help." And he's all nodding to the statue of the Countess and Lord Flood.

And I'm all, "Do you know the first thing that will happen if we let them out?"

And Foo's all, "Jody will totally kick our asses."

And I'm like, *"Oui, mon amour,* epic ass-kickings *pour toi* and *moi.* But you know what's even scarier?"

And Foo's all, "What? What? What?" Because French drives him mad.

So I'm like, "You still have wood!" And I squeezed his unit and ran into the bedroom.

'Kayso, Foo chased me around the loft a couple of times, and I let him catch me twice, just long enough to kiss me before I was forced to slap him—well, you know why—and run away. But as I was prepared to let him think I would surrender to his manly deliciousness, I'm all, "You could turn me to a vamp and I could use my dark powers to scoop Chet's litter box of destruction."

And Foo was all, "No fucking way. I don't know enough."

Then someone started pounding on the door. And not a little "Hey, what's up?" pound. Like there was a big sale on door pounds down at the Pound Outlet. Buy one, get one free at Pounds-n-Stuff.

I know. WTF? Privacy much? Pounding on the love lair.

JODY

It was like perpetual "not quite lunchtime" in her cubicle at the insurance company, back in ancient history, three months ago, before she was a vampire. Every sundown, for about fifteen seconds, Jody awoke and panicked over the hunger and constraint until she was able to will herself into mist and float in what she thought of as the blood dream, a pleasant, ethereal haze that lasted until sunup, when her body went solid inside the brass shell and for all practical purposes, she became dead meat until sundown came round again. But sometime around the end of the first week of freakouts, she realized that she was touching Tommy. That he was in the bronze shell with her, and unlike her, he couldn't go to mist. She should have taught him, she knew, just as the old vampyre had taught her, but now it was too late. Maybe, since she couldn't move enough to tap a message with her finger in Morse code, let alone talk, she could reach out to him, somehow connect with him telepathically. Who knew what kind of powers she might have that the old vampyre had forgotten to tell her about. She concentrated, pushed, even tried to send some sort of pulse to the places where their skin touched, but all she got back was an extended, jagged, electric panic.

Poor Tommy. He was there all right. Alive and mercilessly aware. She tried to reach him until she could bear the weight of her own hunger and panic no longer. "Abby, if I ever get out of here, your narrow ass is mine," she thought before fading to mist and blissful escape.

INSPECTOR RIVERA

It wasn't a homicide, strictly speaking, because there was no body, but there was a traffic enforcement officer missing in action, and it had involved the Emperor and a certain block of light industry buildings and artist lofts south of Market Street that Rivera had flagged for notice if anything happened there. And something had definitely happened here, but what?

He lifted the collar of the empty traffic officer's uniform with the tip of his pen to confirm that the fine gray ash was not on the sidewalk underneath, and it wasn't. Inside the uniform, on the sidewalk at the cuffs and collar of the uniform, yes, but not on the sidewalk under the uniform.

"I don't see a crime," said Nick Cavuto, Rivera's partner, who, if he'd been a flavor of ice cream, would have been Gay Linebacker Crunch. "Sure, something happened here, but it could have just been kids. The Emperor is clearly nuts. Totally unreliable."

Rivera stood up and looked around at the blood-soaked street, the ashes, the still-flashing light on the parking cart, and then at the Emperor and his dogs, who had their noses pressed to the back window of their brown, unmarked Ford sedan. Rivera's flavor was Low-fat Spanish Cynic in an Armani cone. "He said cats did this."

"Well there you go, an Animal Control issue. I'll call them." Cavuto made a great show of flipping open his mobile and punching at the numbers with his thick sausage fingers.

Rivera shook his head and crouched over the empty uniform again. He knew what the powder was, and Cavuto knew what the powder was. Sure, it had taken them a couple of months, and a lot of unsolved murders, and watching the old vampire take enough gunfire to kill a platoon of men, only to survive to kill a half-dozen more people, but they had finally caught on.

"It wasn't cats," Rivera said.

"They promised to leave," Cavuto said, pausing in his display of percussive dialing. "The creepy girl said they left town." *They,* meaning Jody and Tommy, who had promised to leave town and never return. "The Emperor said he saw the old vampire get on a ship—a whole bunch of them sail away."

"But he's totally unreliable," Rivera said.

"Most of the time. This is not—"

Rivera held up a finger to stop him. They had agreed never to use the *v*-word when others were around. "We have to go see the spooky kid."

"Noooo," Cavuto wailed, then caught himself, realizing that for a man of his size, appearance, and occupation, that whining over having to confront a skinny teenage girl was, well—he was being a huge wuss—that's what.

"Man up, Nick, we'll tell her not only does she have a right to remain silent, it's an obligation. Besides, I called in backup."

"I should probably stay in the car with the Emperor. See if he remembers anything else."

Just then there was a commotion at the crime scene tape and a uniformed officer said, "Inspector, this woman wants through. She says she has to see her daughter, who lives in that apartment." The officer pointed to the fire door of the loft where the spooky kid lived with her boyfriend.

An attractive blond woman in her late thirties wearing paisley medical scrubs was trying to push past the officer.

"Let her through," Rivera said. "Look, Nick, an angel come to protect you."

"Oh God save me from fucking neo-hippies," said Gay Linebacker Crunch.

The Further Chronicles of Abby Normal, Miserable, Broken-hearted Emo-ho of the Night

'Kayso, who is outside my door but Baroness Buzzkill herself, the Motherbot, accompanied by those most crapacious homicide cops, Rivera and Cavuto.

So I'm all, "Oh joy, does this caffeine fresh clusterfuck come with donuts?" Which it turned out, it didn't, so really, WTF is the point of bringing cops?

And the Mombot is all, "You can't do this, and who is this boy, and where have you been, and you have no right, and blah, blah, blah, responsibility, worried sick, you're a horrible, horrible person and you ruined my life with your platform boots and your piercings."

Okay, those weren't her exact words, but the subtext was there. And in retrospect, I may have erred in using the "I'm sleeping over at Lily's house" gambit for two months running, when I was, in fact, living in my own *très* cool love lair with a mysterious love ninja. So I decided to turn the tables on her by asking questions, before she got in the rhythm of grilling me and heaping me with mom guilt.

So I'm all, "How did you find me?"

And the dark, Hispano cop steps up, and he's all, "I called her."

So I rolled up in his grill. Well, up in the knot of his tie, because he's taller than me. And I'm all, "I can't believe you ratted me out. You traitorous fuck!"

And the cop gets all chilly and he's all, "I'm not a traitor because I'm not on your side, Allison." Using my day-slave name, just to fuck with me.

So I'm all thinking, *Okay, cop, I can see that you believe that your shit cannot be shaken, and you are totally trying to come off all sly and badass in front of the Mombot so she might do you a good long time?* I know—mating rituals of the ancient and crusty—makes you barf in your mouth a little, huh?

So I go over to the big gay cop, and I'm all soft-spoken little-girl voice, "I thought we were on the same side be-cause—well—because we know about the nosferatu, and all that money you got from his art collection. We're not? I'm crushed." Totally hand to forehead, fake-heartbreak faint-ing. I was going to cry a little, but my mascara was lined up like the spikes on the gates of hell, and I didn't want it to go raccoon on me so early in the day, so only a sniffle. I wiped my nose on the big gay cop's sleeve.

And the Momster is all, "What? What? Nosferatu? What? Money? What?"

And Rivera is all, "Excuse us a moment, Mrs. Green, we need to have a word with Allison."

So the Mombot starts to go into the bedroom and I'm all, "Oh I don't think so. You can wait outside," or something like that, because it turns out I didn't want her to see the inner sanctum of our love nest, because she's a nurse and seeing the dog collars, test tubes, centrifuge, and whatnot might give her the wrong idea. (Foo and I like to get our mad scientist freak on in the privacy of the boudoir.)

So Mom steps outside.

And Foo is all, "Owned, bitches!" And he did a pathetic imitation of my own superb booty dance of ownage, and I was, at once, touched by his support, yet embarrassed by his tragic lack of rhythm and booticuity.

And Rivera is all, "Allison, how did you know about the money and the old vampyre and the yacht and you have no proof and blah, blah, I so can't decide whether I'm the good cop or the bad cop, or if I'm going to still pretend to be bad-ass or totally crap my pants from the verbal death grip you just put on my man sac, blah, blah."

And I'm all, "I know it all, cop," popping the *p* in cop because it makes both of them flinch a little. "You need to exit and take the Mombot home or I will be forced to expose your evil shit to your masters, and not in the fun way."

And the Hispano cop was all chill, nodding and smiling, which harshed my confidence somewhat. And he's all, "That so, Allison? Well, Mr. Wong here is twenty-one, and you are still a minor, so among other things, we can take him in for contributing to the delinquency of a minor, kid-napping, and statutory rape." And he folds his arms all, "Take that, bee-atch." Hip-hop superior.

So I'm like, "You're right, he is totally taking advantage of my innocence. Foo, you ginormous perve!" Then I slapped him, but for the drama, not because he might think I was a slut. "I should have known when you had me shave my va-jay-jay into the shape of a beaver!"

And Foo's all, "I did not!"

"Pervy *and* redundant, don't you think?" I asked the big gay cop, who wouldn't know a va-jay-jay if it bounced up to him and sang the "Star-Spangled Banner." (You ever notice that hardly anything besides the "Star-Spangled Banner" is spangled? There's no, like, the Raisin-Spangled Scone, or the Flea-Spangled Beagle. I'm just saying.) So, I, like, start to pull up my skirt to further freak him out, like I'm going to flash the beav, which was a bluff, because I am totally trimmed bat-shape and dyed lavender and I was wearing my hot-pink fishnets, which are full-on tights and put the PG-13 on my no-no place.

But instead of hiding his head and screaming like a little bitch, which is what I was going for, the big gay cop is across the room and has Foo in handcuffs in like seconds, cranking them down tight.

So Foo is all, "Ow! Ow! Ow!"

And I'm heartsick at his suffering, so I'm like, "Unhand him, you fascist-ass bear."

And Rivera is all, "Allison, we need to come to an understanding, or your boyfriend is going to jail, and even if the charges don't stick, he can kiss his master's degree good-bye."

Powned! I was forced to lower my skirt in defeat. Foo's eyes were all anime-huge and started to get tear-spangled, and my noble love ninja looked all pleading to me like, "Please, do not abandon me, despite my obvious emo tendencies."

So I'm like, "We'll give you a hundred thousand dollars to leave our love lair like nothing happened."

And Rivera is like, "We're not interested in your money."

And gay bear cop is like, "Wait, where did you get that kind of money, anyway?"

And Rivera is like, "Never mind, Nick, it's not about money."

And I'm like, "OMG Rivera, your bad cop skills suck ass. It's always about the money. Don't you have a TV?"

And he's like, "What happened out there this morning?"

And I'm all, "You know, vampyre kitties, meter maid sucked to dust, samurai in orange socks, Abby's kung-fu of solar ass-kicking." Then to Foo: "Foo, the jacket is the sickest shit ever!"

"Which is a good thing," Foo translated for the cops.

And Rivera is all, "Vampyre cats? That's what the Emperor said."

'Kayso, it's clear that the cops have doubts, so I explain the whole battle, and Foo's theory of how Chet is making vampyre kitties, and how we are pretty much fucked nine ways to Kwanzaa because it's the end of the world and whatnot, and there are metric buttloads of kitties in the City, and only two fly, vampyre-frying solar jackets, mine and Foo's, and we are being detained by law enforcement assbags instead of saving humanity.

So Rivera's all, "What about Flood and the redhead? You helped them, right?"

Kudos to Inspector Obvious, we're only living in their loft, spending their money, and hanging our damp towels on their bronzed bodies. I was all, "They left. All the vampyres left. Didn't you talk to the Emperor? He saw them get on a boat at the Marina?"

"The Emperor isn't the most dependable witness," Rivera says. "And he didn't say anything about those two, but I find it hard to believe that a cat, even a vampyre cat, even a gang of vampyre house cats took down a full-grown parking enforcement officer."

So I was like, "Chet is not a normal vampyre kitty. He's huge. More huge than normal. He's getting huger. If you don't let Foo work his mad science skills to cure him, by next week Chet might be dry-humping the Transamerica Pyramid."

Foo was nodding like a manga-haired bobblehead. He was all, "Truth."

The big gay Cavuto cop is all, "Can you do that, kid? Can you put this shit storm back in the box?"

"Absolutely," says Foo, when he totally has no clue how to catch Chet. "I'll need some time, but leave the handcuffs on, because that's how I work best."

Foo can be most sarcastic when faced with day dwellers less intelligent than himself, which is almost everyone.

'Kayso, Rivera takes the sleeve of my jacket and starts turning it over, looking at it, all Neanderthal discovers fire face. And he's all, "Can you make one of these in a leather sport coat? Forty long?"

And I'm all, "Are you coming on to me?"

And he gagged a little (which was mean), and he's all, "No. I am definitely not coming on to you, Allison. Not only are you the most irritating creature on the planet, you are a child."

And I'm all, "A child?! A child?! Do these belong to a child?" And I pulled up my top and flashed him. And not just a flash, a full, glorious boobosity.

And he didn't say anything. So I turned my headlights on Foo and the big gay cop.

And they're all, "Um-uhr-uhr-um—"

I'm like, *"Et tu,* Foo?" Which is Shakespearean for, "You traitor!"

And I ran into the bedroom and locked the door. I was kind of wishing I'd taken a hostage, except really the only weapon I had was a jacket with little light warts all over it, so I was limited to being dangerous to vampyres and emos who get their feelings hurt really easily by my snarky wit.

'Kayso, then I stared into the dark abyss that is the meaninglessness of human existence, because there was nothing on cable. And in searching the depths of my soul, I saw that I must stop using sex as a weapon, and that I must only use my powers of seduction for good, unless Foo wants to do something freaky, in which case, I can have him sign a waiver. Now, I realize that the only way for me to righteously explore my strength as a woman is to become nosferatu. And since the Countess and Lord Flood wouldn't bring me into the fold, I must find my own way to the blood power.

'Kayso, in a few minutes Rivera's at the door all, "Allison, I think you'd better come out here."

And I'm all, "Oh no, Inspector, I can't open the door. I've taken all these pills and everything's all wiggly. You'll have to break the door down."

Then Foo's all, "Abby, please come out. I need you." He used his I'm sad, wounded, and locked in the castle tower with all my powers gone voice, which I didn't even know he had, but it was tragic and I had to come out and humble myself before the cops like a little bitch, despite my new resolve to partake of the dark gift.

So I'm all, "What?"

And Rivera is all, "Allison, we have an agreement with Mr. Wong. He will stay here and work on a solution to the cat problem, and in return for our not filing charges, you both will say nothing to anyone about our previous—uh—adventures, with Mr. Flood, Ms. Stroud, and any other persons of the blood-drinking persuasion. Nor will we mention any funds that may have changed hands, and who may be in possession of said funds. Agreed?"

I'm all, "Sweet!"

"And you have to go home and live with your mother and sister," the evil Hispano cop continued.

And I'm all, "No way!"

And all three of them are shaking their heads at me. And Foo, who is out of handcuffs now, is all, "Abby, you have to go with them. You're still a minor and your mom will chuck a spaz if they don't bring you home."

"And if that happens, we'll have no choice but to drop a hammer on Mr. Wong," said Cavuto.

And Foo's all, "And to defend ourselves we'll have to tell everyone about everything. So we'll all be hosed and meanwhile, Chet the huge shaved cat will own the City, plus our relationship and stuff would be strained."

And by "and stuff," Foo meant that we would lose the love lair and no one would take care of Tommy and Jody, and Foo would have to become love ninja to some big guy in prison. We were owned.

I was all, "I blame my mother."

I offered my wrists to Rivera for the cuffs.

And they were all nodding, and "Sure," and "That works for me." And "Yeah, I'm good with that."

But Rivera didn't put the cuffs on me.

And I'm all, "Can we have a minute to say good-bye?"

And Rivera nods, so I start to lead Foo into the bedroom.

And Rivera is all, "Out here."

So I unzip Foo's pants.

And Cavuto grabs my arm and starts to drag me away, so I was forced to give Foo only a minor good-bye kiss that brushed his lips like a breeze from the tomb and left a little bit of a black lipstick streak on his cheek.

And I'm all, "I will never forget you, Foo. They may tear us asunder, but our love will endure for eternity."

And he's all, "Call me when you get home."

And I'm all, "I'll text you on the way."

And he's all, "Abby Normal, you rock my stripy socks." Which was totally romantic, because he doesn't wear stripy socks. I cried and my mascara melted in sorrow.

Then Cavuto's all, "Oh for fuck's sake." And he starts to lead me out the door, but turns to Foo and goes, "Is that your tricked-out yellow Honda downstairs?"

And Foo is all, "Yeah."

And Cavuto's all, "You know it's full of rats, right?"

And Foo's all, "Yeah."

And so I am a prisoner of the dreaded Motherbot and Foo faces the menace of Chet alone. Gotta jet, my sister, Ronnie, is asleep and I'm going to Magic Marker a pentagram on her shaved head. L8erz.

RIVERA

As they were walking away from delivering Abby Normal and her mother to the apartment building in the Fillmore, Cavuto said, "You know, if I'd had Allison there around when I came out to my dad, I think he would have understood a lot more why I like guys."

"If the vampire cats' victims turn to dust, most won't even be reported unless someone sees the attack," Rivera said, hoping Cavuto's train of thought would head on to the next station.

"She's so obnoxious," said Cavuto. "Like a whole Saturday night drunk tank full of obnoxious packed into one little body."

"Maybe if we get a cadaver dog," said Rivera.

"Okay, but don't bitch about how the car smells later, because I want chili and onions."

"What the fuck are you talking about?"

"Cadaver dogs. You were saying we should go to the ballpark and get cadaver dogs for lunch."

"I was saying no such thing. I was saying we should get a dog that's trained to sniff out cadavers to help us find the clothing of the victims."

"Oh," said Cavuto, who didn't want to think about vampires. "Sure, that makes sense. So, Barney's Burgers for lunch then?"

"You buy," Rivera said, as he popped the locks on the unmarked Ford and climbed in.

They drove eight blocks down Fillmore Street toward the Marina, before Cavuto said, "She's right, you know? I am a bear."

Rivera put on his sunglasses and took a few seconds adjusting them on his face to buy time before he answered with a sigh. "I'm glad you decided to come clean about that, Nick, because observing your six-foot-three-inch, two-hundred-and-sixty-pound, growling gay personage for the last fourteen years would have never betrayed your true identity, given my dull, homicide detective powers of observation."

"Your sarcasm is the main reason Alice left you."

"Really?" Rivera had wondered. Alice had said because he was too much of a cop and not enough of a husband, but he had suspicions about her testimony.

"No, but I'm sure it was on the list."

"Nick, in all our time as partners, have I ever indicated that I wanted to discuss your sexuality?"

"Well, not beyond using it to threaten suspects."

"And have I ever offered to share the details of my sex life with Alice?"

"I just assumed you didn't have one."

"Well, that's not really relevant. I'm just saying, I'm fine with you just the way you are."

"Mantastic, you mean?"

"Sure, go with that. Although I was thinking more of large and furry, yet afraid of tiny girls."

"Well, you can't hit her, she's a kid," Cavuto whined.

They found parking in a garage near Barney's. Rivera pulled into a no-parking spot (because he could) and shut off the engine. He sat back and looked at the wall in front of them.

"So, vampire cats," Cavuto said.

"Yeah," said Rivera.

"We're fucked," said the big cop.

"Yeah," said Rivera.

The Vampire Parrots of Telegraph Hill

A flock of wild parrots lives in the city of San Francisco. They are South American cherry-headed conures—bright green with a red head, a little smaller than a typical pigeon.

No one is quite sure how they came to the City. It's likely that they are the descendants of animals caught in the jungle, then released to the city skies when they proved too wild to be kept as pets. They fly over the northern waterfront of San Francisco, foraging for fruit, berries, and blossoms, from the Presidio at the entrance of the Golden Gate Bridge, over Pacific Heights, the Marina, Russian Hill, North Beach, and all the way to the Ferry Building near the Oakland Bay Bridge. They are social, squawky, silly birds that mate for life and advertise their presence with a cacophony of beeps and cheeps that inspire smiles from residents, bewilderment from tourists, and hunger in predators, mostly red-tailed hawks and per-egrine falcons.

The parrots spend their nights high in the trees of Telegraph Hill, beneath the great concrete phallus of Coit Tower, sheltered from attack from hawks by the evergreen canopy overhead, and from all but the most ambitious cats, by the sheer altitude. But still, they are sometimes attacked, and although gentle creatures, they will fight back, biting with their thick, built-for-seed-crushing beaks.

Which is what happened.

The next morning after he witnessed the cat attack in the SOMA, the Emperor of San Francisco was awakened from a nest he'd made in one of the little stair gardens on Telegraph Hill, to hear parrots squawking in the trees. The sun was just breaking the horizon behind the Bay Bridge, turning the water red-gold under a blue morning mist.

The Emperor crawled out from under a pile of carpet padding, stood, and stretched, his great joints creaking in the cold like ancient church doors. The men, Bummer and Lazarus, poked their noses out of the gray cloak, snuffled the dawn, then, with the call of the parrots, resolved themselves to morning and emerged like urgent butterflies to search for the perfect spot for the first wee of the day.

The three watched as fifty or so squawking parrots circled Coit Tower and headed out toward the Embarcadero, where, suddenly, they all stopped flying, burst into flames, and fell like a smoldering storm of dying comets into Levi's Plaza.

"Well, you don't see that every day," said the Emperor, scratching Lazarus's ears through the bandages. The retriever was a doggy version of *The Mummy*, wrapped ears to tail in bandages after his last encounter with the vampire cats. The vet in the Mission wanted to keep him overnight, but the retriever had never spent a night away from the Emperor since they had found each other, and the vet had no accommodations for a large and burly monarch, let alone a feisty Boston terrier, so the three had bunked together under the carpet pad.

Bummer chuffed, which translated from dog to: "I don't like it."

As the famous frog sang, it's not easy being green.

The Fog Comes on Little Cat Feet and Whatnot

FØØ

Stephen "Foo Dog" Wong's fully bombed Honda drift machine was full of rats. Not completely full, the passenger seat was filled by Jared Whitewolf, Abby's backup BFF. (BBFF, really.)

"Did you have to get all white ones?" Jared asked. He was six foot two, very thin, and paler than Death shagging a snowman. The sides of his head were shaved and in the middle he sported an unlaquered Mohawk, which hung in his eyes unless he was lying on his back or looking up. In addition to a floor-length black PVC cenobite coat, he was currently wearing Abby's thigh-high red platform Skankenstein® boots, which was completely within his rights, as her current BFF. What bothered Foo was not that Jared had on girl's boots, but that he had on the boots of a girl with distinctly small feet.

"Don't those hurt?"

Jared tossed his hair out of his eyes. "Well, it's like Morrissey said, 'Life is suffering.' "

"I think the Buddha said that."

"I'm pretty sure Morrissey said it first—like, back in the eighties."

"No, it was the Buddha."

"Have you ever even seen a picture of the Buddha with shoes on?" Jared asked.

Foo couldn't believe he was having this argument. What's more, he couldn't believe he was losing this argument.

"Well, I have some Nikes upstairs that might fit you if you need to change shoes. Let's get the rats unloaded. I have to get to work."

Jared already had four plastic cages with two white rats in each stacked on his lap, so he unfolded himself out of the Honda and wobbled on the red platforms to the fire door of the loft. "Don't try to paint them black," Jared said, peering into the Plexiglas boxes as Foo opened the door for him. "I tried that with my first rat, Lucifer. It was tragic."

"Tragic?" said Foo. "I'd have never guessed. Put them on the floor in the living room. I'll borrow the truck from work tomorrow and pick up some folding tables to put them on."

In addition to pursuing his degree in molecular biology, and variously rescuing Abby, formulating vampire serum, and tricking out his Honda, Foo still worked part-time at Stereo City, where he specialized in telling people that they needed a bigger TV.

"You still have that job?" Jared said as he stumbled up the stairs. "Abby said you guys have total fuck-you money."

Why did she tell him? She wasn't supposed to tell him. Did she tell him everything? Why did she have to have friends at all? She'd given Jared five thousand dollars of Jody and Tommy's money for Hanukkah—despite the fact that neither one of them was Jewish. "Because I will not let mainstream society make me into the Christmas bitch of the zombie baby-Jebus, that's why," she'd said. "And because he helped me take care of the Countess and Lord Flood when they were in trouble."

"I need to keep my cover," Foo said. "For tax purposes."

That was partially true. He *did* need to keep up his cover, because, like Abby, he hadn't actually told his parents that he'd moved out. They were so used to him being at school, in the lab, or at work, that they hadn't really noticed that he hadn't been sleeping at home. It helped that he had four younger brothers and sisters, who were all carrying insane work and course loads. His parents were all about toil. As long as you were toiling, you were okay. They could smell toil from miles away, or the lack of it. He might be able to get away with living in his own loft with his spooky-sexy girlfriend, and doing bizarre genetic experiments on the undead, but if he quit his job they'd sense it in a second.

It took Foo and Jared twenty minutes to get all the rats up the steps and lined up around the living room.

"We're not going to hurt them, are we?" said Jared, holding up one of the plastic cages so he was eye to eye with its occupants.

"We're going to turn them into vampires."

"Oh, cool. Now?"

"No, not now. For now, you're going to need to feed them and make sure there's a water bottle in each of their cages," Foo said.

"Then what?" Jared asked, tossing his hair out of his eyes.

"Then you can go home," said Foo. "You don't need to observe them full-time until the experiment starts."

"I can't go home. I told my parents I was staying over at Abby's."

Foo was suddenly horrified at the thought of having to spend the night in the loft with a hundred rats, two bronzed vampires, and Jared. Especially Jared. Maybe he'd go home and leave Jared to watch the rats—make an appearance at home for the parents, so as to throw them off the trail of his non-toiling, loft-living, Anglo-girlfriend lifestyle.

"You can stay here, then," Foo said. "I'll be back in the morning."

"What about them?" Jared nodded toward the bronzed figures of Jody and Tommy.

"What about them?"

"Can I talk to them? I didn't get to finish telling Jody my novel." Jared had spent a very long night telling Jody the first part of the novel he was going to write, an erotic horror story that starred himself and his pet rat, Lucifer 2.

"Okay," said Foo. He didn't really like thinking about the two people, well, vampires, but they seemed a lot like people, that he'd helped imprison in a bronze shell. It sort of gave him the willies, and that was highly unscientific. "But no touching," he added.

Jared pouted and sat down on the futon, about the only spot in the entire living-room-kitchen area not covered with plastic rat cages. "Okay, but will you help me get these boots off before you go?"

Foo shuddered. It had been less than an hour since the cops led Abby away and already he missed her like a severed limb. It was embarrassing. How could hormones and hydrostatic pressure make you feel like this? Love was very unscientific.

"Sorry," Foo said. "Gotta jet." A true hero, the kind Abby accused him of being, he knew, would have helped Jared.

JARED

Abby Normal had once offered to pay for a tattoo for Jared that read: *Danger. Do not administer caffeine without adult supervision.*

Jared asked, "Can it be in red? Does it have to be on the forehead? Maybe on the side so I can grow my hair over it if I don't like it. Am I being emo? Do you want to play Bloodfeast on Xbox? They have green fur iPod cases at Urban Outfitters. I love white chocolate mochas. Marilyn Manson needs to be dragged to death behind a clown car. Oh fuck, I'm so allergic to this eyeliner I could cry."

Abby said, "Oh my God, you're like Obnoxious and Annoying had an ass baby!"

"What are you trying to say?" asked Jared.

What she had been trying to say, although she didn't know it at the time, was that under no circumstances should Jared be left alone in an apartment with an abundance of time and espresso, which is what Foo had just done. So after feeding, watering, and naming all the rats (most given French names from Abby's copy of Baudelaire's *Les Fleurs du Mal*), Jared began brewing espressos and was nine demitasse cups into the afternoon when he decided to act out the remainder of his unwritten vampire adventure novel, *The Dark of Darkness,* for a hundred rats caged in plastic and two vampires encased in bronze.

"So the evil Blood Queen dons her chrome strap-on of death and goes after Lucifer 2. But Jared Whitewolf is on her like a fat kid on a cupcake, parrying her blows with his dagger of death, or Dee Dee, as it is known." Jared pirouetted, a move he'd learned in ballet class at age six, and slashed the air, low and fast, with the double-edged dagger held backhand so as to sever his imaginary enemy's femoral artery, a move he'd learned in Soul Assassin Five on the Xbox (although it was harder to do while wearing platform boots than it was in the video game). The dagger was real enough, twelve inches of double-edged high-carbon stain-less steel with a dragon hilt. Jared carried it because he thought it made him look badass when doormen took it away from him at clubs.

"And he strikes her weapon in half!" he said, leaping and bringing the blade around a little too fast. He turned his ankle, lost his balance, and as he fell, the dagger put a deep nick in the bronze statue.

"Ow!" He sat on the floor holding his ankle and rocking back and forth in the yoga position known as the "freaked-out half-lotus." Then he noticed the gash he'd put in the bronze, directly over Jody's right clavicle.

"I'm sorry, Countess," Jared said, still a little breathless from his battle. "I didn't mean to hurt you. It's just that I had to save Lucifer 2. You'd do the same thing for Lord Flood if he was in the story."

Jared buffed at the bronze with his sleeve, but the gash was deep and wasn't going to go away with polishing. "Ab-by's going to kill me. I'll patch you, Countess. Just hang on. Toothpaste. We used it on the wall that time we drank Abby's mom's vodka and played cross-country darts in her living room. Hang on a minute."

Jared let the heavy dagger drop to the floor, climbed to his feet, winced, then limped off to the bathroom to look for toothpaste.

He located a tube of all natural tartar control with bak-ing soda just as the sun dropped under the horizon in the west. Out in the living room, a needle-thin stream of mist began leaking out of the gash he'd made in the bronze statue. Toothpaste probably wouldn't have fixed it.

THE ANIMALS

In the last two months, the Animals, the night stock crew at the Marina Safeway, had hunted an ancient vampire, blown up his yacht, stolen millions of dollars' worth of art, sold it for pennies on the dollar, spent the remaining hundreds of thousands on gambling and a blue hooker, got turned into vampires, were torn apart by zoo animals, then burned up by sunlamps when they attacked Abby Normal, then turned, by Foo, back into seven guys who stocked shelves at the Safeway and smoked a little too much weed. And as it often is with adventurers, after the adventure, they were feeling a little bored, and a little worried that nothing exciting would ever happen to them again.

After you've battled the darkness, then become the darkness, then shagged the darkness, frozen turkey bowling and skiing behind the floor-scrubbing machine just doesn't hold the same thrill. After you've shared a blue prostitute with your buddies to the tune of a half a million dollars, only to have her kill and resurrect you before disappearing into the night, swapping stories of banging babes was a bit of an anticlimax. After all, they worked nights and the oldest of them, Clint, was only twenty-three, so most of their stories were gross exaggerations, wishful thinking, or outright lies anyway. Even crucifying Clint with zip ties on the potato chip rack every other Friday didn't seem fun anymore, and last week they had just left him hanging, thrashing in the Doritos, and went off to stock their aisles before he could even forgive them for knowing not what they did. Tragic, really, to be young, free, and mind-numbingly bored.

So when the Emperor of San Francisco came screaming out of the parking lot and slammed, face-first, into the big Plexiglas front window, rattling the Tic Tacs on every register, each of them dropped what he was working on and headed to the front of the store, hoping in their hearts that something outstanding was coming down.

The seven, the Animals, stood on one side of the big window, while the Emperor pounded on the other, the royal hounds leaping and barking at his side.

"Maybe we should let him in," said Clint, curly-haired, born-again, ex–heroin addict who worked cereal, coffee, and juices. "He seems troubled."

"*Sí*," said Gustavo, the porter, leaning on his mop. "Troubled."

"Seems fucking freaked," said Drew, the Ichabod-Crane-gaunt master of the frozen food aisle and chief medical officer. "Totally fucking freaked."

"What's wrong?" asked Lash, the lean black guy who had become their leader when Tommy was turned into a vampire, largely because he almost had an MBA, but also because he was a black guy and inherently cooler than everyone else.

"Murder, destruction, ravenous creatures of the night, a storm of them," shouted the Emperor. "Hurry, please."

"He always says that," said Barry, the balding fireplug of a scuba diver who also stocked soap and dog food.

"Well, every time he says it, it's kind of true," said Jeff, the tall blond ex–power forward with the blown-out knee (baking supplies and international foods). "I say let him in."

"Look, the retriever is all bandaged up. Poor guy," said Troy Lee, their resident martial arts expert who worked the glass aisle. "Let them in."

"You just want to roll the little one up in a burrito," said Lash.

"Yeah, that's right, Lash. Because I'm Chinese, I have a deep-seated need to nosh house pets. Now why don't you let him in before my inner Chinaman forces me to kung-fu your bitch ass."

Because he understood that he was the leader only so long as he told everyone to do what they wanted to do anyway, and because he had had his bitch ass kung-fued in the past and hadn't cared for it, Lash unlocked the door and let the Emperor in.

The old man fell into the store when Lash opened the door. Bummer and Lazarus stopped barking and bolted by them, and on toward the back of the store.

Jeff and Drew got the Emperor seated on one of the registers and Troy Lee handed him a bottle of water. "Chill, Your Majesty, we've done this before."

"Not like this. Not like this," said the Emperor. "It's a storm of evil. Lock the door."

Lash rolled his eyes. They really had done this before, and the door being locked or unlocked wasn't going to make much difference if a vampire was following the old man.

"We got your back, Highness," Lash said.

"Lock the door," the Emperor moaned, pointing through the window. A fog bank was moving across the parking lot, with rather more intent than one usually expects from a fog bank. A high, yowling screech seemed to come out of the fog in a stream, as if it had been sampled, amplified, and duplicated a thousand times.

The Animals moved to the glass.

"Lock the door, Lash," Clint said. Clint never gave orders.

The edge of the fog bank was boiling with shapes, claws, ears, eyes, teeth, tails—cats formed of fog, rolling in a wave over one another, some materializing partially, only to evaporate and roll back into the cloud, their red eyes moving through the cloud like embers out of a firestorm.

"Whoa," said Drew.

"Whoa," repeated the others.

"Okay, that *is* different," said Troy Lee.

"My friends all over the City are missing," the Emperor said. "Street people. They're gone. Just their clothes and gray dust," the Emperor said. "The cats are killing everything in their way."

"That is fucked up," said Jeff.

"Deeply, deeply fucked up," said Barry, dragging one of the heavy wooden order dividers off the register and brandishing it like a club.

"Lock the fucking door, Lash!" Clint screamed.

"Jesus hates it when you use the *f*-word," said Gustavo, the Mexican porter, who was Catholic and liked to remind Clint when his Jesus was slipping.

The fog washed against the window and claw marks etched the Plexiglas instantly to frost, as if it had all been sanded. The noise was like, well, it was like a thousand vampire cats clawing on Plexiglas—it made their teeth hurt.

"Did anyone bring weapons?" Troy Lee asked.

"I brought some weed," Drew said.

A cat's claw of fog crept under the door and raked the toe of Lash's sneaker. He snapped the lock shut, pulled out the key, and backed away.

"Okay, break time," he said. "Crew meeting in the walk-in."

JARED

Across town, in the bedroom of a fashionable loft, in the fashionable SOMA neighborhood, aspiring rat-shagger, Jared Whitewolf, looked up from rubbing his sore ankle to see a completely naked redhead walk into the room. Her hair hung to her waist in a great curling cape, framing her figure, which was perfect and as white as a marble statue. She held Jared's double-edged dagger in her right hand.

Jared backed up onto the bed in a reverse crab walk. "I, I, I, it, it, it—Abby made me—"

"Chill, Scissorhands," Jody said. "You'd better find some of those blood bags of Steve's fast, unless you'd like to finish high school as a pile of greasy dust. Countess is thirsty."

Being the Chronicles of Abby Normal, in the Double-doomed Doghouse of Despair

Do the condemned in hell know the suffering that is a whole day of mom-guilt heaped like steaming piles of bat guano upon my spiky magenta coif? (I went with magenta spikes with electric violet tips to express my outrage at being dragged from my home and imprisoned with the cruel Mombot and my crapacious little sister, Ronnie.) Evidently, Mother feels that we were too young to move in together only a week after meeting, and live in a stolen apartment with two of the undead and their stupid amounts of cash. Although she doesn't really know about the undead or the cash parts, but she made her point.

'Kayso, I had like put on my red tartan wedding gown with the black veil and resolved myself to an all-day power-pout in the corner of the living room, coming up only to text Foo messages of my agony of missing him and change the channel and whatnot, when Jared called from the land-line at the love lair.

So I'm all, "Speak, corpse-fluffer."

And Jared is all, "OMFG! The Countess is out, and she was naked, but now she's not, and she totally got blood all over your leather corset, and you have to come right now because the rats are freaking out and we need a hacksaw and a file."

And I'm all, "Uh-oh."

And Jared is all, "I know. I know. OMG! OMG!"

And I'm all, "Is she pissed?" Sounding way more chill than I felt.

And Jared pauses for a second like he's thinking it over, then he's all, "She's wearing your clothes and there's blood running all down the front of her and she's nodding and showing her fangs and shit."

So I'm like getting some perspective now—like when you're a kid and you think it sucks that you have to eat hydrogenated peanut butter on your PBJ, and then you see one of those starving commercial kids with the flies in their eyes, who don't even have a sandwich—and you're all, "Well, that sucks." 'Kayso, I'm thinking that maybe being under restriction in the mother unit's Fillmore stronghold isn't so bad when compared to having the Countess busting out her wrath on you for imprisoning her in bronze.

So I'm like, "Sucks to be you, Jared. Byez." And I offed my phone.

So like five minutes go by, which I spend in my corner

going, "Oh shit, oh shit, oh shit," and whatnot, and the land-line rings. And Ronnie is all, "Are you going to get that?" from her room.

And I'm all, "I didn't even know it was hooked up."

And she was all, "It's probably Mom checking up on you, so you might as well get it."

And I'm all, "Ronnie, answer it or I will murder you in your sleep and dump your body in the Bay."

And she's all, " 'Kay."

Then, "It's for you. It's some girl named Jody." And Ronnie is all standing there with her shaved head and her non-existent hip thrown out, like "So there, ho."

And I'm all, "Fucksocks!" And I take the phone and I'm like, "Hi, I have amnesia and don't remember anything for the last two months!" Because what do you say to someone who you had bronzed?

And the Countess is all, "Abby, I'm not angry."

Which was a total lie, because I could hear that she was angry. She had that "I'm not angry" mom voice, even though she's only, like, twenty-six in real years.

"So you're not going to kill me?"

"We'll talk. Right now I need you to get a power drill and a hacksaw with extra blades and come to the loft."

And I'm all, "I don't know where to get stuff like that, and Foo's at work, and I'm on restriction, and I have to go to school tomorrow. I have a test, so I totally can't cut class, and besides, what do you need that stuff for?"

And she's all, "Find the tools and come now. Tommy is stuck in the statue and we need to get him out."

And I'm thinking, Oops. But I'm chill and I'm like, "Can't he get out the same way you did?"

And the Countess is all, "Tommy doesn't know how to turn to mist. That's how I escaped, but Tommy has been trapped in there for—how long, Abby?"

"Oh, like a couple of days. It's all so foggy, after the head trauma."

Then I hear her saying, like, "Jared, come over here. I want Abby to hear your neck snap."

"Okay, like five weeks. Fuck, Countess, overreact much?"

"Come now, Abby."

And she just clicks off.

So I text Foo: COUNTESS OUT, NEED HACKSAW PWRDRILL NOW

And he's all: WTF? WTF? WTF? OUT? WTF? ACE HARDWARE, CASTRO ST

(I know. Four WTFs! Foo has deep intellectual curiosity. Last week he quizzed me for twenty minutes on what it was like to have a clitoris. I just kept saying "nice." I know, I'm such a tard, I couldn't think of anything else. I *so* have to learn French. They have like thirty-seven words for clitoris. They're like snow to Eskimos, only you know, harder to build an igloo out of.)

'Kayso, I text him: KTXBYE <3

And I tell Ronnie to tell Mom that I think I got some anthrax on my toothbrush and I have to go to Walgreens to get a new one so I'll be right back. Then I put on my jacket with the sun warts, in case of vampyre kitties and whatnot, and I take the F car up to Castro Street and go to Ace Hardware. And I'm totally feeling the animosity coming off the Builder Bob guy in the red apron, and I'm like, "What? You've never seen a wedding dress?"

And he's all, "No, I love the dress, the jacket, the whole ensem is fabulous."

And I'm like, "Really? Thanks. Your apron rocks. I need a hacksaw and a power drill."

And he's all, "What's it for?"

And I'm all, "You want a note from my mom? A fucking hacksaw and a power drill. I'm on a schedule."

And he's all, "I asked because we have over thirty different kinds of power drills."

And I'm like, "Oh. I need to release my Dark Lord from the bronze shell in which I imprisoned him."

And he's, "Oh, you should have said so." And he leads me to the drill boutique and I picked out a red and black one that matched my dress, and Bob picked out a hacksaw which totally clashed, but I didn't want to hurt his feelings, so I said it was *très beau,* which is French for sweet.

'Kayso, as I'm paying for my stuff, I go, "So, why are you guys still open at midnight?"

And Bob goes, "Well, you know how it is, you never know when someone is going to need to free their dark lord in the middle of the night, or tie him up."

And I'm all, "Ewww." Because I do not go for that shit. I am only into S&M and bondage as it applies to wardrobe. I tried cutting myself to express my heartbreak over Tommy

(Lord Flood) rejecting me, but OMFG it hurts like flaming fuck. I mean, I'm into self-mutilations as much as the next person—I have eight piercings and five tattoos, some that hurt like double flaming fuck to get, but that was professional, and you can blame someone. In fact, I know a guy in the Haight who will tattoo you for free if you're a girl and you keep yelling at him the whole time, which, it turns out, isn't that hard to do when someone is poking you with an electric needle. When he did my bat wings I screamed at him so much I lost my voice for two days.

'Kayso, I took the F car across town and the three blocks from Market to the loft, but like holding the button on my sun wart jacket in case I got ambushed by Chet and his vampyre kitty pals, because I totally can't run in my wedding dress because the buckles of my motocross platforms get caught in the lace, so it's like, stand and fight or die, bitches! But no vamp kitties came.

Anyway, I make it to the loft and I come in all, "Hey Countess, here's your drill!" All Carebear-on-crack-perky, although that might have been a mistake, because it's a proven fact that it's easier to murder the perky. And I'm sort of, *WTF vampyress*? Because she's not her normal self, which is like hemophiliac hawt, but she's like printer-paper pale. And I totally ignore the fact that she's wearing one of my long skirts and my black bustier without even asking, and it's bustiering her way more than it does me, which is kind of rude. And I'm all, "Countess, are you okay? You look kind of pale."

And Jared is all, "You should have seen her before she drank those blood bags."

And I'm suddenly feeling all poop on a stick, because it's obvious that she's all gone snowflake because she's been locked up without feeding. So I'm like, "Sorry. I just wanted you guys to be together for eternity, and it didn't sound like that's how it was going to happen."

And she's like, "Later, Abby." And she just takes the tools from me and goes over to the statue and starts drilling and sawing and whatnot.

So I'm like, "How did you get out?"

And she's all, "Rat boy was dancing and nicked the casting with his dagger."

And Jared's all, "I wasn't dancing. I had some espresso and I was telling them my novel and I lost my balance on your stupid boots."

And I'm all, "You can't give him caffeine, Countess. His aunt gave him a hundred-dollar Starbucks card for Christmas and we had to have an intervention."

And Jody pauses and looks back at me, her eyes looking all emerald-like, because except for her hair, she has no color in her face and she's like, "Tommy didn't know how to turn to mist, Abby. I never had a chance to teach him before you bronzed us. He's been trapped in here, fully conscious, for five weeks."

And I'm like backing away, because I've seen the Countess pissed off before, like when the Animals kidnapped Tommy and she had to kick their asses to get him back, but now she's all jaw tightened like she's keeping herself from tearing my arms off or something. So I sort of feel for the button on the cuff of my sun jacket. Not like I was going to fry the Countess, because I wouldn't do that, but just for security.

And she just snaps her hand out and before I can move she's pulled the battery out of my inside pocket and ripped off the wire leads. I mean like faster than you can blink.

So I'm like, "I wasn't going to light it up."

And she's all, "Just to be safe."

But I'm not feeling safe. And I can tell that Jared isn't feeling safe because he's sort of sniffling like he's going to start crying.

And Jody is sawing on the bronze like a crazy person—on the side where she used to be, so she doesn't cut Tommy—and finally she has, like, enough sawed away that she can pull a piece away and look in.

And she's all, "Tommy, we're going to get you out of there. I have to be careful, but I'll get you out of there soon."

And Jared is like, "Do you need a flashlight?"

And Jody is like, "No, I can see."

And Jared is all, "Is he dead?"

And right then Jody snaps a hacksaw blade and goes, "Well of course he's dead, he's a vampyre."

And I'm all, "Duh? Tard." As I hand Jody another blade.

I have to say, that for someone with super powers and immortality, the Countess kind of sucks ass with tools. I guess the dark gift doesn't include home improvement skills.

'Kayso, after about an hour the Countess pulls a big piece off the statue, revealing Tommy's face and torso and whatnot, and he's just stuck there, not moving, not opening his eyes, and even whiter than the Countess, kind of a light bruise-blue color.

And Jared is all, "He dead?"

And Jody is like kind of between a scream and a sob, and she's like, "Get me another blood bag, Jared. And Abby, where the fuck are my clothes?" And a little blood tear runs down her cheek.

And I'm like, "Uh-oh." Because now I realize why she's wearing my clothes. When Foo and I moved in we put all of Tommy and Jody's clothes in vacuum bags under the bed. So I'm like, "What do you want to wear, Countess? I'll get it. I mean, you can wear my stuff any time you want, because I am your faithful minion, but you have been endowed by your creator with significantly more boobage and junk in the trunk than me, no offense, and my stuff doesn't exactly fit you. No offense."

And Jared is all, "She had your Emily hoody on over that but it got blood all over it." Not helping at all. "Hey, who wants a latte?"

And the Countess snarled at Jared, full frontal fangs and all. And Jared jumped back and turned his ankle. And I'm like, "Oh shit!"

And she barks, "Blood!"

And Jared and I are all, "Coming right up. Oh shit. Oh shit. Oh shit."

And I bring her the bag of blood and she tears it open with her teeth and just pours it over his lips and in his mouth and nothing happens. And Jody is crying and getting louder and Jared and I are getting more and more freaked out and even all the rats in their little boxes are freaking out and running around in circles and whatnot. And finally Tommy's eyes pop open, and they're like crystal blue, like ice, not like eyes, and he screams, and I swear to fucking zombie Jebus, the whole wall of windows in the loft just shattered in the frames.

So Jared and I are all bent over in the corner, covering our ears, and Tommy comes flying out of the statue. You can hear his leg bones cracking like pretzels as he pulls them out, but he scurries on his hands, knocking rats and furniture every which way, coming right at me, fangs first.

And I go to reach for the button on my sleeve, but he's on me, biting my neck. He's so strong it's like trying to fight a statue, and I can hear Jody screaming, and the skin on my neck tearing in shreds. And my vision is like tunneling down to dark, and I'm thinking, *I'm fucking dying? What the fuck's up with that?*

Then there's this loud clang, like a bell, and I feel Tommy pulled off me. And light sort of comes back on. I can see the Countess standing there, holding Foo's stainless-steel floor lamp like it's a lance, and she's obviously just smacked Tommy with it hard enough to knock him off of me. But instead of going at her, he comes scurrying right back at me, smearing blood all over the floor and everything.

And the Countess catches him by the neck from behind and swings him around and out through the broken windows, and the metal frames and everything go with him.

So there's the scream again, and I'm holding my neck, and I sort of crawl to the big hole that used to be the front wall of the loft, and Tommy is in the middle of the street below, naked, in a big splash of metal and glass, and he's like crawling up the side of a car to his feet.

And Jody's beside me. And she's all, "Tommy! Tommy!"

But he's limping off down the alley across the street, walking like his legs are still broken, but maybe healing or something as he goes, but hurting like holy-fuck.

So Jody takes my head and turns it to the side and pulls my hand away from the bite. And I feel like I'm going to pass out. But she bends down and licks my neck, like three times, then puts my hand back on the wound.

"Hold that. It'll heal in a second." Then she shook me and was all, "Now, where the fuck are my clothes?"

And I'm all, "Under the bed. Vacuum bags."

I think I passed out then, because next thing I remember, the Countess is standing there in jeans and boots and her red leather jacket, and she's stuffing bags of blood into my biohazard messenger bag.

And she's all, "I'm taking this."

And I'm all, " 'Kay." Then I'm like, "You saved me."

"I'm taking half the money, too," she said.

I'm all, "You can't go. Where will you go? Who will take care of you?"

"Like you did?" she says.

"I'm so sorry," I said.

And she's all, "I know. I have to find him. I brought him into this. He never wanted any of this. He just wanted someone to love him."

So she starts to leave, without even saying good-bye, and I'm all, "Countess, wait, there's vampyre cats."

And she stops. And she turns all, "Whaaaa?"

And Jared is all nodding and going, "Really. Really."

And I'm, "Chet turned a bunch of kitties into vampyre kitties. They attacked the Emperor last night and they ate a meter maid."

And she was all, "Oh, for fuck's sake."

And I'm all, "I know, I know."

Then she was gone. And Jared was like in the middle of catching some escaped rats and he's all, "You guys are going to totally lose your security deposit."

Jody is just gone. Gone. On her own in the night. It's like Lord Byron said in that poem "Darkness."

> Darkness had no need
> Of aid from them—
> She was the Universe.
> I'd like to go bone my sister now.

I'm paraphrasing.

Tenderloin

If you're looking for a great taco in San Francisco, you go to the Mission district. If you want a plate of pasta, you go to North Beach. Need some dim sum, powdered shark vagina, or ginseng root? Chinatown is your man. Hankering for stupidly expensive shoes? Union Square. Want to enjoy a mojito with an attractive, young professional crowd, well you'll want to head for the Marina or the SOMA. But if you're looking for some crack, a one-legged whore, or a guy sleeping in a puddle of his own urine, you can't beat the Tenderloin, which was where Rivera and Cavuto were investigating the report of a missing person. Well—persons.

"The theater district seems somewhat deserted today," said Cavuto as he pulled the unmarked Ford into a red zone in front of the Sacred Heart Mission. The Tenderloin was, in fact, also the theater district, which was convenient if you wanted to see a first-rate show in addition to drinking a bottle of Thunderbird and being stabbed repeatedly.

"They're all at their country homes in Sonoma, you think?" Rivera said, with a sense of doom rising inside him like nausea. Normally at this time of the morning, the Tenderloin sidewalks ran with grimy rivers of homeless guys looking for their first drink of the day or a place to sleep. Down here you did most of your sleeping during the day. Night was too dangerous. There should have been a line around the block at Sacred Heart, people waiting for the free breakfast, but the line barely reached out the door.

As they walked into the Mission, Cavuto said, "You know, this might be the perfect time for you to get one of those one-legged whores. You know, with demand down, you could probably get a freebie, being a cop and all."

Rivera stopped, turned, and looked at his partner. A dozen raggedy men in the line looked, too, as Cavuto was blocking the light in the doorway like a great, rumpled eclipse.

"I will bring the little Goth girl to your house and film it when she makes you cry."

Cavuto slumped. "Sorry. It's all kind of getting to me. Teasing is the only way I know to take my mind off of it."

Rivera understood. For twenty-five years he'd been an honest cop. Had never taken a dime in bribes, never used unnecessary force, had never given special favors to powerful people, which is why he was still an inspector, but then the redhead happened, and her *v*-word condition, and the old one and his yacht full of money, and it wasn't like they could tell anyone anyway. The two hundred thousand that he and Cavuto had taken wasn't really a bribe, it was, well, it was compensation for mental duress. It was stressful carrying a secret that you could not only not tell, but that no one would believe if you did.

"Hey, you know why there's so many one-legged whores in the Tenderloin?" asked one guy who was wearing a down sleeping bag like a cape.

Rivera and Cavuto turned toward the hope of comic relief like flowers to the sun.

"Fuggin' cannibals," said the sleeping bag guy.

Not funny at all. The cops trod on. "If you only knew," said Rivera over his shoulder.

"Hey, where is everybody?" asked a woman in a dirty orange parka. "You fuckers doing one of your round-ups?"

"Not us," said Cavuto.

They moved past the cafeteria line and a sharp young Hispanic man in a priest's collar caught their eyes over the heads of the diners and motioned for them to come around the steam tables to the back. Father Jaime. They'd met before. There were a lot of murders in the Tenderloin, and only a few sane people who knew the flow of the neighborhood.

"This way," said Father Jaime. He led them through a prep kitchen and dish room into a cold concrete hallway that led to their shower room. The father extended a set of keys that were tethered to his belt on a cable and opened a vented green door. "They started bringing it in a week ago, but this morning there must have been fifty people turning stuff in. They're freaked."

Father Jaime flipped on a light and stood aside. Rivera and Cavuto entered a room painted sunny yellow and lined with battleship gray metal shelves. There was clothing piled on every horizontal surface, all covered, in varying degrees, with a greasy gray dust. Rivera picked up a quilted nylon jacket that was partially shredded and spattered with blood.

"I know that jacket, Inspector. Guy who owns it is named Warren. Fought in Nam."

Rivera turned it in the air, trying not to cringe when he saw the pattern of the rips in the cloth.

Father Jaime said, "I see these guys every day, and they're always wearing the same thing. It's not like they have a closet full of clothes to choose from. If that jacket is here, then Warren is running around in the cold, or something happened to him."

"And you haven't seen him?" asked Cavuto.

"No one has. And I could tell you stories for most of the rest of these clothes, too. And the fact that clothing is even being turned in means that there's lot of it out there. Street people don't have a lot, but they won't take what they can't carry. That means that this is just what people couldn't carry. Everyone in that dining room is looking for a friend he's lost."

Rivera put down the jacket and picked up a pair of work

pants, not shredded, but covered in the dust and spattered with blood. "You said that you can link these clothes to people you know?"

"Yes, that's what I told the uniformed cop first thing this morning. I know these people, Alphonse, and they're gone."

Rivera smiled to himself at the priest using his first name. Father Jaime was twenty years Rivera's junior, but he still spoke to him like he was a kid sometimes. Being called "Father" all the time goes to their head.

"Other than being homeless, did these people have anything in common? What I mean is, were they sick?"

"Sick? Everyone on the street has something."

"I mean terminal. That you know of, were they very sick? Cancer? The virus?" When the old vampire had been taking victims, it turned out that nearly every one of them had been terminally ill and would have died soon anyway.

"No. There's no connection other than they were all on the street and they're all gone."

Cavuto grimaced and turned away. He started riffling through the clothing, tossing it around as if looking for a lost sock.

"Look, Father, can you make us a list of the people these clothes belong to. And add anything you can remember about them. Then I can start looking for them in the hospitals and jail."

"I only know street names."

"That's okay. Do your best. Anything you can remember."

Rivera handed him a card. "Call me directly if anything else comes up, would you? Unless there's something in progress, calling the uniforms will just put unnecessary steps in the investigation."

"Sure, sure," said Father Jaime, pocketing the card. "What do you think is going on?"

Rivera looked at his partner, who didn't look up from a dusty pair of shoes he was examining.

"I'm sure there's some explanation. I don't know of any citywide relocation of the homeless, but it's happened before. They don't always tell us."

Father Jaime looked at Rivera with those priest's eyes, those guilt-shooting eyes that Rivera always imagined were on the other side of the confessional. "Inspector, we serve four to five hundred breakfasts a day here."

"I know, Father. You do great work."

"We served a hundred and ten today. That's it. Those in line now will be it for today."

"We'll do our best, Father."

They moved back through the dining room without looking anyone in the eye. Back in the car, Cavuto said, "Those clothes were shredded by claws."

"I know."

"They're not just hunting the sick."

"No," Rivera said. "They're taking anyone on the street. I'm guessing anyone who gets caught out alone."

"Some of those people in the cafeteria saw something. I could tell. We should come back and talk to some of them when the priest and his volunteers aren't around."

"No need, really, is there?" Rivera was scratching out numbers on his notepad.

"They'll talk to the paper," Cavuto said, pulling in behind a cable car on Powell Street, then sighing and resolving himself to move at nineteenth-century speed for a few blocks as they made their way up Nob Hill.

"Well, first it will be covered as amusing stuff that crazy street people say, then someone is going to notice the bloody clothes and it's all going to come out." Rivera added another figure, then scribbled something with a flourish.

"It doesn't have to come back to us," Cavuto said hopefully. "I mean, it's not really our fault."

"Doesn't matter if we get blamed," said Rivera. "It's our responsibility."

"So what are you saying?"

"I'm saying that we're going to be defending the City against a horde of vampire cats."

"Now that you said it, it's real." Cavuto was whining a little.

I'm going to call that Wong kid and see if he has my UV jacket done."

"Just like that?"

"Yeah," Rivera said. "If you go by Father Jaime's example, they've eaten about three-quarters of the Tenderloin's homeless in, let's call it a week. If you figure maybe three thousand street people in the City, you're talking about twenty-two hundred dead already. Someone's going to notice."

"That's what you were calculating?"

"No, I was trying to figure out if we had enough money to open the bookstore."

That had been the plan. Early retirement, then sell rare books out of a quaint little shop on Russian Hill. Learn to golf.

"We don't," Rivera said. He started to dial Foo Dog when his phone chirped, a sound it hadn't made before.

"The fuck was that?" asked Cavuto.

"Text message," said Rivera.

"You know how to text?"

"No. We're going to Chinatown."

"A little early for eggrolls, isn't it?"

"The message is from Troy Lee."

"The Chinese kid from the Safeway crew? I don't want to deal with those guys."

"It's one word."

"Don't tell me."

"CATS."

"Did I not ask you not to tell me?"

"The basketball court off Washington," Rivera said.

"Have that Wong kid make me one of those sunlight jackets. Fifty long."

"You get that many lights on you they'll have you flying over stadiums playing Goodyear ads on your sides."

Unlikely Knights

THE EMPEROR

They called it Wine Country. What it was, in fact, was
an area south of Market Street, adjacent to the Tenderloin, where liquor stores sold a high volume, yet small
variety, of fortified wines like Thunderbird, Richard's
Wild Irish Rose, and MD 20-20 (known in the wine world
as Mad Dog, for the propensity of its drinkers to uri-
nate publicly and turn around three times before passing
out on the sidewalk). While Wine Country was technically the SOMA, or the "fashionable" *South of Market
Street* neighborhood, it had yet to draw the young professional crowd that sprayed everything with a shiny coat
of latte and money, as had its waterfront neighbor. No,
Wine Country consisted mainly of run-down apartments,
sleazy residence hotels, deeply skeezy porn theaters, and
old industrial buildings, which now housed mini-storage

units. Oh, and a huge Federal Building that looked like it was being molested by a giant steel pterodactyl, but evidently that was just the government trying to get away from their standard bomb shelter architecture to something more aesthetically appealing, especially if you liked Godzilla porn.

It was in the shadow of that architectural abomination that the Emperor had taken his search for the alpha vampire cat. He and the men didn't spend much time in Wine Country, as he had lost a decade in a bottle somewhere and had since forsworn the grape. But it was his city, and he knew it like the cat-scratch scars on Bummer's muzzle.

"Steadfast, gents, steadfast," said the Emperor, throwing his shoulder against a Dumpster behind a hundred-year-old brick building. Bummer and Lazarus had commenced low, rumbling growls since they'd come into the alley, as if there were tiny semi-trucks idling in their chests. They were close.

The Dumpster rolled aside on rusty wheels, revealing a basement window with a sheet of plywood loosely fitted into it. The building had once housed a brewery, but had long since been refitted for storage, except for the basement, half of which had been bricked off from the inside. But this window had been forgotten, and it led to an underground chamber completely unknown to the police, where William, and other people who succumbed to the Wine Country's charms, would seek shelter from the rain or the cold. Of course, you had to be drunk to think it was a good place to stay. Except for the spot by the window, the basement was completely dark, as well as damp, rat infested, and reeking of urine.

As he pulled away the plywood, the Emperor heard a high sizzling sound, and the smell of burning hair came streaming out the window. Bummer barked. The Emperor turned away and coughed, fanned the smoke away from his face, and then peered into the basement. All over the visible parts of the floor, cat cadavers were smoldering, burning, and reducing to ash as the sun hit them. There were scores of them, and those were just the ones the Emperor could see from the window light.

"This appears to be the place, gents," he said, patting Lazarus's side.

Bummer snorted, tossed his head, and ruffed three times fast, which translated to, "I thought I would enjoy the smell of burning cats more, but strangely, no."

The Emperor got on his hands and knees, then backed through the window. His overcoat caught on the window sill and actually helped him in lowering his great bulk to the floor.

Lazarus stuck his head in the window and whimpered, which translated to, "I'm a little uneasy about you being in there by yourself." He measured the distance from the window to the basement floor and pranced, preparing himself to leap into the abyss.

"No, you stay, good Lazarus," said the Emperor. "I fear

I wouldn't be able to lift you out once you are down here."

With the ashes of burned cats crunching under his shoes the Emperor made his way across the room until he reached the end of the direct light that lay across the floor like a dingy gray carpet. To move farther he'd have to step on the bodies of the sleeping—well, dead—cats, as even in the shadows, he could see that the floor was covered with feline corpses. The Emperor shuddered and fought the urge to bolt to the window.

He was not a particularly brave man, but had an overly developed sense of duty to his city, and putting himself in harm's way to protect her was something he was compelled to do, despite the acute case of the willies that was crawling up his spine like an enormous centipede.

"There must be another entrance," the Emperor said, more to calm himself than to actually impart information. "Perhaps not large enough for a man, or I would have known."

He tentatively nudged a dead cat aside with his toe, cringing as he did it. The vision of the vampire cats engulfing the samurai swordsman filled his head and he had to shake it off before taking another step.

"A flashlight might have been a good idea," he said. He didn't have a flashlight, however. What he had were five books of matches and a cheap, serrated-edged chef's knife that he'd found in a trash can. This would be the weapon he'd use to dispatch the vampire cat, Chet. In his younger, naïve days, last month, he'd carried a wooden sword, thinking to stake the vampires in the heart, movie style, but he'd seen the old vampire nearly torn apart by explosions, gunfire, and spear guns by the Animals when they'd destroyed his yacht, and none of it seemed as effective as had the little swordsman he'd seen in the SOMA. Still, a flashlight would have been nice. He lit a match and held it before him as he moved into the dark, working his foot between cat bodies with each step. When the match burned his fingers, he lit another.

Bummer barked, the sharp report echoed through the basement. The Emperor turned and realized that he'd somehow made his way around a corner and the window was no longer visible. He reached inside his great overcoat and felt for the handle of the chef's knife, which was stuck in his belt at the small of his back. He pushed on, moving into another room, a large one as far as he could tell, but still, to the edge of the match light, the bodies of cats littered the floor, most of them lying on their sides as if they'd just dropped over, or in awkward piles, as if they'd been in the middle playing, or fighting, or mating when something suddenly switched them off like a light switch.

Another distant bark from Bummer, then a deeper one from Lazarus. "I'm fine, men, I'll be finished with this and back out in no time."

Well into his third book of matches, the Emperor saw a steel door, partly ajar. He made his way to it; the dead cats thinned out and then there was a bit of a clearing in the carnage, although only for a foot or two, as if a path had been cleared, but a narrow one. He stood and caught his breath.

He heard men's voices, but coming from back by the window, amid them more barking and now snarling from the men.

"I'm in here!" the Emperor called. "I'm in here. The men are with me!"

Then a distant voice. "Mo-fuckas need to cover this up. The City see it they brick this bitch up, then where we go when it rain?"

There was a thump, then a grating noise, a rusty creaking, and the Emperor realized it was the sound of the plywood being fit back into the window and the heavy Dumpster pushed into place before it.

"Block them wheels," said the voice.

"I'm here! I'm here!" called the Emperor. He gritted his teeth, preparing to run across the deep carpet of cat corpses to the window, but he hesitated, the match burned his fingers, and darkness fell upon him.

THE ANIMALS

"I'm pretty sure it's the Apocalypse," said Clint, not even looking up from his red-letter King James Bible.

The Animals were spread out in various positions around the basketball court, playing HORSE. Clint, Troy Lee, and Drew sat with their backs to the chain-link fence.

Troy Lee was trying to read over Clint's shoulder, Drew was packing pot into the bowl of a purple carbon-fiber sports bong.

Cavuto and Rivera made their way around the outside of the court.

"What's up my niggas!" came a scratchy, wizened voice—totally out of place for the surroundings—like someone smacking a fiery fart out of a tiny dragon with a badminton racket.

Rivera stopped and turned toward a small figure who stood at the foul line dressed in enormous sneakers and an Oakland Raiders hoody big enough for a pro offensive tackle. Except for the cat-rim glasses, it looked like Gangsta Yoda, only not so green.

"That's Troy Lee's grandma," said the tall kid, Jeff. "You have to give her a pound or she's going to keep saying it."

Indeed, she had a fist in the air, waiting for a pound.

"You go ahead," said Cavuto. "You're ethnic."

Rivera made his way to the tiny woman and despite feeling completely embarrassed about it, bumped fists with her.

"Troot," said Grandma.

"Truth," said Rivera. He looked to Lash, who had been the ad hoc leader of the Animals after Tommy Flood was turned vampire. "You okay with this?"

Lash shrugged. "What are you gonna do? Besides, it's prolly the Apocalypse. No time to roll all politically correct up in this bitch when the world is ending."

"It's not the Apocalypse," said Cavuto. "It's definitely not the Apocalypse."

"I'm pretty sure it is," said Troy Lee, looking over Clint's shoulder at Revelation.

They all gathered around the seated Animals. Rivera took out his notebook, then shrugged and put it back in his pocket. This wasn't going to be in any report.

Drew sparked up the bong, bubbled a long hit, then handed it to Barry, the balding scuba diver, who inhaled the extra off the top.

"We're cops, you know?" said Cavuto, not sounding that sure of it himself.

Drew shrugged and exhaled a skunky blast. "S'okay, it's medical."

"What medical? You have a card? What's your condition?"

Drew produced a blue card from his shirt pocket and held it up. "I'm anxious."

"That's not a condition," said Cavuto, snapping the card out of Drew's hand. "And this is a library card."

"Reading makes him anxious," said Lash.

"It's a condition," said Jeff, trying to look somber.

"It's for arthritis," said Troy Lee.

"He doesn't have arthritis. It's not a thing." Cavuto was pulling handcuffs out of the pouch on his belt.

"She does," said Troy Lee, pointing to his grandmother.

The old woman grinned, held up her card, flashed an

arthritic "West Coast" gang sign, and said, "What's up, my nigga?"

"I'm not giving her a pound," said Cavuto.

"She's like ninety. You must. It is our way," said Troy Lee in his mysterious ancient Chinese secret voice. From his sitting position, he bowed a little at the end for effect.

Cavuto had to bend down to give the old woman a pound. "You know you'll never escape the killer cats in those giant shoes," he said.

"She doesn't understand," said Barry.

"No *comprende* English," said Gustavo.

"Cats?" said Rivera. "Your message."

"Yeah, you said to call if anything weird happened," said Troy Lee.

"Actually, we said not to call us," said Cavuto.

"Really? Whatever. Anyway, the Emperor came banging on the store windows last night all freaked out about vampire cats."

"Did you see them?"

"Yeah, there were shitloads. And I don't know how you're going to take them down. That's why it's pretty obvious that it's the Apocalypse."

Clint, the born-again, now looked up. "I figure that the number of the beast is a number of how many. So, there were like six hundred sixty-six at least."

"Although it was hard to count," said Drew. "They were in a cloud."

Rivera looked to Troy Lee for explanation.

"It was like they'd all gone to vapor, like we saw the old vampire trying to do that night we blew up his yacht. Except they were all merged into one, big-ass vampire cloud."

"Yeah, it started coming into the store, even with the door locked," said Jeff, now at the foul line, sinking his fourth swish in a row.

"How'd you stop it?" Cavuto asked.

"Wet towel under the door," said Barry. "It's what you do when you're smoking weed in a hotel and you don't want everyone calling security. You're always supposed to have a towel. I read about it in a guide for hitchhiking through the galaxy."

"Skills," said Drew, a little glassy-eyed now.

"But, if not for the wet towel, it was the Apocalypse," said Troy Lee. "Clint is looking in the book of Revelation for the part about the towel now."

"I hope it's like Thunder Dome Apocalypse," said Jeff. "Not zombies trying to eat your brain Apocalypse."

"I'm pretty sure it's going to be, city-wiped-out-by-vampire-cats Apocalypse," said Barry. "You know, just going on what we know."

"It's not the Apocalypse," said Cavuto.

"So, what happened?" Rivera asked. "The cloud just went away?"

"Yeah, it sort of distilled to a big herd of cats and they went running every which way. But what do we do tonight if it comes back? The Emperor led it right to us."

"Where is the Emperor?"

"He went off this morning with his dogs. Said he thought he knew where the prime vampire cat might be and that he and *the men* would dispatch it and save his city."

"And you let him?"

"He's the Emperor, Inspector. You can't tell him shit."

Rivera looked at Cavuto. "Call dispatch to post a bulletin to call us if anyone sees the Emperor."

"We're not getting off work today, are we?" said Cavuto.

"Take an Apocalypse day," said Barry. "Woo-hoo! Apocalypse day!"

Troy Lee's grandma fired off a barrage of Cantonese to her grandson, who replied with the same. The old woman shrugged and looked up at Cavuto and Rivera and spoke for about thirty seconds, then went and took the ball from Jeff, then shot a complete air ball, at which everyone cheered.

"What? What?" said Cavuto.

"She wanted to know what Barry was woo-hooing about, so I told her."

"What did she say?"

"She said no big deal. They had vampire cats in Beijing when she was a girl. She said their shit is weak."

"She said that?"

"The idiom is different, but basically, yeah."

"Oh good," said Cavuto, "I feel better."

"We need to find the Emperor," Rivera said.

Cavuto pulled the car keys out of his jacket. "And pick up our Apocalypse jackets."

"What about us?" asked Lash.

Rivera didn't even look back when he said, "You guys have more experience fighting vampires than anyone on the planet . . ."

"We do, don't we?" said Troy Lee.

"Oh, we are so fucked," said Lash.

"That's sad," said Drew, repacking the bowl of the bong. "Really sad."

THE EMPEROR

Darkness. He waited a moment, listening to his pulse beat in his ears before striking another match. "Courage," he whispered to himself, a mantra, an affirmation, a sound to keep him from jumping out of his own skin at every creak or rustle in the dark. He lit the match, held it aloft.

He pulled at the big steel door, throwing his weight, and it moved a few inches. Perhaps this was the other way out. It was clear that all these cats hadn't come in through the window, not with the plywood blocking it. He elbowed the door aside, feeling the resistance of a drift of dormant vampire cats piled up against it. When the opening was wide enough to squeeze through, he put his shoulder inside, then paused as the match went out from the movement.

He was inside, and the floor seemed clear at his feet, although it felt as if he was standing on powder. As he lit the next match he hoped to see a stairway, a hallway, perhaps another boarded-up window, but in fact what he saw was that he was in a small storeroom fitted with wide metal shelves. The floor was indeed covered with a thick layer of dust, and among it, rumpled clothing. Ragged overcoats, jeans, and work boots, but also brightly colored satin garments, hot pants, and halter tops, tall platform shoes in fluorescent colors, dingy under the dust and darkness.

These had been people. Homeless people and hookers. The fiends had actually dragged people down here and fed on them—*sucked them to dust,* as the little Goth girl had termed it. But how? No matter how strong or ravenous, the cats were still just housecats before they had turned. And they hadn't seemed cooperative. He couldn't imagine a pack of twenty vampire cats dragging a fully grown person down here. It didn't make sense.

The match burned his finger and he tossed it aside, then pulled the knife from his belt before lighting the next. When the next match flared, he saw something on one of the high shelves at the far side of the room. Something quite a bit larger than a housecat. Perhaps it was one of their victims who had survived.

He adjusted his grip on the knife and moved forward, trying not to cringe as the dusty clothing clung to his feet and ankles.

No, not a cat. At least not a housecat. But it had fur. And a tail. But it was the size of an eight-year-old child, and it was snuggled up against something even larger. The Emperor raised the knife and stepped forward, then stopped.

"Well, you don't see that every day," he said.

The cat thing was spooning the naked form of Tommy Flood.

Being the Chronicles of Abby Normal, Pathetic Failure to All Creatures Great and Small

I have failed as a minion, a girlfriend, and a human being in general, and that doesn't even count Biology 102, which I am still totally failing despite actually going to class twice.

The Countess has been gone for like a week, and no one has seen her or the vampyre Flood. I've gone looking for them, mainly when I'm supposed to be at school. I don't even know where to look. I kind of walk around asking people if they've seen a totally hawt redhead and they either hurry away really fast or, in the case of one guy, who I suspect was a pimp, offered me a thousand dollars to bring her to him if I found her. Then he offered me a job, because he said, "Johns go for that skinny Lolita shit."

And I was all, "Oh, that's very flattering, sir. Thank you. Once I find my friend I will bring her back and we'll both be happy to service the disgusting choads of creepy strangers and hand you all of our money along with any self-worth we might have left."

And he was all, "You do that, little momma. You do that."

Which is just another reason that I need to find the Countess and beg her forgiveness, because my new phone has video and I can't wait to post a clip on my blog of Jody scattering bloody pimp parts all over the Tenderloin. (The Countess has lectured me about respecting myself and how a woman must never sacrifice her dignity to a man unless he gives her jewelry or is a smoking hottie and has a job, so I think there will at least be broken bones and a beating of many colors.)

Evidently there's a shortage of hookers and homeless people in the City, it was on the *Chronicle*'s Web site. They reported it like it was a good thing, VICE ARRESTS DOWN or something, and another article about homeless shelters having plenty of room for the first time, ever. OMFG! They're kitty treats, you douche nozzles! That's why I refused to be on the school paper. Journalists are oblivious to the obvious and they won't even let you say fuck.

'Kayso, when I finally got back to the love lair, the windows were all boarded up with plywood and Foo and Jared had like alphabetized all of the rats and had them stacked up and labeled and whatnot. So, I, like, ran into Foo's arms and kissed him a good long time, then I looked around and I was all:

"They're dead. Our loft is full of dead rats."

And Jared is all, "Not dead. Undead."

So to Foo I'm all, " 'Splain, *s'il vous plaît*."

And Foo's like, "It's amazing, Abby. You just have to inject them with a little vampyre blood and it turns them, but not until you kill them. It took us a while to figure that out."

"So you killed all these rats?"

"I did," goes Jared. "It made me sad, but I'm okay with it now. Science."

"How?"

And Foo says, "Potassium chloride."

At the exact same time Jared says, "With a hammer."

And Jared gets all big scared anime eyes and is like, "Yeah, potassium chloride. That's what I meant."

And I'm all, "You have been killing and vamping rats while the Countess and Tommy are lost and the whole city is papered with missing cat flyers, and like Chet and his minions are eating all the homeless and probably the hookers?"

And they were like, "Well—yeah."

"And I had to work and go to class," says Foo. "And polish my car."

And Jared's all, "And we've been making sunlight jackets for those two cops, which takes like a million little wires." And he, like, points to our coffee table, which is the only surface that doesn't have cages full of dead rats, and there's not even jackets there, just, like, jacket-shaped nets of wire with little glass beads all over them.

And I'm all, "Cops can't wear those. They look like robot lingerie."

And Jared is all, *"Très* cool, *non?"*

"No!" I go. "And do not further endorken the French language by wrapping your disgusting penis port around it. You'll ruin the whole language before I even learn enough to express my deep despair and dark desires *en français,* you rat smasher."

'Kay, I know that was a little harsh, but I was angry, and in my defense, I was grinding Foo's leg a little when I said "dark desires," so I said it with love.

Foo's all, "We didn't have time to actually get jackets. They need to be leather and they're expensive."

So it's clear that despite his mad ninja science skills, even my beloved Foo cannot be left without female supervision. But he *has* been going home lately, and his parents are a bad influence on him.

So I'm like, "I got this. I'll go see Lily."

Lily is my backup BFF. She used to be my BFF, but at the same time I met Lord Flood and the Countess, Lily got a book in the mail at her work, which is Asher's Secondhand, and it convinced her that she is Death, so I'm all, "Whatever, ho."

And she was all, "Free to live my own nightmare, skank."

So we were cool.

'Kayso, I took the 45 bus from the dead-ratted love lair to North Beach. Walking through Chinatown sort of creeps me out 'cause of all the Chinese grandmothers on the street, who I'm pretty sure are talking about me because they think I have ruined Foo with my Gothy-Anglo charms. Also, I get mad dim sum cravings for which I should someday seek treatment, or, like, snacks.

'Kayso, at Asher's, Lily comes out from behind the counter and gives me a hug and a big kiss on my forehead (because she is taller than me in addition to having surplus boobage).

And I'm like, "There's a big violet lip print on my forehead, huh?"

And Lily goes, "Kiss of Death—get used to it, beyotch—matches your hair tips, *très* cute."

So I'm all, " 'Kay." It wasn't really the kiss of Death, but it did match my tips. Then I was all, "Lils, I need men's leather jackets in these sizes." I gave her the note Foo wrote out with the sizes and cut and whatnot.

And she was all, "WTF, Abs? Fifty long? You buying a jacket for an orca?"

"Ginormous gay cop. You got it?"

"Yeah. You wanna smoke a clove?"

And I'm all, "Do you have enough violet lipstick?" Because smoking is, like, the worst for your lipstick and it did match my hair.

And she's all, "Bitch, please." Meaning, *"Do I ever not have enough makeup?"* Which is true, because Lily carries a PVC ROBOT PIRATES messenger bag you could hide a small kid in, only she carries beauty products.

So I was all, " 'Kay."

So Lily and I went out the back door and stared at the Dumpster like it was the very abyss of our despair while we smoked. And I'm just getting ready to tell her about the love lair, and Foo, and vampyre kitties and all, because I've sort of been in boyfriend mode, so, like, out of contact, which Lily totally gets.

And Lil's like, "So, the big gay cop have a Hispanic partner?"

And I'm like, "Rivera and Cavuto. Crusty day dwellers, but Rivera kind of has a secret-agent vibe. You know them?"

And Lily is all, "Yeah, they were here yesterday. Rivera wears expensive suits. Smells good, too. I'd do him."

And I'm like gagging. "Lils, he's like a thousand years old, and a cop. The Motherbot was getting squishy over him. OMG! You're disgusting!"

"Shut up, I'm not saying I'd do him normal. I mean like zombie Apocalypse trapped in the mall right before we have to shoot each other to keep them from eating our brains and turning us to the undead—then I'd do him."

So I'm all, "Oh sure, then." To make her feel better, because she doesn't have a BF and often oversluts to compensate, but I still thought it was disgusting. But to change the subject, I was all, "So what did they want?"

"They were asking all kinds of irrelevant bullshit. Had I seen any strange cats, did I see the Emperor, or some redhead."

And I'm all, *Fucksocks! Fucksocks! Fucksocks!* inside. But on the outside I'm all chill and I'm like, "So, you like didn't know anything, right?"

"No, Asher said a hot redhead came into the store the other night, and then I was on the cable car last night, going down to Max's Deli for a sammy, and I think I saw her going into the Fairmont Hotel. Like a crazy cape of long red curls I would slaughter puppies for."

"Red leather jacket?"

"Sweet red leather jacket."

"You didn't tell them, did you?"

And Lil's all, "Well, yeah."

And I was all, "You traitorous whore!" And I punched her in the shoulder.

In my defense, you're supposed to tell your ex-BFF when you get fresh ink, so the screaming was completely over the top. I had no way of knowing that she had a new tattoo on that shoulder, so her punching me in the boob was totally uncalled for.

So, I'm ouching *très* loud and this Russian lady from upstairs peeks her head out the window and she's all, "Quiet please, is sounding like burning bear out there."

'Kayso, Lils and I start to laugh and say, "Like bear," over and over again until the Russian lady slams the window shut, like bear.

Then it comes back to me and I'm all, "Lils, I have to get those jackets and get to the Fairmont. I have to save the Countess."

And Lily is like, " 'Kay," not even asking details, which is why I love her—she is so nihilist it's, like, not funny.

'Kayso, I take the jackets and catch a cab to the Fairmont, which totally pisses off the cabbie because it's only like six blocks, but when I get to the hotel I'm all, "Fucksocks!" because I'm too late.

JODY

Falling asleep was one of the things Jody missed about being human. She missed the satisfied, tired feeling of falling into bed and drifting off in a dreamy twilight sea of dreams. In fact, since she'd turned, unless she'd just gone too long without feeding, she never even felt tired. On most mornings, unless she and Tommy had been making love, and they went out in each other's arms, she just found a relatively comfortable position and waited for the sun to rise and put her out. Maybe a flutter of an eyelid, lasting a second, then off like a light.

The closest thing to a dream state she'd experienced as a vampire was when she'd gone to mist inside the bronze statue, and even then, the door into dreamland slammed shut at dawn. The constant alertness of being a vampire was, well, it was a bit irritating. Especially since she'd been searching the City for Tommy for a week, pushing her jumped-up senses to their limits, and had to return to the hotel every morning with nothing. Apparently, Tommy had limped down an alley and vanished. She'd checked ev-

eryplace in the City that she'd ever taken him, every place
he'd ever been, as far as she knew, and still there was no
evidence of his having been there. She'd hoped she would
have some special vampire "sixth sense" to help her find
him, like the old vampire who had turned her seemed to
have had, but no.

Now, she was returning to her room at the Fairmont
for the seventh morning. And for the seventh morning she
would put out the "Do Not Disturb" signs, lock the door,
put on her sweats, drink a pouch of the blood she kept
locked in a mini-cooler, brush her teeth, then crawl under
the bed and go over a mental map of the City until dawn
put her out. (Since she was technically dead at dawn, sleeping *on top* of a comfortable mattress was a dangerous luxury, and by climbing under the bed she put one more layer
between her and sunlight, should a nosy maid somehow
find a way into her room.)

Part of her new pre-dawn ritual had been returning to the
hotel a little later each morning; like the skydiver who will
let himself fall closer and closer to earth before pulling the
ripcord to boost the adrenaline rush just a little more. The
last two mornings she'd just been entering the hotel when
the alarm watch she wore, which was set to go off ten minutes before sunrise on any given day, based on an electronic
almanac, had started beeping. She'd bought one for Tommy,
too, and wondered if he was still wearing his. As she strode
down California Street, she tried to remember if he'd been
wearing it when they cut him out of the bronze shell.

Two blocks from the Fairmont her alarm watch went off and she couldn't help but smile a little at the thrill. She picked up her pace, figuring that she'd still be safely inside her room with time to spare before sunup, but she might have to forgo the sweats and the blood snack.

As she came up the steps into the lobby she smelled cigar, and Aramis cologne, and the combination sent an electric chill of alarm up her spine before she could identify the danger. Cops. Rivera and Cavuto. Rivera smelled of Aramis, Cavuto of cigars. She stopped, her boot heels skidding a little on the marble steps.

There they were, both at the front desk, but a bellman was leading them to the elevator. He was taking them to her room.

How? she thought. *Doesn't matter.* It was getting light. She checked her watch: three minutes to find shelter. She backed away from the door, out onto the sidewalk, then began to run.

Normally she would have paced herself so someone didn't notice the redhead in boots and jeans running faster than an Olympic sprinter, but they'd just have to tell their friends and not be believed. She needed cover, now.

She was a block and a half down Mason Street when she came to an alley. She'd survived her first night as a vampire under a Dumpster. Maybe she could survive the day inside one. But there was someone down there, the kitchen crew of a restaurant, outside smoking. On she ran.

No alleys in the next two blocks, then a narrow space between buildings. Maybe she could shimmy down there and crawl in a basement window. She crawled on a narrow, plywood gate and had one foot down before a pit bull came storming down the corridor. She leapt out onto the sidewalk and started running again. What kind of psychopath uses a two-foot-wide space between buildings as a dog run? There should be laws.

This was Nob Hill, all open, with wide boulevard streets, a once-grand neighborhood now made incredibly irritating to a vampire in need of shelter. She rounded the corner at Jackson Street, snapping a heel off her right boot as she did. She should have worn sneakers, she knew, but wearing the high, expensive leather boots made her feel a little like a superhero. It turned out that turning your ankle hurts like hell, even if you're a superhero.

She was up on her toes now, running, limping toward Jackson Square, the oldest neighborhood in San Francisco that had survived the great quake and fire of 1906. There were all kinds of little cubbyholes and basement shops in the old brick buildings down there. One building even had the ribs of a sailing ship in its basement, a remnant built over when the Gold Rush left so many ships abandoned at the waterfront that the City literally expanded over them.

One minute. The shadow of the Transamerica Pyramid was lying long across the neighborhood ahead like the needle of a deadly sundial. Jody did a final kick-sprint, snapping off her other boot heel as she did. She scanned the streets ahead for windows, doors, trying to sense movement inside, looking for stillness, privacy.

There! On the left, a door below street level, the staircase hidden by a wrought-iron railing covered in jasmine. *Ten more steps and I'm there,* she thought. She saw herself jumping the rail, shouldering through the door, and diving under the first thing that would shelter her from the light.

She took the final three steps and leapt just as the sun broke the horizon. She went limp in the air, fell to the sidewalk, short of the stairwell, and skidded on her shoulder and face. As her eyes fluttered, the last thing she saw were a pair of orange socks right in front of her, then she went out and began to smolder in the sunlight.

Alchemy

The Chinese herb shop smelled like licorice and dried monkey butt. The Animals were piled into the narrow aisle between counters, trying to hide behind Troy Lee's grandmother and failing spectacularly. Behind a glass case, the shopkeeper looked older and more spooky than Grandma Lee, which none of them thought possible until now. It was like he'd been carved from an apple, then left on the windowsill to dry for a hundred years.

The walls of the shop were lined, floor to ceiling, with little drawers of dark wood, each with a small bronze frame and a white card with Chinese characters written on it. The old man stood behind glass cases that held all manner of desiccated plant and animal bits, from whole sea horses and tiny birds, to shark parts and scorpion tails, to odd spiky bits that looked like they'd been flown in from another planet.

"What's that?" Drew asked Troy Lee from under a veil of stringy blond hair. He pointed to a wrinkled black thing.

Troy Lee said something in Cantonese to Grandma, who said something to the shopkeeper, who barked something back.

"Bear penis," said Troy Lee.

"Should we score some?" asked Drew.

"For what?" asked Troy.

"An emergency," said Drew.

"Sure, okay," said Troy Lee, then he said something to Grandma in Cantonese. There was an exchange with the shopkeeper, after which Troy said, "How much do you want? It's fifty bucks a gram."

"Whoa," said Barry. "That's expensive."

"He says it's the best dried bear penis you can buy," said Troy Lee.

"Okay," said Drew. "A gram."

Troy passed the order through Grandma to the shopkeeper. He snipped a tip off a bear penis, weighed it, and placed it on the pile of herbs in the sheet of paper he had laid on the counter for Drew. Grandma's paper was much larger, and the shopkeeper had been tottering around the shop for half an hour gathering the ingredients. At one point when the old man was up on the top of the ladder at the far back corner of the shop, the Animals had leapt the counter and laced their arms together as a human rescue net, which served only to scare the bejeezus out of the shopkeeper and set Grandma off in a tirade of Cantonese scolding, to which they all responded like dogs, paying her rapt attention and tilting their heads as if they actually had some idea of what the fuck she was talking about.

Lately the Animals had been all about saving lives. Most of the time, guys their age would be fairly convinced of their immortality, or at least oblivious of their mortality, but since being murdered by a blue hooker turned vampire, then resurrected as vampires, then restored to living by Foo Dog's genetic alchemy, they had been feeling what they could only describe as Jesusy.

"I'm feeling extra Jesusy," said Jeff, the tall jock.

"I always feel extra Jesusy," said Clint, who always did.

"Yeah, extra Jesusy, bitches! Let's go save some motherfuckers!" Lash had shouted, which had sort of embarrassed everyone a little, since they had been sitting around a table in Starbucks at the time, discussing the attack of the cat cloud and the information they'd exchanged with the two homicide cops. "It's up to us," Lash added softly, sort of slinking into his hoody and putting on his shades.

Now they watched as the old shopkeeper folded up Grandma Lee's bundle of ingredients and tucked in the paper so it was as tight as a toothpick spliff, then flipped the package over and wrote some Chinese characters on the back with a carpenter's pencil.

"What's it say?" Barry asked Troy Lee.

"It says, 'vampire cat remedy.'"

"No shit?"

"Yeah. Then there's a bunch of warnings about side ef-fects."

An hour later they were sitting around the Lee kitchen table, waiting for the big twenty-quart soup pot on the stove to come to a boil.

Grandma Lee rose from her chair and tottered over to the stove with her package of herbs. Troy Lee joined her, helped her unwrap the package, and held the paper away from the burner as she scooped handfuls of herbs and ani-mal parts into the boiling water. Foul and magical fumes bubbled out of the kettle, like the flatulence of dragons on a demon-only diet.

"This really going to work, Grandma?" Troy Lee asked in Cantonese.

"Oh yeah. We used it when I was a girl in China and some vampire cats invaded the city."

"And they still have the recipe in a shop down on Stock-ton Street?"

"It's a good recipe." She scooped the last of the package into the water.

"How do you use this stuff, anyway?"

"With firecrackers."

"It's wet, how are you going to use firecrackers?"

"I don't know how, I just like firecrackers."

The Animals covered their noses and started filing out of the kitchen. "That smells like fermented skunk ass," said Jeff.

Grandma said something in Cantonese, followed by

"My bitches," pronounced in frighteningly accentless English.

"What? What'd she say?" asked Jeff.

"She says, 'That's how you know it's a good recipe, gents,'" said Troy Lee.

THE EMPEROR

A dark basement. A thousand sleeping vampire cats. One formerly human vampire. One huge, shaved vampire-cat hybrid. Five matches left. No way out. A half hour, maybe less, until sundown.

The Emperor was not a man to use profanity, but after he assessed his situation and burned his fingers with his fourth to last match, he said, "Well, this blows."

There was no helping it, sometimes a man, even a brave and noble man, must speak the harsh truth, and his situation, did, indeed, blow.

He'd tried everything he could think of to escape the basement, from building a stairway to the window with empty fifty-five-gallon drums, to screaming for help like a man on fire, but even on a platform of oil drums he couldn't find the leverage or the strength to move the Dumpster away from the window.

He could hear Bummer and Lazarus whimpering outside in the alley.

All the other windows had been bricked up, all the steel fire doors were bolted, and, of course, the elevators and

cables were long gone from the shafts (which he'd discovered after an hour prying the doors open with a metal support bar he'd taken off one of the shelves where Tommy
Flood lay curled up with the Chet-thing). A dusty spray of
twilight filtered down the elevator shaft from somewhere
above, and it was by this that the Emperor ascertained that
there was no way to climb the shaft, and that now it was
dangerously close to sundown, as the light had turned a
dim orange color.

He would fight, oh yes, he would not go down without a battle, but even the magnificently agile little swordsman had gone down to the attacking pounce of cats. What
chance did he stand in the dark with only a metal bar? He'd
already checked the empty oil drums for accelerants, hoping he might burn his enemies before they awakened, but
he'd had no luck. The barrels had had dry goods or something solid in them, and even so, he wasn't sure how he'd
avoid being suffocated by burning cat fumes.

Then, in thinking about how he might escape the
flames, it occurred to him how he might escape. He made
his way back to the storeroom where Chet and Tommy
lay, and lit one of his precious matches to get his bearings.
Yes, there was still a bolt on the door, and in addition there
were enough barrels and shelves to construct a barricade
beyond that. The match went out and he felt his way across
the room until he touched Tommy's back—cold flesh. He
took his ex-friend under the armpits and dragged him off
the shelf and across the room, bumping through the door-

way as he went. He shoved the body to the side and cringed with the crunch it made, falling onto the immobile bodies of dead cats.

Back through dark, feeling around until he found Chet's fur. He felt for what he thought were the front paws, then backed across the room again, the huge shaved vampire cat in tow. Chet was lighter than Tommy had been, but not by much, and the Emperor was winded. He couldn't afford to sit. The ray of light in the elevator shaft had gone deep red.

He heard Bummer let out a ruff beyond the window.

"Run, men, away! Go away from this place. I'll find you in the morning. Go!"

He never raised his voice to the men, even when they were in peril, and he heard Lazarus whimper at his command, but then the sound of Bummer growling while being dragged away by the scruff of his neck. He would get the message after a block or so. The men were safe.

He pulled the metal door shut, then yanked on it until he heard a click. Then spent the second to the last of his matches looking at the simple bolt, and taking a last look around the room, trying to memorize the layout of the barrels and shelves that he would have to move in the dark.

As the match burned out, he heard stirring in the room outside. There was a rack of metal shelves to the right of the door. He grabbed them and overturned them in the doorway. Yes, the door opened out, but what could it hurt. The more he put between himself and the vampire cats, the better. He scooped up armloads of the clothing at his feet and tossed them over the shelves, then backed across the room, throwing everything he touched in front of him, as if he were tunneling out the other side. Finally, he crawled up in the heavy shelf where Tommy and Chet had been and crouched, facing the door. He felt for the handle of the kitchen knife that he'd tucked in his belt at the small of his back, drew it, and held it before him.

There were distinct cat noises—yowls, hisses, and me-ows, coming from the room outside. They were awake, up, and moving. There was a tentative scratch at the door, then a whirr of scratching, like someone had turned a power sander on outside, then it stopped as quickly as it had started and all he could hear was his own breathing.

No. There was movement. The slight rustle of cloth, then a low, trilling purr. And it was coming from inside the door, he was sure of it. The Emperor clamped the knife in his teeth and lit his last match. The room was as he thought it would be, a pile of debris and barrels, but swirling out from under shelving in front of the door was a layer of mist, moving across the floor toward him, undulating in tiny waves that approximated the sound of a purr.

Being the Chronicles of Abby Normal, Who, Befouled by the Wicked Taint of Rat Suck, Must Find Her Own Murderer

How could I have known that my own tragic failure karma would reach out its slimy tentacles and engeeken my heroic Foo beyond the limits of our white-hot romance?

'Kayso, I was major freaked about the cops almost getting the Countess and I needed to unburden on Foo, which I didn't have a chance, 'cause, as soon as I returned to the love lair, I ran into the comfort of Foo's arms, and rode him gently to the floor where I French-kissed him until he kinda gagged in ecstasy. Then he just threw me off him, like I was a gob of *Bubblicious* with all the *licious* chewed out of it.

So he's like, "Not now, Abby. We have a crisis."

"You 'bout to have a crisis, nerdslice"—I go in my most authentic hip-hop 'hood-ho accent—"crisis of my boot heel in your man marbles."

And he totally ignores my hurt feelings and is like, "Jared, get the door! She left the door open!"

So Jared goes all stumbling across the loft to the door, and I'm all, "You're stretching out my boots."

And Jared is all, "Rat fog! Rat fog! Rat fog!"

And I'm all, "Don't call me rat fog, bitch. Who held your hair when you drank that whole bottle of crème de menthe and hurled green for an hour?"

And Foo's like, "Abby, look." All pointing to the little plastic cages on the coffee table, which are kind of empty, then at this steam that's running around the outside of the room and blowing out from under the fridge in the kitchen and whatnot.

And I'm, " 'Splain, *s'il vous plaît*."

And Foo's all, "The rats came awake as vampyres at dusk. And Jared and I were feeding them with the blood that Jody left, by filling their little water bottles. But then when we turned around, the ones we were about to feed were out of their cages. And then we saw some of the cages were still streaming fog out, and the fog was going for the blood bags."

"And they bite," goes Jared.

"Yeah, they bite," goes Foo. And he pulls up his pant leg and shows me where he's been bitten like a dozen times.

And I'm like, "You can't go vamp without me."

And he's all, "No, I'd have to have some of their blood in me, and I was careful not to even get any on me."

Then all of a sudden there's a stream of mist coming

up my boot (I was wearing my red Docs) and a little head starts to appear out of it.

Then Foo snags a tennis racket from, like, out of nowhere and smacks the rat head, which goes flying across the room and hits the wall, trailing like a comet tail of mist.

I know! A tennis racket. WTF?

So I'm all, "Where did you get a tennis racket? Is that a secret thing with you?"

"Missing the point," sings Jared, like I'm totally missing the point. "Hello? We need to be freaked out that they're going to eat us, Nurse Oblivious."

And right then the mist starts taking form again and coming at me, and Foo bats another half-mist rat across the room.

So I'm all, "Okay, good point. What are we going to do?" And I, like, gesture at the button on my sun jacket, because Foo has replaced the battery, which is out of a laptop, and I'm ready to toast some rodents.

And Foo's all, "No, not yet. We have to figure out a way to study them. I need to turn them back to rats. And I have to figure out how this mist is manifesting. I mean, technically, it's not possible."

And I'm like, "You mean it's magic?"

"I mean I've never even heard of anything like it in nature."

"Like magic."

He's like, "There's no such thing as magic."

I'm like, "The Countess said it was magic."

He's like, "My grandmother thinks the microwave is magic."

So I'm all, "It's not?"

And Foo's all, "Magic is just science we don't understand yet."

So I'm all, "Told you."

And he like sighs all heavy and does his exasperated science face at me, and he's like, "We have to get them back in their cages. They can't feed when they are in mist form, so we just need to get them feeding and then we can catch them and put them in the cages."

And I'm like, "Can you believe that Tommy couldn't learn to turn to mist in five weeks and your rats did it, like, overnight? He must be a total tard."

"Or we have genius rats," goes Jared, just as Foo is tennis racketing another rat head off his leg.

So I'm all, "Nope, I don't think that's it. Why don't you just put out a little dish of blood and when they turn solid to drink it you can just tennis racket them into a box?"

"We tried that. They figured it out," goes Foo.

And Jared's all, "See. Genius rats."

Then, to Foo, I'm all, "He has a thing for rats."

Foo's like, "Yeah. I got that. They turn back to solid when exposed to UV light, too, but then they start burning."

Then Jared's like, "Once, when Lucifer 2 got stuck in a drain pipe in our garage, we sucked him out with my dad's Shop Vac."

And Foo's like, "That's it. We can suck them up with a Shop Vac."

So I'm like, "That will just blow the mist out the other side?"

"I can put a really weak UV LED in the barrel of the Shop Vac. Maybe that will be enough to turn them solid without burning them. I'll experiment a little while you're gone."

And I'm all, "Foo, you know it makes me hot when you talk all nerdy, but what do you mean, while I'm gone?"

And he's all, "To get the Shop Vac. We don't have a Shop Vac."

So I look at Jared, all wobbly-assed on my Skankenstein® boots, so he's useless, and I'm like, "Well, I'm not dragging a Shop Vac back on the bus or the F car. Give me your car keys."

And Foo's, like, big "OH NOEZ" mouth and anime eyes, like, "Whaaaaa?"

And I'm like, "Unless you really do love your car more than me."

And he's like, " 'Kay." And hands them over. Which, as it turns out, was really poor judgment on his part.

More L8z. Gotta jet. The tow truck is here.

'Kayso, it turns out that driving an actual car is way harder than it is in Grand Theft Auto: Zombie Hooker Smackdown. Even though there was only, like, minor damage, it could have been totally avoided if you didn't have to shift so much. Everything was good going to get the Shop

Vac, because I only used first and second gear. It was coming home, when I started feeling confident and decided to see if there was a third gear, that it went kind of wrong. Still, all the screaming and crying on Foo's part was kind of over-emo, considering that after the tow truck lowered the Honda, you couldn't even see any damage if you didn't crawl under and look at where the fire hydrant had sort of rearranged a couple of wiry-looking things. And Hondas are totally waterproof for the most part, so no biggie, right?

So, it was like this—

I drive totally ninja all the way to the Ace Hardware in the Castro, but I didn't park because it involves backing up, which is not in my skill set. So I'm, like, double-parked, and I run in and this crusty guy behind the counter is all, "You can't park there."

And I'm like, "Fuck off, butt-munch, I have a guy."

'Kayso, I find my gay Builder Bob guy, and he's all, "Darling, how are you? Fab boots!"

And I'm like, "Thanks, I like your apron. I need a Shop Vac."

And he's all, "What size?"

And I'm like, "It needs to hold about a hundred rats."

And he's all, "Girlfriend, we need to party or go shopping and dish."

And I'm, like, totally flattered, because shopping is a sacred thing to gay guys, but I stay on mission, and I'm all, "In red, if you have it." Because red is the new black and because it will match my Docs.

And so we're going to the Shop Vac section, Bob is like, "So, how's the dark lord?"

And I'm all, "Oh, he's gone. He tried to tear out my jugular vein, so the Countess threw him out the window and it hurt his feelings."

So Bob pats my shoulder and goes, "Men. What are you gonna do? He'll be back. The drill worked okay, though?"

And I'm like, "Oh yeah. We got him out, but he broke both his legs because he was kind of eager."

Then Bob gets all protective Daddy-voice on me and is like, "Safety word, sweetheart. Everyone needs a safety word."

So I'm all, " 'Kay."

Then Builder Bob helps me get my Shop Vac into the car, because it turns out that it takes a vacuum big enough to sleep inside to suck up a hundred rats.

'Kayso, then I drove and that thing happened with the car and the cops came and they were all, "You don't have a license and you're not allowed to drive on the sidewalk, blah, blah, oh my God my insipid cop life is so boring I should just eat my gun, bluster, blah, blah."

And I'm all, "Chill, cops. Call my cop minions Rivera and Cavuto, *s'il vous plaît*. They will confirm that I am on a secret cop mission and should not be fucked with by pathetic day dwellers like yourselves." Then I presented them with Rivera's card, which I whipped out of my messenger bag like it was my badge of badassness.

So cop one, who is in charge because he has the car keys,

is all, "I'll check this out, wait here while I go make radio noises in the car like a humongous loser while my wife is home boning some huge stud-muffin."

I'm paraphrasing.

And in like two minutes, up pulls Rivera and Cavuto, and they have a dog now. His name is Marvin, and he's *très* cute. He's all red, and like a Doberman or something badass, but he totally likes me and his little stubby tail was wagging and I let him drink some of the hydrant water out of my hand, and he did, even though there was plenty of water everywhere, but I guess it tasted like street and whatnot.

So I'm like, "Hey, Rivera, tell these douche waffles that you and the ass bear are my bitches."

And Rivera is all concerned quiet cop voice, "She has mental problems."

"Head injury caused Tourette's syndrome," goes Cavuto.

"We'll handle this from here," goes Rivera.

So I got to ride in the back of the cop car with Marvin and the Shop Vac. It was really crowded and Marvin was all doggie licky love face, so my makeup was *très* fucked up by the time we got to the loft.

So I'm all, "Marvin loves me good long time, cops."

And Cavuto's all, "Figures, he's a cadaver dog."

And I'm all, "Sure, just make up things to make yourself sound cooler."

And Rivera's like, "Out. Tell your boyfriend we need

our jackets ASAP. And after you deliver the message, go home. You're supposed to be at your mother's house."

'Kayso, they abandoned me on the sidewalk with my Shop Vac and drove off. I could see little tears of doggie despair in Marvin's eyes.

So I text Foo that I need help getting the Shop Vac up the stairs and he comes down just as the tow truck pulls up, so all the crying and the screaming happens, and Foo is totally inconsolable, even when I offered him a hand job, which is really the best I could do on the sidewalk with people going by and whatnot, but I was rejected, proving, I think, that he really does love his car more than me.

So it's like, *Oh noez!* And an inky-colored despair of rejection enveloped me like the black tortilla of depression around a pain burrito.

I needed to mope and grieve for my lost innocence, but no. We had to fix the vacuum so it would suck vampy rat fog and turn it into vampy rat chunks. So while Foo wired science stuff into the Shop Vac, I had to get Jared down off the kitchen counter, where he had decided to stand and chuck a major spaz because he hit his rat fog tolerance level.

And Jared's all, "Get them off me! Get them off me!" And he's swinging the tennis racket around like a friggin' windmill, when the rat fog isn't anywhere near him, but running around the edges of the room like a steamy baseboard.

And I'm all, "You must chill, Spunk Monkey, my boots are scratching the counters."

Which Jared takes as his cue to start screaming like a little girl. (When Lily and I were going through our Gothic Lolita fashion phase, which we both abandoned later, me because I'd just gotten my lip ring and I kept dribbling lattes on my lacy parts, and Lily because ruffles made her ass look huge, we used to go to Washington Square Park and practice our horrified little-girl screams, but even without practice, Jared was way better than either of us ever was. I think maybe it's his asthma. Me and Lily could pown him at creepy staring, though.)

Anyway, I was just glad that Jody took his dagger away from him, because someone could have lost an eye if he was still holding on to it when I swept his feet out from under him with the same stainless-steel torchiere lamp that the Countess had used on Tommy. (Although it was kind of bent now.)

And he's all, "Ow, ow, ow."

And I'm all, "Your cross-dressing sissy-man kung-fu is no match for my superior household lighting kung-fu."

And he whines like, "I'm going home. You hurt me. You suck. This sucks. I have to go have family dinner—with my family—and I'm going to school tomorrow so you can just fuck off and die, Abby Normal."

And I'm like, "Fine, give me my boots."

And he's like, "Fine."

And I'm like, "Fine."

And it would have been way better if he could have just stormed out right then, but it took us about a half hour to get my boots off of him, with me sitting in the sink and him on the counter, guarding me with the tennis racket, because it turned out that I have a pretty low tolerance for rat fog trying to bite me, too.

'Kayso, we got my boots off of Jared and he decided to stay and help because it turns out that even a stream of biting rat fog is more fun than family dinner. So Foo had the Shop Vac all scienced up with sunlight LEDs and whatnot and he turns it on and starts sucking in the mist with most awesome suckage. (Gay Builder Bob rocks hardware!) And it's so cool, because we can see the fog go in—then we can hear the thump as the sun LED turns the rats to solid again and they hit the inside of the plastic drum.

And Foo is all yelling over the motor, "We may have to unload and put them in their boxes before we get too many. We don't want to open this and try to deal with a hundred rats."

And I'm all, "Why don't we just leave them in there until sunup and then they'll all be asleep?"

And Foo looks at me, all surprised, and I'm like, "Shut up. I can be smart *and* hawt."

And he's all, " 'Kay," which I don't know whether he meant sarcastically, or that I couldn't be smart, or that I wasn't hawt. But I never found out, because right then the Shop Vac starts making this, *foof-thoop splat* noise, and Jared lets loose with his little-girl scream.

And it turns out that the exhaust of the Shop Vac is blowing vampy rats out the back side, which is the *foof-thoop* noise,

and splattering them against the wall, which is the *splat*.
And with every one, Jared is eeking. So it's like, *Foof-thoop-
splat-eek! Foof-thoop-splat-eek! Foof-thoop-splat-eek!* I know!
It would make a totally cool industrial beat for a dance
groove. But I didn't sample it because there was stuff happening.

And Foo is all, "Pick them up and put them in their
boxes. Seal them with duct tape."

'Cause it turns out that vampy rats are pretty durable,
and after they splat and slide down the wall, they are starting to pull themselves together again and sort of limp away,
but slow enough to catch. But they're still all squishy and
whatnot.

So Jared and I just turn to Foo and give him our best,
"Bitch, please," look.

So Foo's all, "Okay, then, you work the hose."

And I'm all, "Sure, now you want me to work your
hose—"

And he's all, "Abby, please!"

Up until then I thought Foo was the most chill love
ninja in the Bay Area, but it turns out that if his science
gets a little sideways he goes to pieces. So I take the hose
and start doing the rat suck, while Foo finds some rubber
gloves and a spatula to scrape up the splatter pets.

Then Jared gets the idea of shooting the rats right into
their little plastic cages, which, as it turns out, kind of
works after we blast a couple of them through the plastic
and he starts holding the boxes against a pillow he tapes on

the wall. And Foo starts duct taping on the lids before the vamp rats can pull themselves together.

Then I'm all, "You know, if we could use this to shoot tiny dogs at the vamp kitties, we'd be finished with this nonsense in a day or two."

And Foo and Jared both roll their eyes at me like I'm high or something, when they are the ones sealing in mashed rats for freshness. 'Kayso, by, like, midnight, we have all the rats boxed again, and most of them are kind of fixed, but some of them are still pretty fucked up from the flight, and Jared is all, "I'm going home. I have issues."

Which I know probably means that he is going to go home and break the news to Lucifer 2 that they are no longer BFFs because Jared has lost his rodent wood forever due to our night of rat carnage, which is a good thing, I guess.

Then Foo is like, "I have to go, too. I have to meet with my academic advisor in the morning, and I have to prepare, then I have work in the afternoon."

And I'm all, "You can prepare here."

And Foo's like, "I don't think I can." And he looks away.

I was going to tell him that I had decided to become a creature of the night, but they were bailing on me, so I was all, "Fine. You two run along. I'll stay here."

And Foo was like, "Wait until dawn, then give each of them a water bottle of blood. They'll heal. But make sure you tape their cages back up so they can't escape. Blah, blah, biology, science, behavior, science word, science word, blah, blah."

So I kissed him like it was the last time, and went into the bedroom to lie down and wait until dawn, but there was like this huge maze made out of wood on our bed, so I went back out into the living room and chilled with the rats on the futon until dawn. I couldn't sleep anyway, because I was thinking of all the people I was totally going to get revenge on when I was nosferatu, after I found Jody and Tommy and rescued them, of course.

'Kayso, like the Terminator (the liquid one, not the one that was governor), I will rise from the wreckage of my own metallic spooge to conquer all who oppose me. I know what I have to do. When Foo is at work, and Jared is at school, I shall use the blood that is blessed with the dark gift and become nosferatu. So suck it, bitches!

'Kayso, at dawn, when all the rats stopped scrambling around in their little cages, I found one of the syringes that Tommy had gotten from the needle exchange program when he was pretending to be a junky, and I drew blood from the most healthy vamp rat we had. Then I had to decide to drink it or inject it, and after a while, I decided to inject it, which it turns out works just like in the movies and hurts way less than getting your eyebrow pierced.

So then I lay down and waited for the vamping to come on. I thought about Foo, riding the BART all the way back to his parents' house in the Sunset instead of staying with me, and how that was kind of an assbag move on his part.

And I thought of our time together, over six weeks, and how it would be hard on him when I was a superior creature of unspeakable evil and supernatural beauty. And I thought that maybe the Countess and Flood and I might have to live together in a *ménage à trois*, and Foo and Jared might have to be our bug-eating minions, like Renfield in Dracula, except Foo would still have his fly manga hair and I would do him occasionally out of pity.

And I cried a little, over the loss of my humanity and whatnot, because I realized that as soon as I was done saving Tommy and Jody, and enslaving Foo and Jared, I was going to sneak into Mr. Snavely's living room one night—come in as mist under the door—then form into my most awesome alabaster naked badassness and freak him completely the fuck out for failing me in Biology, and that it would be kind of an inhuman thing to do. And as I grieved, I fell into the deep sleep of the undead.

I know. *Très* awesome.

But no! Now I'm awake, and it's still light out, and the vamp rats are still out and I don't have super powers and my evil is still totally speakable. Fucksocks! I forgot, I have to die before I change. I looked all over for that potassium chloride stuff that Foo said they killed the rats with, but all I found was the hammer, and I was all, "I don't think so." So I went up to Market Street and thought I'd throw myself in front of a bus, but then, what if they left my body out in the sun and I burned up? So that was out. So then I was like, "Oh, duh, cut your wrists?" But it hurt like holy fuck, so I only kind of cut one wrist a little bit, and I bled for like a half hour and I wasn't even light-headed, so I was all, "Fuck this fun-free circus, I need an accomplice."

So I called the suicide hotline.

And I'm all, "I need help."

And the guy is all, "What's your name?"

And I'm all, "You don't have caller ID? What kind of lame hotline is this?"

And he's all, "It says here that your name is Allison. Are you okay, Allison?"

And I'm all, "No, I'm not okay. I'm calling the suicide hotline."

And he's all, "You don't want to commit suicide, Allison."

And I'm all, "Exactly, doofasaurus, I need someone to take me out. I need it to be quick, private, painless, and it shouldn't fuck up my hair too much."

And he's like, "But there's so much to live for."

So I'm like, "You're burning my minutes, fuckstick. I need a number for a hit man or one of those Kevorkian doctors."

And he's all, "I can't help you with that."

So I'm all, "Loser!" And I offed my phone.

I can't believe it, but it turns out that the Motherbot was right. Sometimes, the only people you can trust are family. (" 'Scuse me, I barely suppressed a rainbow yawn when I typed that.) So here I am, waiting for my little sister, Ronnie, to get home from school so she can murder me, then hide my body under the bed until I return as the true Mistress of the Greater Bay Area Dark. This will be my last entry as a mortal. I have to go pick out an ensem for my death.

I wonder how she'll do it? It better be painless or the first thing on my undead to-do list will be to open a bottle of Whoop-Ass P.M. on little sister.

The Samurai of Jackson Street II

Katusumi Okata had lived among the gaijin for forty years. An American art dealer, traveling through Hokkaido in search of woodblock prints from the Edo period, had come into Katusumi's father's workshop, seen the boy's prints, and offered to bring Okata to San Francisco to create prints for his gallery on Jackson Street. The printmaker had lived in this same basement apartment since. He'd once had a wife, Yuriko, but she had been killed in front of him on the street when he was twenty-three, so now he lived alone.

The apartment had a concrete floor covered by two grass mats, a table that held his printmaking tools, a two-burner stove, an electric kettle, his swords, a futon, three sets of clothes, an old phonograph, and now, a burned-up white woman. She really didn't go with anything else, no matter how he arranged her.

He thought he might make a series of prints of her—

her blackened, skeletal form posed about the apartment like some demon wraith from a Shinto nightmare, but the composition wasn't working. He walked up to Chinatown and bought a bouquet of red tulips and put them on the futon beside her, but even with the added color and design element, the picture wasn't working. And she was making his futon smell like burned hair.

Okata was not used to company, and he wasn't sure how to keep up his end of the conversation. He had once made friends with two rats who came out of a hole in the brick wall. He had talked to them and fed them on the condition that they not bring any friends, but they hadn't listened and he was forced to mortar up the hole. He figured they didn't speak Japanese.

To be fair, however, she wasn't doing very well holding up her side of the conversation, either—lying there like a bog person dipped in creosote, her mouth open as if in a scream of agony. He sat on a stool next to the futon with his sketch pad and a pencil and began to sketch her for a print. He had very much admired the great cape of red curls that streamed out behind her when he'd seen her on the street, and he was sorry that all but a few strands had burned away in the sun. A shame. Perhaps he could draw the red curls in anyway. Make them swirl around the blackened rictus like one of Hokusai's waves.

He knew what she was, of course. He was still healing from his encounter with the vampire cats, and it took no little bit of sketching to fill in the details, especially as her fangs were pointing prominently at his ceiling right now and they were far too long and sharp to be those of a normal burned-up white girl. He filled three pages with sketches, experimenting with angles and composition, but on the fourth page he found that a sadness had overcome him that he could not chase away with the moment created in making a drawing.

Katusumi retrieved his wakizashi short sword from the stand on his work table, unsheathed it, and knelt by the futon. He bowed deeply, then put the point of the sword on the pad of his left thumb and cut. He held his thumb over her open mouth and the dark blood dripped over her teeth and lips.

Would she be like the cats? Savage? A monster? He held the razor-edged wakizashi ready in his right hand, should a demon awake. But if he'd been able to raise his beloved Yuriko, even as a demon, wouldn't he have? All the years that had passed, kendo training, drawing, carving, meditating, walking the streets unafraid, alone, hadn't they all been about that? About making Yuriko live? Or not living without her?

When the burned-up girl jerked with a great, rasping intake of breath, cinders cracked off her ribs and peppered the yellow futon and water began to flow from the swordsman's eyes.

RIVERA AND CAVUTO

Marvin the cadaver dog took them to the Wine Country. There they found Bummer and Lazarus, the Emperor's dogs, guarding a Dumpster in an alley behind an abandoned building. Marvin pawed the Dumpster, and tried to stay on task while the Boston terrier sniffed his junk and the golden retriever looked around, a little embarrassed.

Nick Cavuto held the lid, ready to lift it. "Maybe we should call the Wong kid and see if our sunlight jackets are done, then open it."

"It's daylight," said Rivera. "Even if there are, uh, creatures in there, they'll be immobile." Rivera still had a very difficult time saying the word "vampires" out loud. "Marvin says there's a body in there, we need to look."

Cavuto shrugged, lifted the lid of the Dumpster and braced himself for a wave of rotten meat smell, but there was none.

"Empty."

Bummer barked. Marvin pawed at the side of the Dumpster. Lazarus chuffed, which was dog for, "Duh. Look behind it."

Rivera looked in. Other than a couple of broken wine bottles and the rice part of a taco combo plate, there was nothing in the Dumpster, yet Marvin still pawed at the steel, which was the signal he had been trained to give when he'd found a corpse.

"Maybe we should give Marvin a biscuit to reset him or something," said Rivera.

"No corpse, no biscuit, that's the rule," said Cavuto. "We all have to live by it."

At the mention of a biscuit both Bummer and Marvin stopped what they were doing, sat, looked dutiful and contrite, and gave Rivera the "I need and deeply deserve a biscuit" look. Frustrated with what biscuit whores his cohorts were, Lazarus went to the side of the Dumpster and started pawing the space between it and the wall, then tried to stuff his muzzle in behind it.

Cavuto shrugged, pulled on a pair of form-fitting mechanics gloves from his jacket pocket, and pulled the cement blocks from under the Dumpster's wheels. Rivera watched in horror as the realization hit that he was probably going to get Dumpster schmutz, or worse, on his expensive Italian suit.

"Man up, Rivera," Cavuto said. "There's police work to be done."

"Shouldn't we call some uniforms in to do it? I mean, we're detectives."

Cavuto stood up and looked at his partner. "You really believe the movies when James Bond kills thirty guys hand to hand, blows up the secret lair, gets set on fire, then escapes under water and his tux doesn't even get wrinkled, don't you?"

"You can't just buy one of those off the rack," Rivera said. "It's a high-tech fabric."

"Just give me a hand with this thing, would you?"

Once the Dumpster was in the middle of the alley, the three dogs more or less dogpiled in front of the boarded-up window, Marvin doing his highly trained, "There's a dead guy in here, give me a biscuit" paw scrape, Bummer barking like he was announcing the big sale event down at Yapmart and everything had to go, and Lazarus rolling out a long, doleful howl.

"Probably in there," said Cavuto.

"Ya think?" said Rivera.

Cavuto was able to work his fingers between the sheet of plywood and the window frame and pulled it out. Before he could even set it aside Bummer had leapt through the window into the darkness. Lazarus pawed the windowsill, then leapt after his companion. Marvin, the cadaver dog, backed away, then ruffed twice and tossed his head, which translated to, "No, I'm good, you guys go ahead, just give me my biscuit. I'll be over here—well, would you look at that—those balls definitely need some tongue attention. No, it's okay, go on without me."

Marvin had a nose that could distinguish as many different odors as the human eye could colors, in the range of sixteen million distinct scents. Unfortunately, his doggie brain had a much more limited vocabulary for giving name to those scents and he processed what he smelled as: *dead cats,* many, *dead humans,* many, *dead rats,* many, *poo* and *wee,* many flavors, none fresh, and *old guy who needs a shower*; none of which would have given him pause. The smell that he couldn't file, that he didn't have a response for, that stopped him at the window, was a new one: *dead, but not dead*. Undead. It was scary, and licking his balls calmed him and kept his mind off the biscuit that they owed him.

Rivera shone his flashlight around the room. The basement appeared empty but for piles of debris and a thick layer of dust and ash over the floor, textured with the paw prints of hundreds of cats. He could see the movement of Bummer and Lazarus just at the edge of the flashlight's beam. They were scratching at a metal door.

"We'll need the crowbar out of the car," said Rivera.

"You're going in there?" asked Cavuto. "In that suit?"

Rivera nodded. "There's something down there, one of us has to."

"You're a goddamn hero, Rivera, that's what you are. A real, dyed in the worsted wool and silk blend hero."

"Yeah, there's that, and you can't fit through the window."

"Can too," said Cavuto.

Five minutes later they were both standing in the middle of the basement, fanning their Surefire ballistic flashlights through the dust like they were wielding silent light sabers. Rivera led the way to the steel door that the hounds were going at as if someone had duct taped it to a fox.

"You guys, shut up!" Rivera snapped, and much to his surprise, Bummer and Lazarus fell silent and sat.

Rivera looked back at his partner. "That's spooky."

"Yeah, and praise Willie Mays that's the only spooky thing going on here." Cavuto was a deeply religious San Francisco Giants fan and genuflected whenever he passed the bronze statue of Willie Mays outside the ball park.

"Good point," said Rivera. He tried the door, which didn't budge, but it was clear from the arc plowed into the dust and ashes that it had been opened recently. "Crowbar," he said, reaching back.

Cavuto handed him the crowbar and at the same time drew his gun from his shoulder holster, a ridiculously large Desert Eagle .50-caliber automatic.

"When did you start carrying that thing again?"

"Right after you said the *v*-word out loud at Sacred Heart."

"It won't stop them, you know."

"It makes me feel better. You want to hold it while I pry the door?"

"If there's a—one of them—in there, they'll be dormant or whatever you call it. It's daytime, they can't attack."

"Yeah, well, just in case they didn't get the memo."

"I got it." Rivera fit the crowbar in the door jamb and threw his weight against it. On the third push, something snapped and the door scraped open an inch. Bummer and Lazarus were up instantly, with their noses in the gap. Rivera looked back at Cavuto, who nodded, and Rivera pulled the door open and stepped away.

A pile of shelving and junk blocked the doorway, but Bummer and Lazarus were able to thread their way through it and were in the room, barking in frantic, desperate yelps. Through a gap in the junk, Rivera played the beam of his flashlight around the small storeroom, over barrels, shelving, and piles of dusty clothing.

"Clear," he said.

Cavuto joined him in the doorway. "Clear, my ass." The

big cop kicked his way through the barricade, holding his flashlight high in one hand and the Desert Eagle trained on a row of barrels on the right side of the room, where Bummer and Lazarus were currently indulging a hurricane-level doggie freakout.

Rivera followed his partner into the room, then approached the barrels while Cavuto covered him. Beyond the barking, he heard a faint metal tapping coming from one of the barrels. The barrel was upside-down and had held some kind of solid, the label said something about water-filtering mineral. It was sitting on its lid, which was only partially crimped on.

"Something's in there."

"Plug your ears," said Cavuto, cocking the hammer on the Desert Eagle, and aiming for the center of the barrel.

"Are you high? You can't fire that thing in here."

"Well there's can't and there's shouldn't. I probably *shouldn't* fire it."

"Cover me, I'm pushing it over."

Before Cavuto could answer Rivera grabbed the edge of the barrel and shoved with all his might. It was heavy, and fell hard. Bummer and Lazarus rocketed around to the exposed lid and were pawing at it.

"Ready?" said Rivera.

"Go," said Cavuto.

Rivera kicked the edge of the lid and it clanked off, then landed with a dull thud in the thick dust on the floor. Bummer rocketed inside while Lazarus frisked back and forth outside.

Rivera drew his weapon and moved to where he could look into the barrel. He was met first by a gray storm of hair, then two crystal blue eyes set in a wide, weathered face.

"Well that was unpleasant," said the Emperor, around the sloppy bath of dog spit he was receiving from Bummer.

"I'll bet," said Rivera, lowering his weapon.

"I may require some assistance extricating myself from this container."

"We can do that," said Cavuto. Cavuto was fighting back a very bad case of the empathy willies, imagining himself spending a night, maybe longer, upside-down, shoved inside a barrel. He and the Emperor were about the same size. "You in pain?"

"Oh no, thank you, I lost the feeling in my arms and legs quite some time ago."

"I'm guessing you didn't get in there on your own, did you?" said Rivera.

"No, this was not my doing," said the Emperor. "I was roughly handled, but it appears to have saved my life. There wasn't enough room in the barrel for any of them to become solid. There were hundreds of the fiends around me. But you saw them as you came in, I'm sure."

Rivera shook his head. "You mean the cats? No, there are tracks everywhere, but the place is empty."

"Well that's not good," said the Emperor.

"No, it's not." Rivera was distracted. He'd been playing his flashlight beam around the room, looking for something to help them get the Emperor out of the barrel. He stopped the beam on a spot by the shelves where the dust hadn't been stirred by their rescue efforts. There, as clearly as if it had been made in plaster of Paris to send home for Mother's Day, was a single human footprint. "That's not good at all," he said.

From outside the window Marvin barked three times quickly, which Rivera thought was a warning, but translated from dog to: "Hey, can I get a friggin' biscuit out here, or what?"

Head in the Clouds and Vice Versa

TOMMY

It was the words that brought Tommy back. For a week with the clutter of vampire cats, and for several weeks before, while trapped inside the bronze statue, the words had left Tommy. His mind had gone feral, as had his body after he escaped. For the first time since Jody had turned him, he turned to his instincts, and they had led him to the huge, shaved vampire cat Chet and his vampire progeny. Running with them he learned to use his vampire senses, had learned to be a hunter, and with them, he took blood prey for the first time: mice, rats, cats, dogs, and, yes, people.

Chet was the alpha animal of the pack, Tommy the beta male, but Tommy was quickly reaching a level of where he would be a challenge to Chet's position. Ironically, it was Chet who led him back to the words, which led him back to his sanity. In the cloud, merged with the other animals, he felt what they felt, knew what they knew, and Chet knew words, put words to concepts and experiences the way a human did, the very thing that had kept Tommy from being able to turn to mist in the first place. As a human, with grammar hardwired into his brain, he put a word to everything, and as a writer, if he couldn't put a word to an experience it had no value for him. But to become mist, you simply had to *BE*. Words got in the way. They separated you from the condition.

Feline Chet had not been a creature of words, as his kitty brain was not wired to file that kind of information, but as a vampire, a vampire sired by the prime vampire, his brain had changed, and concepts carried words for him now. As the cloud of hunters was streaming under the door to attack the Emperor (toward the smell of dog and recognition, for Chet had known the Emperor in life) the word "dog" fired across Chet's kitty mind, and in turn across the minds of all of the hunters, but for Tommy, it was transformational, as words, meaningless to the cats, cascaded across his mind, bringing with them memories, personality, identity.

He materialized out of the cloud in the dark storeroom, where he could see the Emperor in heat signature, huddled in a corner, holding his knife at the ready. Even if the room had been light, Tommy moved so quickly it would have been hard for the Emperor to see what was happening. The vampire scooped up the old man, stuffed him into the barrel, crimped on the lid with a grip that crushed the metal edges, then placed the barrel so the weight would rest on the lid. Instinct and experience told Tommy that the hunters wouldn't find enough space inside to materialize as a whole, so even though the barrel was not air tight, the Emperor would be safe as long as the lid remained intact. There wasn't enough room in there, literally, to swing a cat, and that would save the old man.

Tommy melted back into the cloud and moved out of the room, trying to will the concept of danger to the rest of the hunters, putting an image to Chet's word "dog" that the kitty minds would recognize, and slowly, the vampire cloud, its various tendrils having tested the room for prey and finding none accessible, snaked back under the door and away to look for blood that wasn't sealed so tight or smelled quite so dangerous.

They streamed up the elevator shaft, through the building, and out onto the street, where a few cats and Tommy solidified and dropped out of the cloud. Tommy, self-conscious now, looked around, realizing that he was naked. Everything he'd experienced from the time he'd been released from the bronze shell was a sensory blur in his memory, now that he was thinking in words again. But he remembered the Emperor, who had been one of the first people he'd met in the City, and who had been kind to him; had in fact gotten him his job at the Safeway, where he'd met Jody.

Jody. Both words and instinct overwhelmed him at the thought of her, memories of joy and pain as pure as the hunter state of mind. He searched in a whirlwind of words and images for a way to contain her. Jody. *Need*. That was the word.

He'd need clothes and language to move in the world where he'd find Jody. He didn't know why he knew that, but he knew it. But first he needed to feed. He loped down the sidewalk after the hunter-cloud, tuned again for prey, and for the first time in weeks, the word *blood* lit up in his brain.

The words brought him back.

THE NOTORIOUS FOO DOG

"Your car's all fucked up," explained Cavuto.

"I know," said Stephen "Foo Dog" Wong. He stood aside and the two policemen walked by him into the loft. "Your jackets are done."

"Your apartment's all fucked up, too," observed Cavuto, looking at the plywood fastened across the front of the loft where the windows used to be.

"And full of rats," added Rivera.

"Dead rats," said Cavuto, shaking one of the plastic boxes with the lid taped on. The rat inside rolled around like—well—like a dead rat.

"They're not dead," said Jared. "It's daytime. They're undead." Jared wore a SCULL-FUCK SYMPHONY band T-shirt, over skin-tight black girl's jeans, with flesh-colored ACE elastic bandages running from midcalf to the midsole of his black Chuck Taylors. His Mohawk had been lacquered into magenta Statue of Liberty spikes.

Cavuto looked at him and shook his head. "Kid, even in the gay community there are limits to tolerance."

"I hurt my ankles," whined Jared.

Foo nodded. "We've had a few rough days."

"I gathered," said Rivera. "Where's your creepy girlfriend?"

"She's not creepy," said Jared. "She's complex."

"Home," said Foo.

"As was agreed in her black covenant with you," said Jared, as ominously as he could manage.

"Did you get an English accent all of a sudden?" asked Cavuto.

"He does that when he wants to sound more Gothic," said Foo. He was trying to stand in front of the ruins of the bronze statue of Jody and Tommy, but since it was twice his size, he only drew attention to it.

Rivera pulled a pen from his jacket and ran it over the sawed edges of the bronze shell and pulled it back with the red-brown clot on it. "Mr. Wong, what the hell happened here?"

"Nothing," said Jared, without an English accent.

Foo looked from one inspector to the other, hoping they would see how hopelessly smarter he was than them, and give up, but they wouldn't look away. They just kept looking at him like he was in trouble. He went to the futon that served as their couch, pushed a bunch of boxes of undead rats to the floor, sat down, and cradled his face in his hands.

"I thought I'd found some kind of scientific bonanza, a

new species, a new way for a species to reproduce—hell, maybe I have, but everything's so out of control. The fucking magic!"

Rivera and Cavuto moved to the middle of the room, and stood over Foo. Rivera reached down and squeezed his shoulder. "Focus, Stephen. What happened here? Why is there blood all over that statue?"

"They were in there. Tommy and Jody. Abby and I had them bronzed when they were out during the day."

"Then they never left town like you said?" asked Cavuto.

"No, they had been in there all the time. Abby said that it wouldn't be bad for them, that when they were in mist form it was like they were dreaming. Mist form! What the hell is that? It's not possible."

"And you felt bad so you cut them out?" said Rivera.

"No, Jared let Jody out."

"Totally by accident," said Jared. "She was kind of a bitch about it, too."

Foo explained about Jared releasing Jody, Abby and Jody releasing Tommy, Jody throwing Tommy through the windows, and Tommy running off into the night, naked.

"So he's out there," Foo said. "They're both out there."

"We know," said Cavuto.

"You do?" Foo looked up for the first time. "You knew?"

"She was seen at the Fairmont Hotel, and we found bags of blood in a room there. We'll find her. But the Emperor saw Tommy Flood, naked, sleeping with all the vampire cats. He said that the one cat, Chet, isn't really a cat any-more. Explain that, science boy."

Foo nodded. "I figured something like that might hap-pen. The rats are smarter."

"That helps," said Cavuto.

"No, what I've found is that the vampire blood carries characteristics of the host species. The further from the prime vampire, the old vampire that turned Jody, or that's who we think is the prime vampire, the less change takes place. Abby said that Chet was turned by the prime vam-pire, so he's picking up human characteristics. He's going to be stronger, bigger, smarter than any of the cat vam-pires. He's turning into something new."

"Something new?"

"Yeah. We found it with the rats. The first ones I turned from Jody's blood are smarter than the ones I turned from those rats' blood. Each generation away from her is less and less intelligent. I mean, we haven't had time to really test them, but in just the amount of time it takes them to learn the mazes, it's clear that the innate intelligence is higher in those closer to the human vampire sire. And they're stron-ger, because Jody was only one generation from the prime vampire. I thought I'd figured an algorithm that described it, but then they all turned to mist and merged and fucked up everything."

"Sure," said Cavuto, "we'll nod and act like we have some idea of what you're talking about until you tell us what the hell you're actually talking about."

Foo got up and waved for them to follow him into the bedroom. There was a plywood maze that covered the entire bed, with small blue LEDs dimly lighting every intersection. A sheet of Plexiglas covered the top.

"The UV LEDs are to keep them from turning to mist and escaping the maze," Foo said. "It's not enough to hurt them, just keep them solid."

"Oh good, a toy city," said Cavuto. "We have time for this."

Foo ignored him. "The rats who were turned from Jody's blood learned the maze more quickly, and remembered it faster than the ones turned from rat blood. It was consistent, until they all got loose and merged into a single cloud. After that, they all knew the maze, even if we had never put them in it."

Rivera bent down and pretended to be examining the maze. "What are you saying, Stephen?"

"I think that they share a consciousness when they are together in mist form. What one knows, the others know. After they had merged, they all knew the maze."

Rivera looked at Cavuto and raised his eyebrows. "The Emperor thought that Tommy Flood was in the same cloud as the vampire cats."

"We're fucked," said Cavuto.

Rivera looked at Foo for confirmation. "Are we fucked?"

Foo shrugged, "Well, from what I could tell, Tommy wasn't really that bright."

Rivera nodded. "Uh-huh, and if your girlfriend didn't have a crush on him, would we be fucked?"

Foo flinched a little, then recovered. "I think they'd be limited by the brain capacity of the species, so the vampire cats would be still be cats, but they'd be very smart. Chet, on the other hand—"

"We're fucked," said Cavuto. "Say it."

"Scientifically speaking, yes," said Jared, who stood in the doorway of the bedroom.

"How do we stop them?" asked Rivera.

"Sunlight. UV light will do it," said Foo. "You have to find them while they're dormant or they'll just run away. They're not invulnerable to physical damage. If they're dismembered or decapitated it will kill them."

"You did experiments on that?" asked Cavuto.

Foo shook his head. "We had some accidents when we were trying to get them back in their cages, but I'm basing that hypothesis on Abby's description of the swordsman who showed up in the street."

"He sounds badass," said Jared. "Did you find him?"

Cavuto took Jared by a hair spike, steered him into the corner, faced him there, then turned back to Foo. "So, these jackets you made us, they'll take them out?"

"If you're close enough. I'd say they're lethal to about twelve feet. I suppose I can rig something higher intensity, like a high-capacity UV laser flashlight. You could cut them down from a distance with something like that."

"Light sabers!" said Jared, his voice going up. He hopped around in excitement, then winced at the pain in his ankles. "Ouch."

"That's it," said Cavuto. "You're too much of a nerd to

be gay. I'm contacting the committee. They'll revoke your rainbow flag and you will not be permitted anywhere near the parade."

"There's a committee?"

"No," said Rivera. "He's fucking with you." Rivera turned back to Foo. "What about something that will work on a wider basis—like a vaccine or something?"

Foo thought for a second. "Sure, what is it, Tuesday? I'm curing Ebola in the morning, but I can work on your vampire vaccine after lunch."

Rivera smiled. "People are dying, Steve. Lots of people. And the only people who have a chance to stop it are in this room."

"Not you," Cavuto said to Jared.

"Bitch," Jared replied.

"I'll work on it," said Foo. "But it's not as bad as you think it is."

"Brighten our day, kid," said Cavuto.

"They can't all handle it. Four out of every ten animals that are turned vampire don't survive to the second night. They either just break down on the spot—sort of decay from the inside, or they go crazy—it's like the heightened senses overwhelm them and they just have sort of a seizure that scrambles their brains and they end up with no survival instincts. They don't feed or hide from the light. The first sunrise after they're turned burns them up. It's like accelerated evolution, taking out the weak the very first day."

"So you're telling me what?"

"The cat cloud won't grow exponentially. And the only way it will pass to other species is if they bite their attacker during the attack and ingest vampire blood—that's why you haven't had any more human vampires."

"Then why no dog vampires?" asked Cavuto.

"I'm guessing the cats tear them apart before they change," said Foo. "I'm not a behavioral guy, but I'd guess there's no brotherhood among vampires. If you're a vampire cat, you're essentially still a cat. If you're a vampire dog, you're still a dog."

"Except for Chet," said Rivera. "Who is kind of a cat plus something else."

"Well, there *are* anomalies," said Foo. "I told you, this is very fuzzy science. I don't like it."

Rivera's phone chirped and he flipped it open and looked at the screen. "The Animals," he said.

"And?" asked Cavuto.

"They're at a butcher shop in Chinatown. They say they have a way to kill the vampires but they can't find them."

"We can take them Marvin. Tell them we're on the way."

Rivera held the phone like it was a foul dead thing. "I don't know how."

Foo snatched the phone out of Rivera's hand, nine-keyed a message, hit SEND, and handed it back. "There, you're on the way. I thought you said the only people who could fix this were in this room."

"They are, and now they're leaving."

"Don't forget your sun jackets," said Jared. "We charged the batteries and everything. Do you think you'll be able to turn them on, or should I come along to help?"

"He's a kid." Rivera grabbed Cavuto's arm. "You can't hit him."

"That's it, kid. You're out of the tribe. If I hear you've touched a penis, even your own, I'm sending you to butch lesbian jail."

"They have that?"

Rivera looked past his partner at Jared and nodded, slowly, seriously.

ЌATUSUϻI ϕЌATA

The burned-up white girl was not healing very quickly and Okata was running out of blood. All he seemed to do was watch her, sketch her, and squeeze his blood into her mouth. While her red hair had returned, and most of the ash had flaked away to reveal white skin underneath, she was still wraith-thin, and she only seemed to breathe two or three times an hour. During the day, she didn't breathe at all, and he thought that she might be dead forever. She had not opened her eyes, and had made no sound except a low moan when he was feeding her, which subsided as soon as he stopped.

He was not feeling well himself, and on the second day he became light-headed and passed out on the mat beside her. If she did come alive as a demon, he'd be too weak to defend himself and she would drain the last drops of his life. Strangely, he was not okay with that. He needed to eat and recover and she needed more blood.

"We will have to find a balance," he said to the white girl in Japanese. He had been talking to her more lately, and found that he no longer flinched at the sound of his voice inside the little apartment that had been without a human voice for so long. A balance.

When it was light and she had been still for an hour, he locked up his little apartment, took his sword, and walked into Chinatown, feeling ashamed of the little, old-man steps he was taking because he had become so weak. Perhaps he would actually go into a restaurant and have some tea and noodles, sit until his strength returned. Then he would find a better way to feed the burned-up white girl.

He only spoke a dozen words of Cantonese, despite having lived near Chinatown for forty years. They were the same dozen words he spoke in English. He told his students at the dojo it was because Bushido and the Japanese language were inseparable, but in fact, it was because he was stubborn and didn't really like talking to people. His words were: *hello, good-bye, yes, no, please, thank you, okay, sorry,* and *suck my dick.* He made it a rule, however, to only say the last three in junction with *please* and/or *thank you,* and had only broken that rule once, when a thug in the Tenderloin tried to take his sword and Okata forgot to say please before fracturing the man's skull with the sheathed katana. *Sorry,* he'd said.

It had been over a week since Okata had been to the dojo in Japantown. His students would think he was testing them, and when the time came to face them, he would say through his translator that they should learn to sit. Should learn patience. Should anticipate nothing. Anticipation was desire and didn't the Buddha teach that desire was the cause of all suffering? Then he would proceed to trounce each and every one of them with the bamboo *shinai* as an object lesson in suffering. *Thank you.*

He didn't care much for prepared Chinese food, but Japantown was too far to walk, and Japanese food in his neighborhood was too expensive. But noodles are noodles. He'd eat just enough to get his strength back, then he would buy a fish, maybe some beef to help replace his blood, and take them home and prepare them.

After he slurped down three bowls of soba and drank a pot of green tea at a restaurant named Soup, he made his way to the butcher. Near the old man who sat on a milk crate playing a *Gaohu,* a two-string, upright fiddle that approximated the sound of someone hurting a cat, the swordsman passed two policemen, who had paused as if considering whether they should give money to the old fiddler or whether it might not be better for everyone if they just Tased him. They smiled and nodded to Okata and he smiled back. They were mildly amused by the little man in the too-short plaid slacks, fluorescent orange socks, and an orange porkpie hat, who they had seen walking the City since they were boys. It never occurred to them that he was anything but an eccentric street person, or that the walking stick with which he measured his easy strolls, wasn't a walking stick at all.

It took considerable pointing and pantomime to get the Chinese butcher to understand that he wanted to buy blood, but once he did, Okata was surprised to find out not only was it available, but it was available in flavors: pig, chicken, cow, and turtle. Turtle? Not for his burned-up white girl. How dare the butcher even suggest such a thing? She would have beef, and maybe a quart or two of pig, because Okata remembered reading once that human flesh was called "long pig" by Pacific island cannibals, so pig blood might be more to her liking.

The butcher taped the lids on eight, one-quart plastic containers containing all the nonturtle blood he had, then carefully stacked them in a shopping bag and handed them to a woman at the cash register. Okata paid her the amount on the register, picked up the bag, and was pocketing the change when someone tapped him on the shoulder.

He turned. No one there. Then he looked down: a tiny Chinese grandmother dressed in thug-wear that made her look vaguely like a hip-hop Yoda. She said something to him in Cantonese, then said something to the butcher, then to the woman behind the counter, who pointed at the shopping bag, then she said something else to Okata. Then she put a hand on his shopping bag.

"Thank you," Okata said in Cantonese. He bowed slightly. She didn't move.

Being confronted by a Chinese grandmother while shopping in Chinatown was not unusual. In fact, more than once he'd had to push through a dog pile of Sino-matrons to simply buy a decent cabbage, but this one seemed to want what Okata had clearly already purchased.

He smiled, bowed again, just slightly, said, "Good-bye," and tried to push past her. She stepped in front of him, and he noticed, as he should have before, that a whole group of young men stepped in behind her; seven of them, Anglo, Hispanic, black, and Chinese, they all looked slightly stoned, but no less determined.

The old lady barked something at him in Cantonese and tried to grab his bag. Then the young men behind her stepped up.

THE ANIMALS

"Have you been washed in the blood?" said Clint, the born-again ex-heroin addict to the detectives as they entered the butcher shop. He grinned over his shoulder. Clint was splattered head to toe with blood. Everyone in the shop was splattered with blood except the two uniform cops, who were trying to keep the three groups—the customers, the butchers, and the Animals—separated. They had the Animals lined up opposite the counter, facing the wall, their hands restrained with zip ties.

"Inspector, these guys say they're supposed to meet you here," said the younger of the uniforms, a gaunt, Hispanic guy named Muñez.

Rivera shook his head.

"He started it," said Lash Jefferson. "We were just minding our own business, and he rolled up on us all badass."

Rivera looked at the Asian officer, John Tan, who he'd worked with before when investigating a murder in Chinatown and had needed a translator. "What happened?"

Tan shook his head and pushed his hat back on his head with the end of his riot baton. "Nobody's hurt. It's beef and pig blood. The butcher says these guys attacked a little old Japanese man, a regular customer, because he had bought the last of the beef blood."

"We needed it for bait," said Lash. "You know, Inspector, like beer for slugs." He winked.

"You attacked an old man because he bought the last cow blood?" asked Cavuto.

"He attacked us," said Troy Lee. "We were just defending ourselves."

"He had a sword," said Drew, who turned back around quickly.

Officer Tan rolled his eyes at Rivera. "The butcher says the old man had a stick of some kind. He used it to defend himself."

"Just because he didn't draw it out of the scabbard doesn't meant it wasn't a sword," said Jeff, the tall, blond jock.

"It was a battle of honor," said Troy Lee.

"One little old guy with a stick, seven of you?" said Rivera. "Honor?"

"He told my grandma to suck his dick," said Troy.

"Still," said Cavuto.

"But she said okay," Troy said.

"That shit is just wrong," said Lash.

Grandma, who was standing with the other outraged, blood-splattered customers across the butcher shop, fired off a volley of Cantonese at the policemen. Rivera looked to Officer Tan for translation.

"She says she misunderstood what he was saying because his accent was so bad."

"Don't care," said Rivera. "Where's the guy with the alleged stick?"

"He ran out before we got here," said Tan. "We called in backup, but we put the responding unit on finding the victim, when these guys didn't resist."

"*Resistance is futile,*" said Clint in a robot voice.

"I thought you were Christian," said Cavuto.

"What, I can't love Jesus *and Star Trek*?"

"Oh for fuck's sake. Rivera, let's just arrest these morons and—"

Rivera held up his hand for silence. "Officer Tan, I'm afraid I do need them. You have their names if the stick guy shows up and wants to press charges. Have all those people leave their names with the butcher. These guys will pay for their dry cleaning."

"Yes, sir," said Tan. "They're all yours. You want me to clip the restraints?"

"Nope," said Rivera. "Come along, boys." He led the Animals, their hands cuffed behind their backs, out of the butcher shop and into the flow of the Stockton Street sidewalk—a river of people.

"You'd better bring Troy Lee's grandma," said Lash, rolling to the side as a vendor with a handtruck full of crates bumped by.

"Yeah, Grandma has a secret weapon," blurted out Troy Lee.

"I heard," said Cavuto.

Jeff, the tall jock, said, "Hey, did anyone wonder why a little old Japanese guy would need eight quarts of animal blood?"

Being the Chronicles
of Abby Normal, Nosferatu

Well, that was dramatic. Ronnie is all crying and cowering in the other room because I drank a little of her blood. Fuck's sakes, you mopey emo-toy, cowboy the fuck up, you have quarts! What did she expect, she got to kill me, that's not free? I'm not like some easy death slut who lets you kill her for nothing, I am nosferatu, bee-yotch. That shit has a price. Her blood totally tastes like zit cream, too. I almost hurled.

I know, *très* cool, *non*? So, now that I am a dark and beautiful creature of unspeakable evil, I think I'm going to start a pay-subscription blog. Except I can only, like, advertise *darkness and unspeakable evil,* because I'm totally starting from the beginning on the beauty. First, all my tattoos are totally gone. Gone! Like wiped off. After I succumbed to the dark gift by taking a whole bottle of the Motherbot's sleeping pills, Ronnie hid me under a pile of blankets and stuffed animals in her room, and when I awoke at sundown and crawled from my sepulcher of Carebears and Muppets and whatnot, all my tats totally wiped off. Like the ink was pushed out on top of my skin. Now Ronnie has an Epileptic Elmo with more of my ink on him than I have. And my piercings healed up. My bars and rings are all in the carpet.

Boobs? Still pathetic. I had so hoped to swoop down on Foo and totally flash my awesome vampyre cleavage on him. You know, like put on a bustier and really squish the girls out the top, then be all: BAM! "Check it out, Foo. Cower before killer décolletage, and beg me to let you rub your handsome ninja face on it." But no! Now he'll be all, "Oh, it looks like you dropped a couple of dimes down your shirt, vamp child. Can I help you with those?"

So I suffer.

And you can't get implants. I saw what happens when the Animals' blue hooker turned vampyre. You wake up and your implants are on the floor and you're all, "Hey, I blew like a hundred strangers to get those." I'm only estimating. I'm sure the number of strangers will vary depending on prevailing suck and surgical rates in your area. (You acquire arcane medical knowledge when your mother is a nurse.) You can't have stuff removed either, you know, if that might be needed.

Even my makeup is ruined from where Ronnie tried to smother me with a pillow, so that's going to take like an hour to fix. I had heard that sometimes even when you overdose on a whole butt-load of drugs, you don't always die because your heart won't stop, which is why you're supposed to put your head in a plastic bag. But I didn't want to because I had done Cleopatra eye makeup that was *très* elegant so I would look hawt for my resurrection. So Ronnie was supposed to put her hand over my mouth and nose, just until I stopped breathing, then like fix my lipstick if it smeared. Because otherwise I'd be all *girlfriend in a coma* for weeks while the Motherbot whined about how she couldn't unplug me because of her guilt for treating me like an assbag and how she had never appreciated my dark complexity and inner beauty and whatnot, and I have too much shit to do for that.

But Ronnie didn't even wait for me to pass out. I had just taken the pills with some Sunny D (because the nosferatu love us some irony), and I laid down on the floor like we had planned, so Ronnie could just roll my body under the bed to hide me from the deadly rays of the sun and Mom. So I'm grieving for the loss of my mortality and whatnot, when Ronnie, like, just throws a pillow on my face and sits on it. And I'm all, "Wait, wait, mmphff, mmphf."

And then she burned one—right in my face—one of those foul, vegan farts—because she's been a vegan ever since she had head lice and we shaved her head. (I don't know why. Something about garlic and parasites. She's insane.) 'Kayso, I decided that I could wait to receive the dark gift, and that Ronnie would have to die as soon as I got her off me. So she, like, burns another one! And she's skinnier than me. I don't know how she could even have it in her. And she's laughing so hard that she falls off of me and I make my move.

'Kayso, I'm chasing her around the house, going, "I'm going to peel off your skin and make it into boots and step in dog shit with them," and other basic super-villain threats, and then things got all wiggly and the last thing I remember is I walked into the sliding glass doors to the balcony and kind of bounced off. And so tragically, I died young, and no one was there to grieve for me or shed tears for me or kiss my cold, lifeless lips and whatnot.

But now I'm undead awesome. I think with practice, I will make a super, super-villain, and really, I'm okay with that, because there won't be any student loans like there would have been with my other career choice of tragic romantic poet.

'Kayso, now I must fix my makeup and pick an ensem and then wander the lonely night, searching for the Countess and the vampyre Flood, and maybe drop by the love lair to totally overwhelm Foo with my haunting and eternal but still small-chested beauty.

Kthxbye. Being immortal rocks! I can type like demon speed! Fear me! L8z.

THE EMPEROR

The Emperor and the men shared a submarine sandwich on a bench by Pier Nine in the bright noonday sun as they watched a dark knife of a yacht glide into dock. She was just short of the length of a football field, all black, with stainless-steel trim—what the Emperor imagined a starship might look like if it were driven by sails. The sails on her three stainless-steel masts were mechanically furled into black carbon fiber shrouds, and the curved windows of her cockpit and cabin were blacked out. There were no crewmen on the deck.

In all his years on and around the sea, the Emperor had never seen anything like it.

Bummer flattened his ears and growled.

"Easy, little one, it's only a sailing ship, and a beautiful one at that," said the Emperor, although he thought it quite strange that there was no crew on deck to secure the mooring lines. A ship of that size, and more important, of that expense, would usually have half a dozen or more tying her up, but once parallel with the dock, attitude jets along the sides opened in the hull and gently pushed her into the dock. Jets on the far side pushed back so she stopped within six inches and hovered there, the jets firing just as needed to keep her from drifting. Three hundred feet of steel and carbon fiber, probably over twelve hundred tons, parked as easily and somewhat more smoothly than a Mini Cooper at a strip mall.

Bummer ran to the edge of the breakwater and let loose with machine-gun volley of yapping, which translated, "Bad boat, bad boat, bad boat, bad boat."

A barking fit from his bug-eyed companion was nothing out of the ordinary, and normally the Emperor would have let it pass with a calming word, but there was still half a submarine sandwich to be eaten, and something had to be very much amiss for Bummer to leave the scene of a sandwich.

Now Lazarus sniffed the chill wind coming off the Bay and whimpered, and tossed his head, then looked back at the Emperor, which translated from dog to, "Smells undead, boss."

The Emperor didn't understand what his companions were saying to him, but he suspected. He just wasn't ready to hear it. It had only been a few hours since the two police inspectors had dropped him off at the St. Francis Yacht Club, where the members allowed him and the men the use of the outer showers, and one of the members had purchased this lovely sandwich and presented it to them in thanks for their service to the City. Only an hour since he'd actually managed to straighten his neck out, after spending the better part of a night upside-down in a barrel. And only now, after a walk along the waterfront and a good meal, was the pain in his knees and shoulders starting to subside. He wasn't ready to go back into battle.

"I am a selfish old man," he said to the men. "A coward, worried for my own comfort, when my people are threatened. I am afraid." But even as he said it, he was rising on his creaky knees, pushing himself up on the walking stick he'd retrieved only this morning from the Yacht Club, where he'd left it for safekeeping. The handle was carved out of ivory into the shape of a polar bear, and it fit the Emperor's hand like it had been made for him, although it had been a gift from a nice young man named Asher, who owned the secondhand store in North Beach, but that's another story. He wished there had been a blade in it, like the cane young Asher carried. Alas, he would have to face the black ship with only a stick, a sandwich, and his intrepid furry companions.

He puffed himself blowfish style and headed up the dock, Bummer and Lazarus following along behind him, ears lowered, trailing a two-part growling harmony. A few people had gathered along the fence at the breakwater, and were pointing to the great ship. It wasn't so unusual that one might bring his day to a full halt, but if you were in the middle of a run or a brisk walk and needed a reason for a pause, the black ship would certainly fire the imagination long enough for you to catch your breath.

Once at the ship, the Emperor was unsure of what to do. There was really no reason beyond Bummer's behavior to justify boarding her. And this ship was not of his city, therefore he could not claim dominion over it. He could hear the attitude jets firing just under the water, sporadically, to keep the ship in place. It was only a step, albeit a long step, and he'd be standing on the deck at her prow. Perhaps, having made the leap, a further course of action would occur to him. He backed up on the dock to take a run at it, or as much of a run as his advanced age and boiler-tank bulk would allow him, but as he announced "two" on his countdown to launch, a tanned face surrounded by a tangle of blond dreadlocks popped up over the rail of the cockpit and a young man called, "Irie, mi crusty uncle, bringing us the jammin' grinds, yeah? I and I tanks ye colossal, but please to be waiting on the dock."

And the Emperor stopped. Bummer and Lazarus even stopped growling and sat and turned their heads in the manner of a doggie listening for a "food" word amid a recitation of *The Iliad*.

The young man vaulted over the black cowling of the cockpit and landed on the lower deck, his bare feet barely making a thump. He was lean and muscular, tanned a café au lait color, with a tattoo of a humpback whale on his right pectoral muscle. He wore board shorts, despite the chill Bay air, a gold ring in his nose, and a series of them chasing down the rim of each ear. His dreadlocks fanned out around his head and shoulders as if they might be sun serpents looking for a way to escape.

He leapt the gap to the dock, dazzled a blindingly white grin, and snatched the remains of the sandwich out of the Emperor's hand. "Ah, Jah's love on ye, Uncle, bringing de rippin' grinds to I'n'I after so long at sea."

Bummer barked and growled. The Rasta-blond had their sandwich.

"Ah, me doggie, dreadies," said the Rasta. "Jah's blessings on ye." He knelt and scratched Bummer behind the ears.

The stranger smelled of coconut oil, weed, and the undead, and Bummer was going to bite him as soon as he was finished having his ears scratched.

"I'n'I be Pelekekona Keohokalole. Call him Kona, for

short. Pirate Captain and lion of the briny science, don't cha know?"

"I am the Emperor of San Francisco, protector of Alcatraz, Sausalito, and Treasure Island," said the Emperor, who couldn't bring himself to be impolite to the smiling stranger, despite the black ship. "Welcome to my city."

"Ah, many tanks, Bruddah. Much respek on you, yeah? But you can't be going on that *Raven* ship, no. She kill you, brah. Automatic-kine kill. Dead, dead, too. Not walkin' around dead like them below."

"It goes without saying," said the Emperor.

FØØ DØG

The rats had been up and moving for about an hour when Foo heard the key in the front door. He put the soldering iron he was using in the wire holder and was turning toward the door when she was on him. He felt his vertebrae crack as her legs wrapped around him and he went over backward. Something caught the back of his head and something wet and coppery was shoved into his mouth: tongue.

Panic vibrated through him and he felt he might suffocate, but then the smell: a mix of sandalwood perfume, clove cigarettes, and caffè latte. Amid the panic, he'd sprung a first-rate erection, which he thrust against his attacker in defense.

She pushed away and twisted up a handful of his shirtfront as he gasped for breath.

"Rawr!" she rawred.

"I missed you," said Foo.

"Your suffering has only begun," Abby said. She wore a red tartan miniskirt over a black leotard with a low swooping neckline, a spiked dog collar, and her lime-green Converse Chuck Taylors, which she sometimes referred to as her "forbidden love Chucks" for no reason that he could ever figure out.

"You're kind of crushing my ribs."

"That is because I am nossssssss-feratu and my powers are legion and stuff! *Très* cool, huh?"

Foo realized then that she had actually done it—she had somehow managed to change herself into a vampire. Her nose, eyebrow, and lip rings were gone, the piercings healed. The spider tattoo on her neck was gone as well. "How?" he asked, immediately trying to calculate her odds of survival. He'd talked to her yesterday on the phone and he was sure she would have mentioned the transition if she'd made it already, so she was in her first twenty-four hours. She might still be one of the ones who went insane and self-destructed, and even though Abby was short neither on insanity or self-destruction, it didn't mean he shouldn't try to save her.

She kissed him again, hard, and as nice as it felt, he was hyper aware of whether she had broken the skin on his lips, or hers. So far, so good. She pushed him back, but then caught the back of his head again so it didn't bang the floor. She actually seemed a little more considerate now that she was dead, although not that much quieter.

"Be patient, my love ninja, I will use you like the delicious manga-haired man-whore that you are, but first we have to try out my powers. Let some of the rats out of their cages and I will command them with my vampire psychic thoughts. I'll see if I can get them to clean the kitchen."

Okay, maybe they weren't out of the insanity woods quite yet, Foo thought. He said, "Yes, and then we'll see if we can get bluebirds to tie a ribbon in your hair."

"Snark not, Foo! You must obey me! I am the Countess Abigail Von Normal, queen bitch of the night, and you are my groveling sex slave!"

"Are you a countess or a queen? You said both."

"Shut up, grommet, before I suck you dry!"

"Okay," said Foo. A wise man picks his battles.

"Not that way, Foo. I mean that I will dominate you and you will do my bidding!"

"Which will be different from any other day, how?"

"Cease your banality and nerdardious questions, Foo. You are totally harshing my heady power over the night."

"It sounds like you bought a flashlight."

"That's it. I am going to beat your ninja ass." She leapt off of him and made the "crouching tiger, rip your heart out" kung-fu posture that everyone who has seen a martial arts movie knows.

"Wait! Wait! Wait!"

" 'Kay," said Abby, relaxing to the much less danger-ous "slouching tiger chillin' with a bag of Cheetos" stance, which is known by all who have ever snacked.

"You need to feed, get your strength up first," said Foo. "You're a vampire noob. You need to grow into your powers."

"Ha," said Abby. "You speak like a mortal who can't possibly grasp the depth of the dark gift. I jumped over a car on the way here. And I totally ran faster than the F train. My Chucks are still warm with residual speediness. Go ahead, feel them. Lick them, if you must. Even now I can see this aura thing around you, which is like bright pink, and doesn't go with your fly hair and manly bulge."

Foo looked down. Yes, his bulge was betraying him. He said, "You should take it slow, Abby."

"Oh yeah, watch this!" In an instant she was across the loft at the kitchen counter, and in another instant she had shot back across the living room and hit the plywood covering the windows.

There was nothing Foo could do. She might have lifted the couch, leapt up fifteen feet, and grabbed the open ceiling beams, or even turned to mist, if she'd figured out how to do that, but what she had decided to do to show her powers was blast through the quarter-inch plywood and land catlike on the street below. And that would have been badass, to be sure.

What Abby didn't know was that while she'd been gone, the window guy had called, and he wouldn't be able to come out to fix the windows for two weeks, so Foo had replaced the quarter-inch plywood with three-quarter-inch plywood, and instead of it just being tacked at the corners with small nails, he had screwed it down with stainless-steel screws, so as not to leave any vapor gaps for the rats to make an escape.

Foo cringed and covered his eyes.

She was fast, and preternaturally strong, but ninety pounds of vampire is still only ninety pounds.

Did she hit the plywood Wile E. Coyote style, then slide down? Wah-wah-wah. Oh no.

She hit the plywood, which bent precipitously, then splintered a bit before springing back and rocketing her all the way across the loft to the back wall, and there, she made a petite Goth girl impression in the sheet rock before falling forward, flat on her face, and saying, "Fucksocks," into the rug.

"You okay?" asked Foo.

"Broken," said Abby into the rug.

He knelt over her, afraid to turn her head to see what damage she might have done. "What's broken?"

"Everything."

"I'll get you some blood out of the fridge. You should heal pretty fast."

" 'Kay," said Abby, still face-down, not having moved since the initial impact. "Don't look at me, okay?"

"No way," said Foo, already in the kitchen. He took one of the plastic pouches of blood from the fridge and worked it back and forth. "Just a second. Don't move, Abs, you might have broken bones." He quick-stepped into the bedroom, grabbed a capped syringe off the cabinet where he kept the chemicals, flipped off the cap, and injected the sedative into the bag.

"Here you go, baby. Just drink this and you'll be fine."

Ten minutes later he heard someone coming up the stairs and realized that Abby had forgotten to lock the door.

Jared bounded into the loft, stopped when he saw Foo kneeling over the prostrate Abby, who had a sizable pool of blood around her head, and began screaming.

"Stop screaming!" barked Foo. "It's not her blood."

Jared stopped screaming. "What did you do to her?"

"Nothing, she's fine. Would you move the maze off the bed and help me get her in there?"

Sometime during the debacle, Abby's skirt had flipped up and Jared pointed at an oblong lump that ran across her bottom and partly down her leg under the black leotard.

"What's that? Did she poop herself?"

"No," said Foo, wishing he didn't know what it was, but he had already checked for himself. "It's a tail."

"Whoa. Weird."

"Yeah," said Foo.

Wide Awake in Sucker-Free

Okata scraped the last few drops of blood from the container into the burned-up white girl's mouth. He'd managed to save two of the eight quart containers, but it wasn't going to be enough, he could tell, and after the fight at the butcher shop and his escape, he knew he wasn't strong enough to give her any more of his own blood. She'd need more, and he was going to have to start thinking of her as something besides the "burned-up white girl." She was starting to resemble a real person now, more than a person-shaped cinder. A very old, very scary dead person, to be sure, but a person nonetheless. Her red hair nearly covered the pillow now, and she'd moved, if only a little, closing her mouth after the last drops of blood went in. No ash had flaked away with the movement. Okata was glad. Her exposed fangs made him a little uneasy, but now she had lips, sort of.

He picked up his sketch pad from the floor, moved to the end of the futon to get a different angle, and began drawing her, as he'd been doing every hour or so since he'd returned from the butcher. He was still covered with the blood that had splashed on him during the fight, but it had long since dried and except for washing his hands so he could work, he'd forgotten it. He finished the sketch, then moved to his workbench, where he transferred a refined version of the drawing to a piece of rice paper so thin it was nearly transparent. He would replicate this drawing four more times, then each would be glued to a woodblock and carved away to make the plate for a different line or color.

He looked over his shoulder at her, and felt a tremor of shame. Yes, she looked like a person now, an old, desiccated grandmother, but he shouldn't leave her like that. He took a bowl from the shelf above his little kitchen sink, filled it with warm water, and then knelt by the side of the futon and gently sponged the last patina of ash from her body, revealing the blue-white skin underneath. The skin was smooth, like polished rice paper, but pores and hair follicles were forming as he wiped the ash away.

"Sorry," he said in English. Then in Japanese he said, "I have not been mindful, my burned-up *gaijin* girl. I will do better."

He went to the cabinet under his workbench and removed a cedar box that looked like it might have been fashioned to hold a set of silverware. He opened the lid and removed the square of white silk, then stood and let the garment fall open to its full length. Yuriko's wedding kimono. It smelled of cedar, and perhaps of a bit of incense, but mercifully, it didn't smell of her.

He laid the kimono out next to the burned-up girl, and ever so slowly, he moved it under her, gently worked her skeletal arms into the sleeves, then closed the robe and tied it loosely with the white obi. He arranged her arms at her sides so they looked comfortable, then picked up a small flake of dried blood that had fallen from his face onto her breast. She looked better now. Still wraithlike and monstrous, but better.

"There you go. Yuriko would be pleased that her kimono helped cover one who had nothing."

He returned to his workbench and began the drawing for the block that would carry the yellow ink for the futon, when he heard movement behind him and wheeled around.

"Well, don't you look yummy," Jody said.

TOMMY

Tommy spent the early evening in the library, reading *The Economist* and *Scientific American*. He felt as if all the words were bringing him back from the animal realm to being a human being, and there were plenty of words in those magazines. He wanted his full powers of speech and human thought before he confronted Jody. He also hoped that his memory of what had happened would come back with his words, but that didn't seem to be working. He remembered a red blur of hunger in his head, being thrown through a window and landing on the street, but between that and the time when his words returned in the basement, with the Emperor, he could remember very little. It was as if those experiences—hunting, finding shelter of darkness, snaking his way through the City in a cloud of predators gone to mist—were filed in a part of his mind that locked as soon as the ability to put words to senses returned. He suspected that he may have helped Chet kill people, but if that was the case, why had he saved the Emperor?

Fortunately, he hadn't lost the ability to turn to mist, which was how he'd obtained the outfit he was wearing now. The whole ensemble—khaki slacks, blue Oxford-cloth shirt, leather jacket, and leather boating moccasins—had been on display in a window at a men's store on Union Square, suspended by monofilament fishing line into the shape of a casual cotton ghost that was haunting other, equally stylish but substanceless marionettes around some deck chairs and artificial sand. Just after the dinner hour, when the store was at its busiest, Tommy streamed in under the door, into the outfit and became solid. With a quick crouch, he snapped all the monofilament line and walked out of the store fully dressed, bits of fishing line curling in his wake. It would, he thought, have been the smoothest, most audaciously cool thing he had ever done, if it hadn't been for the straight pins that had fastened the shirt to the slacks. But after a minor fit on the sidewalk as he yanked the pins out of his back, hips, and abdomen, while rhythmically chanting, "Ouch, ouch, ouch, ouch," he returned to the calm and casual cotton-clad vampire aspect he'd been going for. He waited until he was at the library, in the stacks, before he pulled the piece of cardboard out of his collar and yanked off various tags and threads. Fortunately, there had been no anti-theft tags on the display outfit.

Now he was ready, or as ready as he was going to get. He had to go to Jody now, hold her, tell her he loved her, kiss her, shag her until all the furniture was broken and the neighbors complained (undead predator or not, he was still nineteen and horny), then figure out what they were going to do about their future.

As he walked back through the Tenderloin, dressed in his "please rob me" white boy outfit, a jittery crackhead in a hoody that had once been green, but now was so dirty it was shiny, tried to rob him with a screwdriver.

"Give me your money, bitch."

"That's a screwdriver," Tommy said.

"Yeah. Give me your money or I'll stab you with it."

Tommy could hear the tweaker's heart fluttering, smell the acrid stench of rotting teeth, body odor, and urine on him, and could see an unhealthy, dark gray aura around him. His predator mind flashed the word "prey."

Tommy shrugged. "I'm wearing a leather jacket. You'll never get a screwdriver through it."

"You don't know that. I'll get a running start. Give me your money."

"I don't have any money. You're sick. You should go to the hospital."

"That's it, bitch!" The crackhead thrust the screwdriver at Tommy's stomach.

Tommy stepped aside. The tweaker's movements seemed almost comically slow. As the screwdriver went by, Tommy decided it might be best if he took it, and he snatched it away. The robber lost his balance and tumbled forward into the street and lay there.

With the flick of his wrist, Tommy threw the screwdriver onto the roof of a four-story building across the street. Two guys who had been standing in an alley a few feet away, thinking about taking the robbery over from the crackhead, or at least robbing him if he was successful, decided they would rather go see what was happening on the next block.

Tommy was a half a block away when he heard the uneven, limping footsteps of the crackhead coming up behind him. He turned and the crackhead stopped.

"Give me your money," said the tweaker.

"Stop robbing me," said Tommy. "You don't have a weapon and I don't have any money. It's totally not working for you."

"Okay, give me a dollar," said the crackhead.

"Still don't have any money," Tommy said, turning his pants pockets inside out. A note from inspector 18 fluttered to the sidewalk. He heard movement above—claws on stone—and cringed. "Uh-oh."

"Fifty cents," said the crackhead. He put his hand in the pouch pocket of his hoody and pointed his finger like it was a gun. "I'll shoot."

"You have got to be the worst armed robber ever."

The crackhead paused for a second and pulled his gun-posed hand out of his pocket. "I have my G.E.D."

Tommy shook his head. He thought he'd left the cats behind, but the felines either still had some connection to him, or there were so many of them now that there was nowhere in the City you could go where they wouldn't be hunting. He didn't relish trying to explain the whole phenomenon to Jody. "What's your name?" he said to the crackhead.

"I'm not telling you. You could turn me in."

"Okay," Tommy said. "I'll call you Bob. Bob, have you ever seen a cat do that?" Tommy pointed up.

The crackhead looked up the side of the building to see a dozen cats coming down the bricks, face-down, toward him.

"No. Okay, I'm not robbing you anymore," said the tweaker, his attention taken by the clutter of vampire cats descending on him. "Have a nice evening."

"Sorry," said Tommy, meaning it. He turned and jogged up the street to put some distance between himself and the screaming, which only lasted a few seconds. He looked back to see the crackhead gone. Well, not really gone, but reduced to a pile of gray powder amidst his empty clothing.

"It's how he would have wanted to go," Tommy said to himself.

He would have thought the cats would go for the two in the alley, but now they were taking the people right out on the open street. He was going to have to get Jody and talk her into leaving the City, like they should have in the first place.

He jogged the twelve blocks to the loft, careful not to run so fast that he might be noticed. He tried to look like a guy who was just late getting home to his girlfriend, which, in a way, he was. He waited outside the door for a moment before pushing the buzzer. What was he going to say? What if she didn't want to see him? He didn't have any experience to draw on. She'd been the first girl he'd had sex with while sober. She was the first girl he'd ever lived with. She was the first to take a shower with him, to drink his blood, to turn him into a vampire, and to throw him broken and naked through a second-story window. She was his first love, really. What if she sent him away?

He listened, looked at the plywood still over the windows, sniffed the air. He could hear people inside, at least two, but they weren't talking. There were machines running, lights buzzing, the smell of blood and rat whiz wafting under the door. It really would have felt better if there were romance in the air, but, well, okay.

He ran his fingers through his hair, snatched away the last strands of fishing line trailing from his clothes like errant crystal pubes, and pushed the button.

FΦΦ

Foo had just placed the vials of Abby's blood in the centrifuge when the buzzer on the intercom went off. He flipped the switch, then looked over at Abby, lying on the bed. She looked so peaceful, undead and drugged and not talking. Almost happy, despite having a tail. But the police wouldn't understand. He ran into the living room and shook Jared out of the game-induced trance he had entered on his game console. Foo could hear the death-metal sound track coming from Jared's headphones, tinny screeching and tiny chainsaw rhythms, like angry chipmunks humping a kazoo inside a sealed mayonnaise jar.

"Whaaa?" said Jared, yanking out his earbuds.

"Someone's at the door," whispered Foo. "Hide Abby."

"Hide her? Where? The closet is full of medical crap."

"Between the mattress and the box springs. She's skinny. You can mash her in there."

"How will she breathe?"

"She doesn't need to breathe."

"Sweet."

Jared went for the bedroom, Foo for the intercom.

"Who is it?" he said, keying the button. He really should have installed a camera. They were easy to wire and he got a discount at Stereo World. Stupid.

"Let me in, Steve. It's Tommy."

Foo thought for a second he might pee a little. He hadn't finished building the high-intensity UV laser, and Abby hadn't worn her sun jacket. He was defenseless.

"I can see why you might be mad," said Foo, "but it was Abby's idea. I wanted to turn you back to human, like you wanted." *Oh fuck, oh fuck, oh fuck.* Tommy was going to kill him. It would be humiliating. The guy didn't even have an undergrad degree. He was going to be murdered by an undead Anglo liberal-arts tard who quoted poetry.

The buzzer went off again. Foo jumped and keyed the intercom.

"I didn't want to do it. I told her it was cruel to put you guys in there."

"I'm not mad, Steve. I need to see Jody."

"She's not here."

"I don't believe you. Let me in."

"I can't, I have things to do. Scientific things that you wouldn't understand. You have to go away." Okay, now he was a tard.

"I can come in, Steve, under the door or through the cracks around the windows, but when I go back to solid, I'll be naked. Nobody wants that."

"You don't know how to do that."

"I learned."

"Oh, that's cool," said Foo. *Oh shit, oh shit, oh shit.* Could he get the door shut and duct taped before Tommy could ooze in. The great room was already taped up to contain the rat fog.

"Buzz me in, Foo. I have to see Jody and I have to feed. You still have some of those blood pouches, right?"

"Nope. Sorry, we're all out. And Jody's not here. And we've installed sunlamps all over the loft, Tommy. You'd be toast." He did have some blood bags. In fact, he still had some of the ones with the sedative in it that he'd used to knock Abby out.

"Steve, please, I'm hungry and hurt and I've been living in a basement with a bunch of vampire cats and if I turn to mist my new outfit is going to get stolen while I'm up there snapping your neck with my junk hanging out."

Foo was trying to think of a better bluff when a dark sleeve shot by him and he heard the door lock buzz downstairs. He looked up at Jared. "What the fuck have you done?"

"Hi," Tommy said in Foo's ear.

"He sounded so sad," Jared said.

THE OLD ONES

At sundown the three awoke inside a titanium vault under the main cabin and checked the monitors that were wired like a nervous system to every extremity of the black ship.

"Clear," said the male. He was tall and blond and he'd been lean in life, so he remained so, *would* remain so, forever. He wore a black silk kimono.

The two females cranked open the hatch and climbed out into what appeared to be a walk-in refrigerator. The male closed the hatch, pushed a button concealed behind a shelf, and a stainless-steel panel slid across the hatch. They walked out of the fridge, into the empty galley.

"I hate this," said the African female. She had been Ethiopian in life, descended from royalty, with a high forehead and wide eyes that slanted like a cat's. "It was to this face that Solomon lost his heart," Elijah had told her, holding her face in his hands as she died. And so he called her Makeda, after the legendary Queen of Sheba. She didn't remember her real name, for she had worn it for only eighteen years, and she had been Makeda for seven centuries.

"It's different," said the other female, a dark-haired beauty who had been born on the island of Corsica a hundred years before Napoleon. Her name had been Isabella. Elijah had always called her Belladonna. She answered to Bella.

"It's not *that* different," said Makeda, leading the way up a flight of steps to the cockpit. "It seems like we just did this. We just did this—when?"

"A hundred and fifty years ago. Macao," said the male. His name was Rolf, and he was the middle child, the peacemaker, turned by Elijah in the time of Martin Luther.

"See what I mean," said Makeda. "All we do is sail around cleaning up his messes. If he does this again I'm going to have the boy drag him out onto the deck during the day and video it while he burns. I'll watch it every night on the big screen in the dining room and laugh. Ha!" Although the oldest, Makeda was the brat.

"And what if we die with the sire?" asked Rolf. "What if you wake up in the vault on fire?" He palmed a black glass console and a panel whooshed open in the bulkhead. The cockpit, big enough to host a party for thirty, was lined in curving mahogany, stainless steel, and black glass. The stern half was open to the night sky. But for the ship's wheel, it looked like an enormous Art Deco casket designed for space travel.

"I've died before," said Makeda. "It's not that bad."

"You don't remember," said Bella.

"Maybe not. But I don't like this. I hate cats. Shouldn't we have people for this?"

"We had people," said Rolf. "You ate them."

"Fine," said Makeda. "Give me my suit."

Rolf touched the glass console again and a bulkhead opened to reveal a cabinet filled with tactical gear. Makeda pulled three black bodysuits from the cabinet and handed one each to Rolf and Bella. Then she slid out of her red silk gown and stretched, naked, her arms wide like Winged Victory, her head back, fangs pointed at the skylight.

"Speaking of people," said Bella. "Where's the boy? I'm hungry."

"He was feeding Elijah when we awoke," said Rolf. "He'll be along."

Elijah was kept below in a vault similar to their own, except the prime vampire's vault was airtight, locked from the outside, and was fitted with an airlock system so the boy could feed him.

"Irie, me undead dreadies," said the pseudo-Hawaiian as he came up the steps, barefoot and shirtless, carrying a tray of crystal balloon goblets. "Cap'n Kona bringin' ya the jammin' grinds, yeah?"

The vampires each spoke a dozen languages but none of them had the slightest idea what the fuck Kona was talking about.

When he saw Makeda stretching, the blond Rastafarian stopped and nearly dumped the goblets off the tray. "Oh, Jah's sweet love sistah, dat smoky biscuit givin' me da rippin' stiffy like dis fellah need to poke squid with that silver sistah on de Rolls-Royce, don't you know?"

Makeda fell out of her "Nike" posture and looked at Rolf. "Huh?"

"I think he said he would enjoy violating you like a hood ornament," said Rolf, taking a snifter from the tray and swirling dark liquid under his nose. "Tuna?"

"Just caught, bruddah," said Kona, having trouble now balancing the tray while trying to hunch to conceal the erection tenting his baggies.

Bella took her snifter from the tray and grinned as she turned to look out the windscreen at the City. The Transamerica Pyramid was lit up in front of them, Coit Tower just to the right, jutting from Telegraph Hill like a great concrete phallus.

Makeda took a slinky step toward Kona, "Should I let him rub oil on me, Rolf? Do I look ashy?"

"Just don't eat him," Rolf said. He sat in one of the captain's chairs, loosened the belt of his black kimono, and began working the Kevlar bodysuit over his feet.

"Quaint," said Makeda. She took another step toward Kona, held her bodysuit before her, then dropped it. In an instant she had gone to mist and streamed into the suit, which filled as if a girl-shaped emergency raft had been deployed inside. She snatched the last goblet out of the air as Kona flinched and dumped the tray.

"Will you oil me up later, Kona?" Makeda said, standing over the surfer now as he cowered.

"Nah need, matey, you shinin' plenny fine. But dat other ting bein' a rascal fo' sure." He held his hand to his chest and ventured a glance up at her. "Please."

"It's your turn," said Bella with a smile, her lips rouged with tuna blood.

"Oh, all right," said Makeda. "But use a glass."

Kona reached into the pocket of his baggies and came out with a shot glass, which he held with both hands before his head like a Buddhist monk receiving alms.

She pushed her thumb against one of her fangs, then let the blood drip into Kona's shot glass. Ten drops in, she pulled her thumb away and licked it. "That's all you get."

"Oh, mahalo, sistah. Jah's love on ya." He drained the blood then licked the shot glass clean, as Makeda watched and sipped her tuna blood. After a full minute, with the ersatz Hawaiian still lapping away at the glass, his breath heaving like he was hoisting the anchor by hand, she took the shot glass and held it away from him. "You're done."

"Bug eater," Bella said, disgusted. Now she was in her own bodysuit and had drained her goblet of blood.

"Oh, I think he's cute," said Makeda. "I may let him oil me up yet." She ruffled Kona's dreadlocks. He was staring blankly into space, his mouth open, drooling.

"Just don't eat him," Rolf said.

"Stop saying that. I won't eat him," said Makeda.

"He's a licensed captain. We need him."

"All right. I'm not going to eat him."

Bella walked over, yanked a dreadlock from Kona's head, and used it to tie back her own, waist-length black hair. The surfer didn't flinch. "Bug eater," she repeated.

Rolf was back at the cabinet, snapping together various bits of weaponry. "We should go. Grab a hood, gloves to go with the sunglasses. Elijah said they had some sort of sunlight weapons."

"This is different," said Bella, gathering all the high-tech kit from the weapons cabinet, as well as a long overcoat to cover it all. "We didn't have all this in Macao."

"As long as you're not bored, darling," said Rolf.

"I hate cats," said Makeda as she pulled on her gloves.

Carpe Noctem

MARVIN

Marvin the big red cadaver dog had done his job. He sat and woofed, which translated from the dog meant, "Biscuit."

Nine vampire hunters paused and looked around. Marvin sat in front of a small utility shed in an alley in Wine Country, behind a particularly nasty Indian restaurant.

"Biscuit," Marvin woofed. He could smell death amid the curries. He pawed the pavement.

"What's he doing?" said Lash Jefferson. He, Jeff, and Troy Lee carried Super Soakers loaded with Grandma Lee's Vampire Cat Remedy, other Animals had garden sprayers slung on their backs, except for Gustavo, who thought that making him carry a garden sprayer was racial stereotyping. Gustavo had a flame thrower. He wouldn't say where he got it.

"Second Amendment, *cabrones*." (The guy who sold Gustavo his green card had included two amendments from the Bill of Rights and Gustavo had chosen Two and Four, the right to bear arms and freedom from unreasonable search and seizure. [His sister Estrella had had seizures as a child. *No bueno*.] For five bucks extra he threw in the Third Amendment, which Gustavo bought because he was already sharing a three-bedroom house in Richmond with nineteen cousins and they didn't have any room to quarter soldiers.)

"That's his signal," said Rivera. He was wearing his UV-LED leather jacket and felt like a complete dork. "When he sits and does that with his paw he's found a body."

"Or vampire," added Cavuto.

"Biscuit," woofed Marvin.

"He's fucking with you," said Troy Lee. "There's nothing here."

"Maybe in the shed," said Lash. "There's no lock on it."

"Who would leave anything unlocked in this neighborhood?" asked Jeff.

"Biscuit please," woofed Marvin. They had an agreement: As consideration for finding dead things, the cadaver dog, heretofore referred to as Marvin, shall receive one biscuit. There was some flexibility, however, and Marvin understood that in this case, they weren't looking for dead humans, but dead cats, and despite their inherent tastiness, Marvin was not to eat the findees. "Biscuit," he rewoofed. Where was the biscuit? It had been months since he'd led them to the dead things. (Well, it seemed like months. Marvin wasn't very good with time.)

"Open it," said Troy Lee. "We'll cover you."

Rivera and Cavuto moved to the shed, which was aluminum and had a roof shaped like an old-fashioned barn's. The Animals moved in a semicircle and trained their weapons on the shed. (Grandma Lee had stayed home to watch wrestling on TV when she realized there weren't going to be any firecrackers.)

"On three then," said Rivera.

"Wait," said Cavuto. He turned to Gustavo. "No *fuego. Comprende*? Do not fucking light up that flamethrower."

"*Sí*," said Gustavo. They had tested the flamethrower on the basketball court in Chinatown. It had a fairly short, wide spray. In other words, if Gustavo used it in the alley he would probably fry them all.

Barry turned and sprayed the flamethrower's pilot light with a stream of vampire cat remedy. The flame went out with a sizzle. "Okay, go."

"On three, then," said Rivera. They all raised their weapons.

"One," Rivera nodded to Cavuto and grabbed the switch to his jacket LEDs.

"Two." Troy Lee crouched and aimed his Super Soaker to the center of the doors, ready to strafe in any direction. Cavuto drew his Desert Eagle, cocked the hammer, and thumbed off the safety.

"Three!"

The cops threw open the doors and lit up their jackets, the Animals leaned in.

Six surprised kittens and a mother cat looked out from a box set on stacks of five-gallon detergent buckets.

They all looked around, not saying anything. The Animals lowered their weapons. The cops turned off their jackets.

"Well, that's embarrassing," said Troy Lee.

"Biscuit," Marvin woofed.

They all looked at Marvin. "You suck, Marvin," said Cavuto. "Those are normal cats."

Marvin didn't understand. He had followed the trail, he had made the signal when he came to the end of the trail. Where was his biscuit?

"Bad dog, Marvin," said Lash.

Marvin growled at him, then turned to Rivera and woofed, "Biscuit." He was not a bad dog. It wasn't his fault that no one had taught him how to point up. It wasn't his fault they weren't looking up, past the top of the shed, up the wall, to the roof, four stories up. Couldn't they hear them?

"Biscuit," he woofed.

CHET

Chet watched the vampire hunters moving below. He understood what they were doing and how badly they were doing it. The other cats had moved away from the edge of the roof, the smell of flame, the sunlight jackets, and the dog had made them weary. A few of them were survivors of the encounter with the little Japanese swordsman, and Asians in general still freaked them out a little. Although they couldn't see the life auras that a human vampire could, it was still in their instinct as predators to take the weak and the sick, and the group below appeared to be neither.

Chet, on the other hand, was less and less of a cat every night. He was bigger than Marvin now, and had lost most of his cat instinct, and whatever he was now, it wasn't a cat. Although he was still a predator, words kept invading his mind, sounds that produced pictures in his mind. Abstract concepts whirled around in sound and symbols. His kitty brain had been rewired with human DNA, and what had resulted was not only an alpha predator, but a creature with the capacity for revenge, mercy, and conscious cruelty.

Chet watched the group below move out of the alley, led by Rivera and trailed by Barry, the bald, portly scuba diver of the Animals. The kitty part of Chet's brain saw Barry's bald spot like a ball of yarn, teasing him to attack. He needed to get it. He went to mist and snaked down the side of the building. He liked climbing face-down, especially since he had grown thumbs, but stealth was the only way to pick off the last one without facing the whole group in combat.

He rematerialized in front of Barry, on his hind feet, and before the hapless grocery clerk could call out, Chet thrust his entire paw into his mouth and unsheathed his claws. There was only a slight gurgling sound, and Clint, the born-again, who had been walking ahead of Barry, turned to see only an empty alley behind him.

Chet was already three floors above him on the wall. Barry dangled from Chet's claws, twitching, as the huge, shaved vampire cat drank his life away.

TOMMY

"Foo," Tommy said, right in Foo's ear. "I want you to remember, before you move, at all, that I was the one who wore your sun jacket to rescue Jody from Elijah. So if I see you even look like you're going to touch a switch of any kind, I'm going to tear that arm off, okay?"

"I didn't want to put you in the statue," said Foo for the third time.

"I know," Tommy said. "Where's Jody?"

"She went looking for you."

Jared started to back away from the door into the kitchen area.

"You too, Jared. If I don't see your hands for one second, I'm taking them off so I don't have to worry about it."

Jared waved his hands in front of him like he was drying his nails. "Whoa, badass much? I'm the one that let you in. I was going to get you some blood."

"Sorry, stress," Tommy said. He had Foo by the throat, but lightly.

"Give him the one that's already opened," Foo said.

"The one with the drugs in it?" asked Jared.

Foo flinched as if waiting for the sound of his neck snapping. "Yes, that one, you fuckwit."

"I'm good for now," Tommy said. Then to Foo, "Jody went where to find me?"

"Just out. Right after she got you out of the shell. She took half the money and most of the blood. Abby said that she was at the Fairmont, but Rivera and Cavuto found her. We don't know where she is now."

"Where's Abby?"

"She's at her mom's," said Foo.

"No, she's not." Tommy choked him a little. "She's here. I can smell her." He cocked his head. "I don't hear her heartbeat. Is she dead?"

"Kind of," said Jared. "She is nossssss-feratu. That's how she says it. I'm so jealous."

"Did I do that?"

"No," said Foo. "She did it herself. You were out of your mind, and you bit her, but Jody pulled you off of her and threw you through the windows. You don't remember?"

"Not much. Probably a good thing for you, too."

"She's under the mattress," Jared said. "Foo made me hide her there."

"I'm going to change her back. I told you I could do it and I can. I'm already working on her batch of serum."

"And she saw Jody last?"

"Her friend Lily saw Jody coming out of the Fairmont

a few nights ago. Abby went there to find her and saw Cavuto and Rivera."

"Then we don't know if they found Jody while she was
out?"

"They didn't. They didn't say anything when they came
to get their jackets."

"Their jackets? Sun jackets? You gave them sun jackets?"

"I have to do what they want. They were going to take
me in for statutory rape and contributing to the delinquency of a minor."

"Really? Have they met Abby?"

"Truth," said Foo, as wistfully as you can when you're
being choked.

"Tommy, let me change you back. It's what you wanted.
I can do you and Abby at the same time."

"No. And you're not changing her. Wake her up."

"What? Why?"

"Because I'm going to go look for Jody and I'm taking
Abby with me. I'm not leaving her here with you guys."

"Why? She's my girlfriend. I wouldn't hurt her."

"She's my BFF," said Jared. "He's the one who can't be
trusted."

"I'm taking her with me. I'm not going out there without someone watching my back. Haven't you ever seen a
horror movie? When you split up and go off by yourself,
that's when the monster gets you."

"I thought in this movie you were the monster," Foo
said.

"Only if you don't do what I say," Tommy said, a little surprised to hear himself say it. "Wake her up, Foo."

JØDY

The last thing she remembered before burning up were the orange socks. And here they were again, fluorescent orange, highway safety orange socks, at the base of a tiny, blood-encrusted man who was fussing about at some sort of workbench.

"Well, don't you look yummy," she said, and she was surprised at the sound of her own voice: dry, weak, and ancient.

The little man turned, startled at first, but then he composed himself, bowed, and said something in Japanese. Then, "Sorry," in English.

"It's okay," she said. "This isn't the first time I've woken up in a strange man's apartment where I can't remember how I got there." This was, however, the first time she remembered where she had been on fire at the end of the night. Before it had gone quite that far, the girls she worked with held a lunchtime intervention in which each told her, frankly and sincerely, as people who loved her, that she was a drunken slut who took all the hot guys at the TGIF bar crawl every week and she needed to knock it the fuck off. So she did.

Now, as in those days, she was disoriented, but unlike those days, it didn't even occur to her to be afraid.

The little Japanese man bowed again, then took a square-pointed knife from his workbench and approached her shyly, his head down, saying something that sounded very much like an apology. Jody held up her hand to wave him off, say, "Hey, back off there, cowboy," but when she saw her hand, an ash-white desiccated claw, the words caught in her throat. The little man paused just the same.

Her arms, her legs? She pulled up the kimono—her stomach, her breasts—she was shrunken, like a mummy. The effort exhausted her and she fell back into the pillow.

The little man shuffled forward and held his hand up. There was a bandage on his thumb. She watched as he raised his hand, pulled off the bandage, and put the point of the knife to the wound that was already there. She caught his knife hand and ever so gently, pushed it down.

"No," she said, shaking her head. "No."

She couldn't imagine what her face might look like. The ends of her hair were like brittle red straw. What must she have looked like before he had done this, done this too much, she could see.

"No."

With him close, she could smell the blood on him. It wasn't human. Pig. It smelled of pig, although she didn't know how she might know that. When she had been at her best she would have smelled blood on someone just walking by on the sidewalk. It wasn't only her strength that was gone, her senses were nearly as dull as when she had been human.

The little man waited. He had bowed, but did not rise up again. Wait, he held his head aside, his throat open. He was bending down so she could drink. Knowing what she was, he was giving himself to her. She touched his cheek with the back of her hand and when he looked she shook her head. "No. Thank you. No."

He stood, looked at her, waited. She smelled the dried blood on the back of her hand, tasted it. She had tasted it before. She felt something tacky in the corner of her mouth—yes, it was the pig blood. The hunger wrenched through her, but she fought it down. He had fed her his own blood, obviously, but also pig's blood. How long? How far had he brought her?

She gestured for him to bring her paper and something to write with. He brought her a sketch pad and a broad square carpenter's pencil. She drew a map of Union Square, then drew a crude figure of a woman and wrote down numbers, many numbers, her sizes. What about money? Rivera would have her things from the room, but she had hidden most of the money in another spot. From the brickwork in the apartment, the window frames, the angle of streetlights coming down from above, she guessed she was in a basement apartment right near where she'd been running on Jackson Street. Nowhere else in the City looked like this, was this old. She pointed to herself and the little man and then to the map.

He took it from her and drew an *X*, then quickly drew a stick version of the Transamerica Pyramid. Yes. They were on Jackson Street. She wrote a "*$*" where she'd hidden the money, then scratched it out. It was hidden in a locked electrical junction box high on a roof, where she had been able to climb easily, two floors above the highest fire escape. This frail little guy would never get there.

The little man smiled and nodded, pointing to the dollar sign. He went to his workbench, opened a wooden box, and held up a handful of bills. "Yes," he said.

"Okay, then, I guess you're buying me an outfit."

"Yes," he said.

She made a drinking gesture, then nodded. He nodded and held up the knife again.

"No, you can't afford it. Animal." She thought about making a piggy sound, but wasn't sure that might not give him the wrong idea, so she drew a stickman on the sketch pad, then Xed it out and drew a first-grade stick piggy, a stick sheep, and a Jesus fish. He nodded.

"Yes," he said.

"If you bring me a Christian petting zoo I'm going to be disappointed, Mr.—uh—" Well, this was embarrassing. "Well, you're not the first guy I've ever woken up with whose name I don't remember." Then she stopped herself and patted his arm. "I'm sounding really slutty, I know, but the truth is I used to be afraid to sleep alone." She looked around the little apartment, at the meticulously arranged tools on the workbench, the one pair of little shoes, and the white silk kimono he had wrapped her in.

"Thank you," she said.

"Thank you," he said.

"My name is Jody," she said, pointing to herself. She pointed to him, wondering if that might not be rude in his culture. But he had already seen her nude and burned up, so perhaps they were past formality. He seemed okay with it.

"Okata," he said.

"Okata," she said.

"Yes," he said, with a big smile.

His gums were receded, which made him look like he had big horse teeth, but then Jody touched her tongue to her fangs, which it seemed were not retracting in her new, dried-up state, and she realized that she should probably be less judgmental.

"Go, okay?" She pointed to the sketch pad.

"Okay," he said. He gathered up his things, put on his stupid hat, and was ready to leave, when she called to him.

"Okata?"

"Yes."

She made a face-washing gesture and pointed to him. He went to the little mirror over the sink, looked at himself covered with blood, and laughed, his eyes crinkled into high smiles themselves. He looked over his shoulder at her, laughed again, then scrubbed his face with a cloth until he was clean and went to the door.

"Jody," he said. He pointed to the stairs outside. "No. Okay?"

"Okay," she said.

When he was gone, she crawled from the futon and stumbled from there to the workbench, where she rested before trying to move farther, to look at Okata's work. Wood block prints, some finished, some with only two or three of the colors on them, proofs perhaps. They were a series, the progression of a black, skeletal monster against a yellow futon, then the gradual filling in of the figure. The care, wrapping her in the kimono, feeding her his blood. The last print was still in the sketch stage. He must have been working on it when she awoke. A sketch on thin rice paper had been glued to the wood block and he was carving away the material for the outline—the black ink in the other prints. They were beautiful, and precise, and simple, and sad. She felt a tear rise and turned so as not to drip blood on the print.

How would she tell him? Would she point at the first sketch, the one where the figure looked like a medieval woodcut of Death himself, and point to his frail chest?

"The first thing I noticed when I saw you was the life aura around you, and it was black. That's why I wouldn't let you give me your blood, Okata. You are dying."

"Okay," he would say. "Thank you," he would say, with his newly found grin.

Being the Chronicles of Abby Normal: Oh Day Dwellers Doth Betray Me?

My heart has been torn asunder, and I am faced with the revelation that my most awesome-haired mad scientist of passion may in fact be an uncaring assbag who has sullied my innocence and whatnot and then cruelly cast me aside. So, that sucks.

'Kayso, like it says in the Bible, "with great power, comes great responsibility," which I totally learned by pushing my vamp abilities too far in trying to show off for Foo by diving through our boarded-up windows. So I was "doh," and I passed out—real passed out, like head-injury passed out, not vampyre passed out. But in my unconsciousness, Foo and Jared gave me blood, and I healed, so when I woke up in the bedroom, I came leaping out into the living area, my claws ready to rend flesh and kick ass.

And I was all, "Rawr!"

And who do I see there but the vampyre Flood, my

most recently escaped master gone mad, who has never even seen me in this outfit, let alone as a vamp.

So I was all, "Rawr!" hoping my fangs were showing.

And he was all, "Hi, Abby."

And I was all, "Rawr! Fear me!"

And he was all, "That's not a thing. Saying *rawr* is not a vampyre thing."

And I'm like, "It is too. I'm totally showing my animal power and fierceness."

And he's like, "No, you're not, you're just saying *rawr* in a big voice. It's not a thing."

"It *could* be a thing," I go, in my defense.

And Jared is like, "I don't think it's a thing, Abs."

And I'm like, "Well then how about I drain you until you're dust and put you in the cat box, Jared? Is that a vampyre thing?"

And he was all, " 'Kay. I'm sorry. *Rawr* is totally a thing."

So I looked at Flood with pity, having humiliated him on the field of battle. But it is in the gentler monster that humanity is revealed, so I'm like, "It's a thing for some of us. So, check it, I'm nossssss-feratu. Like you, only, you know, not fashion retarded. Speaking of, why do you look like the window at Banana Republic?" Flood was always sort of jeans and flannel before, like he was caught in some '90s grunge vortex, but now he was like linen and tan leather.

And Flood's like, "I was running around the streets na-ked until a few hours ago."

And I was like, " 'Kay. My bad."

So he's all, "Abby, we need to go. I need to find Jody and I need your help."

And then Foo, who has been doing science stuff in the kitchen, comes over and he's like, "Abby, I can switch you back. I can switch you both back. I already have Tommy's serum made from before."

And I'm like, "You are *très* cute when you're threatened." And I jump over there and kiss him deeply—like I can hear a couple of his vertebrae crack. But then I go to slap him, so he won't think I'm a slut, and Tommy catches my hand.

And he's all, "Abby, you have to stop doing that. You could kill him."

I'm like, "Really?"

He's all nodding. And Foo's all mouthing "thank you" to him, like I don't have vampyre hearing and don't know that he's being a total little bitch about it. So I, like, turn on Foo and go, "Rawr."

I don't care what Tommy says, Foo trembled in fear.

And Tommy's like, "Let's go, Abby." Like Foo hasn't said a word.

And I grab my *Pirate Bunny* messenger bag and start to pack in my laptop and charger, and Flood is all, "Leave that here."

And I'm like, "How will I express my angst and dark inspirations and whatnot?"

And Flood is like, "I thought we'd go suck the blood out of some people."

And I was like, " 'Kay, but I'm still taking my laptop. I have to do my blog. I have subscribers." I do. Well, *a* subscriber.

And he's like, "If we have to go to mist you'll lose it."

And I'm like, "You don't know how to do that."

And he's all, "I do now."

And I'm all, "Teach me. I didn't go to ancient evil vampyre school like you."

And he's like, "I'm nineteen, remember? I went to public school. In Indiana."

And Foo's like, "You're only nineteen? You're not even old enough to drink?"

And Jared is like, "Shut up. He's her dark lord. Our dark lord."

And Foo's like, "Fine. Go. Be careful. Text me. I'll be here trying to save the world."

And Tommy's all, "I'm just going to try to save the woman I love, and that's as good as the world to me."

And I was like—nothing. I just looked at Tommy. But I would have done him on a bed of carpet tacks right then.

So outside the love lair, which is technically not mine and Foo's anymore, now that the rightful owners are not imprisoned in bronze, I go, "So, where do we start?"

And Flood is all, "We start by finding a safe place to sleep during the day."

And I'm all, "The love lair. Foo and Jared will be our minions and whatnot."

And he's like, "The last time I went out there I woke up inside a statue, and the last time you were up there your love ninja gave you blood with a sedative."

And I'm all, "No."

And he's all, "Yeah."

And I'm all, "Foo, you crapacious little geek! Can I go slap him around a little?"

And Flood is all, "He was going to change you back. To save you."

And I go, "Without even asking? I think not, noble vamptard. As soon as we find the Countess I'm coming back. There will be screaming."

And Flood's like, "You don't have any confrontation issues, do you?"

And I'm all, "No, I'm very insecure, actually, but I have found that if you roll up screaming like a madwoman, hair on fire, guns blazing, no one is going to mention the zit on your forehead." Which is totally true.

"Okey dokey," goes the vampyre Flood. "We'll look for someplace low or high. Low is probably safest, we can look for maintenance closets in the BART tunnels, but that keeps us out of the north end of the City, because there's no subway there. High, harder to find a place, but it gives us more choice, and it's less obvious, if Rivera and Cavuto are looking for us. There are a lot of utility sheds and meter shelters on roofs."

So I'm like, "Are we going to sleep together?"

And Flood's like, "No, but we'll be dead in the same space."

And I was thinking, "How romantic," but I go, "Let's get high."

And Tommy's all, "I think that's a good idea. Jody lived in the north end of the City and so did I. It makes sense that's where she'd go. We need to get into the upper floors of a tall building and look down on other roofs, look for a shed or something. Climbing up won't be a problem. You can tell if there's people in it by looking for heat. You know you can see heat now, right?"

And I'm like, "I was figuring that it was that or that every lightbulb was leaking into the sky. But how do you know all this other stuff?"

And Tommy's like, "I have no idea."

And I was like, "If we find a roof shack with a pigeon coop by it we'll have snacks when we wake up." I know, perky. I must resist the perky. Must resist the perky.

So, like, an hour later we've found our sweet roof grave on a building in the financial district, and Flood and I are walking up Powell Street, toward California and the Fairmont, where the Countess was last seen. And we are totally alive with the night. There's like two cities in the City. I didn't see it before. There's like the indoor city, the daytime city, with people inside of apartments and restaurants and offices, and they have, like, no fucking clue about the outside city. And there's the outside city people, who are in the streets all the time, and who know every hiding place, and every tree, and where it's dangerous, and where it's just creepy. The outside city people live on, like, a different plane of existence, like they don't even see the inside people either. But when you're a vampyre, the two cities are all lit up. You can hear the people talking and eating and watching TV in their houses, and you can see and feel the people in the streets, behind the garbage cans, under the stairs. All these auras show, sometimes right through walls. Like life, glowing. Some bright pink, like Foo's, some sort of brown, or gray, like on the AIDS vet panhandling at the corner of Powell and Post. And I'm totally losing my ability to appear bored, because it's fucking awesome. I'm trying to be chill for Flood, but I want to know.

So I'm like, "What's with the pink ring around people?"

And he's like, "It's their life force. You can tell how healthy they are by it. You'll be able to smell if they're dying, too, but you won't know that right away."

I know, whoa. So I'm like, "Whoa."

And he's all, "You see it for a reason."

And I'm like, " 'Splain, *s'il vous plaît.*"

And he's all, "Because you're only supposed to take the sick, the dying. It's part of our predator nature. I didn't know that before I—I was lost, but I know it now."

I know, whoa. So I'm like, "Okay, how do you turn to mist?"

And he's like, "It's mental. Completely. You can't think about it, you just have to *be.*"

And I'm like, "You're fucking with me, aren't you?"

And he's all, "No, if you think, it doesn't work. You have

to just be. Words get in the way. I think that's why the cats do it instinctively. That's the key. Instinct. I don't function well on instinct. I'm a word guy."

And I'm all, "I'm a word guy, too," like a total dwee-bosaurus. I know. How is it that I, acting Mistress of the Greater Bay Area darkness, can be reduced to spewing nano-brained beauty-queen dialog when I should be enjoy-ing the heady power of my vamp immortality? Simple, I am a romance slut, and there's nothing I can do about it. If a guy does or says something romantic, I'm all, "Oh, please excuse me, kind, sir, let me dial down my IQ and oh, if it would please sir, may I offer you this moist, yet helpless va-jay-jay that seems to have lost its way." I was clearly born in the wrong time. I should have been born in *Wuthering Heights* times. Although if I was Cathy, I would have hunted down that Heathcliff guy and beat him with a riding crop like a sado-hooker with his Black Card on file. Just sayin'.

So there's nothing at the Fairmont. We talk to the bell-man and the guy at the concierge desk, who talks to the front-desk guy who says that he's not at liberty to talk about guests, when I whip a hundred-dollar bill on him and he says "the redhead" never showed up again after the day the cops came around asking for her. He said the cops took a cooler from her room.

And Tommy's like, "She just vanished."

And I'm all, "Do you want to get coffee? I have a bag of blood and ten thousand dollars in my messenger." The nosferatu can totally drink lattes as long as they put some blood in it, unless they're lactose intolerant.

And he stops and looks at me. He's like, "Really, ten thousand? Think that will be enough?"

And I'm like, "Well, you'll have to drink the cheap stuff, but I like to drink my lattes directly out of the veins of a toddler, and those little fuckers aren't cheap."

And he's like, "Okay, you just completely creeped me out."

So I'm all, "You suck at this. Let's go get coffee and do some vamp stuff, like beat up some pimps and whatnot."

"Since when is beating up pimps a vampyre thing?"

"Since I was looking for the Countess and they kept trying to recruit me because I'm am so awesome sexy that desperate losers will totally pay to do me, which is flattering and whatnot, but I still kind of feel like they would have taken advantage of me because of my youth and naivety."

"So you want to go beat them up."

"I want to try that kung-fu thing where you tear their heart out and show it to them while it's still beating. *Très* macabre, *non*? Plus, I'll bet the look of surprise on their faces will be worth it. Did you do that when you were out slaughtering people with Chet?"

"I don't remember any of that. I don't remember slaughtering people."

"That's why the pimps were trying to recruit me. You and Chet ate all their hos."

"You make it sound so sordid."

"Okay, you make eating hos sound pretty. Talk poetry to me, writer boy."

And he looks all heartbroken and whatnot. And he's like, "That's what Jody calls me."

And I'm like, "Sorry. Where do you want to look for her now?"

"I don't know. What time is it?"

And I look at the watch that the Countess gave me, and I'm all, "A little after one," in my *I am total poop on a stick* voice.

"Polk Street."

And I'm all, "Why Polk Street?"

He's like, "Because I'm out of ideas and we need to resort to magic."

And I'm like, "Sweet! Let's rock the dark magic!" I was tempted to do a booty dance of total dark magic celebration, but I thought it might reveal my secret.

'Kayso, we roll into this coffee shop on Polk Street, and it's all full of hippies and hipsters and couples on dates and drunks sobering up and whatnot. And everyone turns and looks at us. I'm about to chuck a spaz, because I realize that I haven't fixed my makeup since I bounced my face off the plywood in the love lair.

So I'm all, "Tommy, psssssst, do I look like a cannibal corpse on crack?"

And he stops and looks at me for a second, and he's like, "No more than usual."

And I'm all, "Do I have raccoon eyes?"

And he's like, "You've kind of taken your broken clown look to the next level, with the crusted blood around your mouth. You look cute."

Flood can be very sweet for a doofus from Indiana. I felt like I had made the right decision to choose him to be my Dark Lord, even if he was only nineteen instead of five hundred.

So I feel like I should say something nice back, so I'm like, "You're not as pathetic in those clothes." Then I realize that didn't sound as nice as I liked, so I'm all, "I want a triple soy latte with type O in it while we're waiting for magic and whatnot."

And Flood is all, "She's here."

I know. I'm like, "Whaaaa?"

'Kayso, Flood sends me for coffees and says he'll meet me at a table in the back, so when I show up, he's sitting with this ginormously fat gay guy, wearing a purple silk wizard robe with silver stars and moons on it, and his head is shaved and there's a pentagram tattooed on it, just like I drew on Ronnie's head with a Magic Marker. I know! And he has a crystal ball on his table on a stand made out of dragons, and a sign that says MADAME NATASHA, FORTUNES TOLD $5.00, ALL PROCEEDS GO TO AIDS RESEARCH.

And so I come up and Flood is all, "Madame Natasha, this is my minion, Abby Normal."

And I'm all, *"Enchanté,"* in, like, perfect fucking French. "Most fly eye-liner, Madame." He had like spider fake lashes and glitter liner out to his ears.

And Madame Natasha is all, "Oh, sweet of you to say, child. Your ensem is *très chic* as well. But you should have a jacket, little thing like you could freeze in the fog."

And I'm all ready to throw down anti-mom *you're-not-the-boss-of-me-talk* on him, then I'm kinda okay with it. Like maybe I would get along with the Motherbot better if she were a ginormous gay guy.

And I sit down next to Madame Natasha, because Flood is, like, in the client seat, and Flood's all, "Madame Natasha told my fortune when I first came to town, and said that I would meet a girl, but the death card kept coming up, so she couldn't figure it out." Then he turns to Madame and is like, "You were right on the money, I ended up meeting a dead girl."

And Madame's all, "Oh my," and she pulls this little fan out of one of her chins and starts fanning herself.

'Kayso, I pull out the bag of blood and squeeze a little into my coffee, then into Flood's, and he's all, "Abby, put that away."

And I'm all, "Why?"

And he's all nodding toward people, who are totally not looking at us now, but like really reading or texting hard. And he's like, "They'll freak."

And I'm like, "Oh bitch, please. They all saw my eye makeup, they saw how I'm dressed, they saw my dark and mysteriously colored hair, and they think I'm just trying to freak them out by pretending to pour blood in my coffee. So they are all furiously not freaking out so as to not give me the satisfaction because then they wouldn't be sophisticated City peeps. This is not my first funeral, Red State."

"Oh, I like her," goes the Madame. "She's got spunk."

And Flood is like, "Okey dokey."

And I'm like, "If you keep saying 'okey dokey' I will be forced to replace you as my Dark Lord."

And Madame is all, "It does sound a little corn-fed, love."

And Tommy is all, "Never mind how I talk. You remember, right, Madame? You remember me?"

And the Madame is all "Oh, yes, yes, I do now. You were the one who had achieved Olympic levels in masturbation, weren't you?"

And Flood was all, "Uh, no, that part was someone else, uh—"

So, like, the master needed a hand, if you know what I mean, so I was like, "Oh chill, it's a stress thing, everyone does it. I'm flicking the bean under the table right now just to dial the tension back a little. Yes. Yes. Yes! Oh-zombie-jeebus-fuck-me-Simba-lion-king-hakuna-matata! Yes!" So I spaz-gasmed a little and kind of slid down in my seat breathing hard. Then I like look up at the Madame with one eye and I'm like, "They're freaking out now, aren't they?"

And she just kind of nodded with big eyes and whatnot. So, you know, embarrassment for my Dark Lord totally diverted. But this one crusty day dweller is all looking up from his *Wall Street Journal* at me with a disgusted face, so I'm all, "Rawr."

And Flood looks at me.

And I'm like, "Shut up, it's a thing. He shouldn't even be allowed out at night, using my dark without permission." So I rawred Wall Street again for eavesdropping.

So we sort of drank our coffee for a while and Madame looked at her cards and then, like, looked up seemed disappointed that we were still there, but Flood was on it.

He's all, "The woman you told me I would meet, I met her. We live together."

And the Madame holds up her hand, which means, "shut the fuck up" in fortune-teller language. And she looks at her cards some more. Then she looks at her tip jar.

Then Flood looks at me and like does the tip jar nod. So I pull a hundred out of my messenger bag and drop it in the jar.

And Flood's like, "Abby!"

And I'm like, "Hello, woman you love? You want to bargain hunt?"

And he's all, " 'Kay."

So Madame Natasha puts down a few more cards, and goes, "A redhead."

And we're all, "Yeah."

And she's all, "She's hurt, but she's not alone."

And we're all, "Uh-huh."

And she lays out about six more cards, and she goes, "That can't be right."

And Flood is like, "If you're getting the dead thing again, that's okay, we've worked through that."

And Madame is like, "No, it's not that." And she shuffles the cards, not cool, like a dealer, but gentle, and every which way on the table, like she's really trying to confuse the cards.

Then she lays them out again. And her eyes are getting bigger as she goes—each card, bigger eyes—until she lays down the last in her pattern and she's all, "Oh my."

And we're all, "What? What?"

And she's, "This has never happened, in thirty years of consulting the cards."

And we're, "What? What?"

And she's, "Look."

There were fourteen cards on the table. All kinds of pictures and numbers. And I'm like, ready to go, " 'Splain, please." But then I see what she's big eyes about. They are all the same suit. So I'm, "They're all swords."

And she's like, "Yes. I'm not sure how to even interpret this."

And I'm all, "She's hurt, she's not alone, and all the cards came up swords?"

And she's, "Yes, dear, that's what I just said, but I don't know what it means."

And I'm, "I do. Can you do them again?" And I slap another hundred in her jar.

And she's, " 'Kay."

Then she lays them all out again, and this time there's a lot of swords, but also other cards. And I'm, "Well?"

And she's all, "In this configuration, the swords signify

north, but also, the air, a sailing ship perhaps. It doesn't make sense."

And we're like, "What? What?"

And she's like, "A sunken ship?"

And I'm like, "It makes total sense."

And Flood is like, "It does?"

And I'm like, "Stay right there, Madame. We may be back."

And Flood is like, "What? What?"

And I'm all, "I forgot to tell you about the little guy with the sword."

And he's like, "You really adjust to this magical stuff fast, Abby."

And I'm like, "Are you trying to say I'm perky? Because I'm not. I'm complex."

I am. Shut up, I am.

He's looking at me right now, like we should be going. Even though I am typing at awesome speed. Okay, that's it, dude, you're harshing the depth out of my literature. I'm coming. What a whiner. Gotta go. We're going to run out of dark. Byez.

THE OLD ONES

Makeda put on the glasses and watched the bricks at the corner of the building light up. They'd find the cats by behavior, because even vampire cats are cats, and they marked their territory. Elijah had told them where it had started and where it was likely to move. The special sunglasses, combined with their vampire vision, allowed them to see the phosphorus expelled in the cats' urine as glowing. They could even see a half-life, of sorts. Something marked days ago would glow much dimmer than something marked only a few hours ago.

"That way," said Makeda.

Rolf cocked his head toward the boarded-up loft apartment on the second floor. "That's the loft where Elijah said he turned the first cat. There are people up there. Sounds like two."

"That's also where he was fried by a jacket covered with sun lights," said Makeda. "I say we clean up the cats first, they're less tricky."

Rolf nodded to Makeda, who bolted down the alley without another word. They followed the trail, a mark here and there, many blocks until they reached the Mission, where the trail started to sunburst out.

"I don't know which way to go," said Bella. "We need to get a vantage point."

Rolf looked around and spotted the tallest building in the area. "How about that one, the one that looks like a robot pterodactyl is perched on it? He pointed to the black glass Federal Building.

Makeda said, "It's an abomination."

"Said the abomination," snarked Rolf. "I'll go. I have to go up solid, I need the glasses." He shrugged off his overcoat and dropped his weapons on top of it.

"Well go to mist if you lose your grip," said Makeda. "I'll catch your glasses. If you fall off of that thing solid we'll have to scrape you into a bag to get you back to the ship."

He grinned, showing his fangs, then started a steady climb up the sheer corner of the building.

Bella pulled a pack of cigarettes from her jacket, shook one out, lit it, then blew a long stream of smoke up after Rolf. "What if Elijah lied about turning more humans? He's lied before."

When they'd retrieved the old vampire from the City initially he'd brought along a blond vampire woman, claiming she was the only one. She hadn't survived the first month at sea. *Weak vessels,* they called her type.

"He didn't admit turning the cat, either, until we found the news stories on the Internet."

"We need to talk to him again when we get back to the ship, if there's time."

Rolf thumped to the pavement beside them. "That way. About six blocks. There's a sunburst pattern that's centered there and spreads out ten blocks or so in every direction. I could actually see a hundred or so cats on a roof there."

"Let's go, then," said Makeda.

"That's not all," said Rolf. "There is a group of men hunting them. Eight of them."

"How do you know they're hunting the cats?"

"Because two of them lit up their coats. If I hadn't been wearing the glasses I'd be blind. They're wearing the sun jackets that Elijah warned us about."

"Well, fuck," said Makeda. "That's eight more we have to kill."

"At least," said Rolf. "How much time before daylight?"

"Two and a half hours," said Bella, checking her watch. "Don't we have a sniper rifle on the ship?"

"Somewhere," said Rolf.

"Well, they can't turn on a sun jacket if they're dead before we're within five hundred yards."

"Messy," said Makeda. "Bullets leave bodies."

"I'd rather have to dispose of a couple of bodies than get fried by a sun jacket," said Bella, taking charge now. "Rolf, you and I will go after the cats. Take out as many as we can. Makeda, follow the hunters, keep your distance, see where they go, and meet us back at the ship. Tonight cats. Tomorrow night, humans."

"I hate cats," said Makeda.

"I know," said Bella.

"There's something else," said Rolf. "There was something else on the roof with the cats. Something bigger."

"What do you mean 'something'?" asked Makeda.

"I don't know," said Rolf, "but it wasn't putting out any heat, so it's one of us."

Hunters

TOMMY AND ABBY

Somehow it had seemed to make sense that he follow Abby's interpretation of Madame Natasha's reading, but now, standing on the dock by the black ship, with the night almost gone, he wasn't so sure.

"You think she's in there?"

"She could be. I saw in the City Blog that this ship arrived—there was a picture, and it looked cool, and—oh, I don't know, I'm new at this. You can't expect me to be good at everything. Why don't you go all misty and sneak aboard?"

They heard bare feet on teak and suddenly a gorgon of blond dreadlocks popped up over the top of the smooth black carbon fiber of the cockpit.

"Irie bruddah. Irie sistah. Howzit?" A young man, very tan, heat coming off him, but with a thin black ring inside his life aura.

Abby elbowed Tommy and he nodded to show he'd seen it.

"What did he say?" Tommy asked.

"I don't know," Abby said. "It sounds Australian. If he goes off about going *down under* to have a go on his *dirigity-doo* I'm going to kick him in the kidneys with my forbidden love Chucks."

"Okey dokey," Tommy said.

The blond guy held up a pair of night-vision binoculars, looked quickly through them, then set them down again. "Shoots! You be deadies! Jah's love to ya, me deadies!"

He vaulted up over the edge of the cockpit, landed on the deck eight feet below, then jumped over to the dock. He was very fit, very muscular, and smelled of fish blood and weed.

"Pelekekona called Cap'n Kona, pirate of the briny science, lion of Zion, and dreadie to deadies of the first order, don't you know."

He extended his hand to Tommy, who shook it, tentatively. "Tommy Flood," Tommy said, then, because he felt as if he should have a title, added, "writer."

Then the blond Rasta man took Abby in his arms, hugged her, and kissed her on both cheeks, then let his hands linger on her back and slide down. He let go when she bent one of his fingers back, driving him to his knees. "Back off, you fucking hemp Muppet! I am Countess Abigail Von Normal, emergency backup mistress of the Greater Bay Area darkness."

"Countess?" Tommy said out of the corner of his mouth.

"And a slim and delicious deadie biscuit, too, as fine as a snowflake, yeah," said Kona. "No harm, me deadies, I'n'I have grand Aloha for ya, but can't bring ya on the ship. That *Raven* ship will kill ya dead for good, don't cha know. But we can chant down Babylon right here, mon." He produced a pipe and lighter out of the pocket of his baggies. Out of the other he pulled a sterile lancet, the kind diabetics use to poke their fingers for blood tests. "If one of me new deadie dreadies would donate to a mon's mystic. Jus' a drop two."

Abby looked at Tommy. "Renfield," she said, rolling her eyes.

Tommy nodded. She was talking about Renfield, the crazed blood slave of Dracula in the original Bram Stoker novel. The original "bug eater."

"Maybe we can help you with that," Tommy said.

Abby said, "You're not worthy of our aid, not worthy to be free, and we would surely both be tools, to help you, vampire fool." She curtsied. "Baudelaire, *Les Fleurs du Mal.* I'm paraphrasing, of course."

"Nice," Tommy said. She knew her romantic poetry, not very well, or accurately, but she knew it.

"Ah, mon, I tried dat paraphrasing in Mexico one time. The boat, she stop too quick and dis brutha drop out da sky like one rock. No mon, Kona doan like de heights."

"Not parasailing, you imbecile, paraphrasing."

"Oh. Dat diffren."

"Ya think," said Abby.

Tommy said, "Kona, I will give you a drop of blood, but first, are you saying that this ship belongs to vampires?"

"Ya mon. Me deadie masters, mon. Powerful old."

"Are they on the ship now?"

"No, mon. They here to fix up this calamity. Vampire cats dat old one leave."

"Just the cats?"

"No mon, dey clean it all up. All the peoples have seen them, or know about it. They cleaning house, brah."

Abby shook her head like she had water in her ears. Tommy knew how she felt. "So, these old vampires are here to take out witnesses and whatnot, and they left you in charge of this ship? Just you?"

"Oh yeah, sistah. Kona *ichiban* top-rate pirate captain of briny science."

"Why would they do that? You're not even trying to keep a secret."

Kona let his good-time bravado slip, his shoulders slumped, and when he answered, the breezy island bullshit accent was gone, "Why would anyone believe a word I say?"

"Good point," Tommy said.

"And besides, you two already knew about vampires. No heat in the night-vision goggles."

"Also a good point," Tommy said. "So these are the vampires who came to get Elijah?" Abby had told Tommy that the Emperor had seen Elijah and the hooker, Blue, leaving with three vampires, taking a small boat out into the fog off the St. Francis Yacht Club.

"Ya, mon. Dat old bloodsucka be locked up below now, air tight. Dat buggah stone crazy, him."

Tommy expected a chill of sorts, but instead of alarm, he felt his senses and mental acuity almost tightening down. There was no flight response, only fight. That was new.

He said, "So Elijah, the hooker, and how many others?"

"Just the three, mon. No hooker. She second gen vamp, mon. They doan make it long. Curl up and die for good, she."

Abby stepped up and tried to grab Kona by the throat, but her hand was too small and she just ended up knocking him over on the dock. "What the fuck, what the fuck, what the fuck, what the fuck are you talking about, Medusa?"

"Oh, dey doan tink Kona know, but only dem vamps Elijah make live long time. How 'bout a drop of Zion, now, brah?" Kona held the lancet out to Tommy.

Tommy was stunned. "One more thing. Why would they bring the ship back here? They had to know that we blew up Elijah's yacht."

"Ya mon, but the *Raven,* she ain't like dat. She protect herself." Kona held up his arm and Tommy noticed for the first time he was wearing something that looked like a dog's shock collar on his wrist. "If I doan have dis here on, da *Raven* kill Kona dead dead, too. She knows. She knows them three. Anyone else, she send to Davy Jones."

Tommy took the lancet from Kona, unwrapped it, and pricked his finger with it.

"Not going to happen," Abby said, catching Tommy's hand as he was holding his bleeding finger out to Kona. "You are not getting dirty hippie mouth on you. You might be dead but you can catch heinous hacky-sac rot from someone like him."

"Gentle down, biscuit, Kona has him feelings, too."

She reached into her messenger and came out with a retractable pen. She unscrewed it, squeezed Tommy's blood into the cap, then handed it to Kona. "There."

The Rasta man sucked at the pen so hard he nearly aspirated it, then sat back on the dock and dazzled a wide, white grin. "Ya mon, takin' the ship home to Zion."

Abby's cell trilled. She checked the screen, said, "It's Foo," then answered and turned away.

Tommy could hear Foo Dog on the phone, begging Abby to come back to the loft right away. He shifted his focus to Kona. "Why?" he asked.

"Shoots, brah, a mon love his blood ganga, so jumpin' ship be powerful hard, but when I sign on the *Raven* ship she have a crew of twenny. Dey say dem boys leave, but they ain't jumpin' ship when we out to sea five days. Dat Makeda deadie, full on African biscuit, too, she eatin' me shipmats, Jah's mercy. Only Kona left now."

"You? You're the only crew on a ship this size?"

"Ya mon. That *Raven,* she sail herself."

Abby turned around. "We have to go."

"What?" Tommy asked.

"Foo said all the rats are dead. All of them."

Tommy didn't understand. He looked at the sky, which was starting to lighten. "We can't get over there now."

Abby checked her watch. "Fucksocks! Sunup in thirty."

RIVERA

The sky was lightening behind the Oakland hills and the pink light reflected in the glass front of the Marina Safeway made it appear to be on fire. The Animals stood around their cars, unslinging the tanks and Super Soakers of Grandma Lee's tea. Clint had Barry's spear gun, and was holding it as if it were a holy relic.

"We're out," said Lash Jefferson. "What are we going to tell Barry's mom? We don't even have a body."

Rivera didn't know what to say. He hadn't thought of the Animals as people, really. It was wrong in so many ways he didn't have time to count them up. Not just endangering the public, but actively drawing citizens into a secret operation that got them killed. Amid all the unreal things that had happened, having Barry plucked out of their ranks was too real. Too wrong.

"I'm sorry," Rivera said. "I thought we were prepared for them. They're just cats."

"The Emperor told you that it wasn't just a cat," said Jeff, the big ex-power forward. He was scratching Marvin's ears and the cadaver dog was smiling.

Rivera shook his head. It was the Emperor. He was a loon. How could you know that *that* part of the story was true?

"Did he have a wife, girlfriend?" asked Rivera. "We could put together some money for her."

"No, he didn't have a girlfriend," said Troy Lee. "He worked graveyard shift like the rest of us. Got high in the morning, slept until time to go to work at eleven. Girls won't put up with that shit."

The other Animals nodded, sadly, for Barry and for themselves.

"You can't quit now," said Cavuto. "You don't even know if your spray works. Don't you want to see? Get revenge?"

"What's the up side?" asked Lash.

"You save the City."

Lash slammed the car door. "We have two hours to get our whole night's work done. You guys need to roll out of here."

Rivera said, "Can we have a couple of those sprayers, then? And you guys should keep them with you. We know that Chet retraces his territory. You might be territory now."

Clint reached into the back of his Volkswagen, grabbed a Super Soaker, and threw it to Cavuto.

"Great," said the big cop, "I'm going to save the friggin' world with an orange squirt gun."

"Okay, in the car, Marvin," said Rivera. He opened the rear door of the Ford and Marvin leapt in. "Call us if you need us."

The two cops drove off. On the roof of the Safeway, the vampire Makeda checked her watch and squinted at the eastern sky, which was threatening sunrise.

ΦҚATA

Okata had never been to the Levi's store on Union Square, yet that's what the burned-up girl had drawn on the map, so that is where he went. It appeared to be a good place to find blue jeans. He handed a young girl the list the burned-up girl had given him. He paid in cash and left fifteen minutes later with a pair of black jeans, a cotton chambray shirt, and black denim jacket. The next mark on his map was the Nike store, and he left there with a pair of women's running shoes and a pair of socks. Then, about a block along the way to his next marker, he turned, went back to the Nike store, and bought a pair of running shoes for himself. They were bouncy and light and on his way to the next mark, he started skipping, but then caught himself and returned to deliberately pacing out his steps with his sheathed sword. People might ignore a tiny Japanese man in an orange porkpie hat and socks, with a sword, but if you went around expressing unrestrained joy, they would have you in a straitjacket before you could belt out a verse of "Zippity Do-Dah."

Next Okata found himself in the very soft and satiny world of a Victoria's Secret boutique. It was nearly Valentine's Day, and the entire store was festooned in pink and red, with very tall mannequins standing around in very small swaths of underwear. It smelled of gardenias. Young women moved back and forth, trailing bits of silk, not really talking, each entranced with her own decoration, in and out of fitting rooms, back to shelves, touching, feeling, stroking the lace, the satin, the combed cotton, then moving on to the next soft scene. He imagined that this must be what it was like in the control room for a vagina. He was an artist, and had never been in a control room, nor a vagina for nearly forty years, but he was sure he remembered it having a similar sensation. This was embarrassingly public, though, and he sat on a round red velvet settee to conceal the sudden memory rising in his trousers.

He was approached by a petite Asian girl with a name tag. He gave her his list and said, "Please," and was shocked out of his fuzzy, separate world when she answered him in Japanese.

"Is this for your wife?" she asked.

He didn't know what to say. She was there in the room with him, this young girl, in a vagina control room with him and his distant erotic memories. He could feel his face go hot.

"A friend," he said. "She is sick and sent me here."

The girl smiled. "She seems to know exactly what she wants, and her sizes are here, too. Do you know what color she likes?"

"No. Whatever you think is best," he said.

"You wait here. I'll go get some samples and you can pick."

He wanted to stop her, or bolt out the door, or crawl under the cushion of the settee and hide his embarrassment, but gardenia was in the air like opium, and there was music playing with the rhythm of slow sex, and the young women moved like diaphanous ghosts around him, and his shoes were very, very comfortable, so he watched the young girl picking out pairs of bras and panties, gathering them like rose petals to be sprinkled over a snowy path to heaven.

"Does she like basic black?" said the girl, noticing all the black denim peeking out of the Levi's bag.

"Red," Okata heard himself saying. "She likes red, like rose petals."

"I'll wrap these up for you," she said. "Will this be cash or charge?"

"Cash, please." He handed her two hundred dollars.

He waited on the settee, willing away his whereabouts, the smell and the music, the women moving, and thought about kendo exercises, training, and how tired—how really exhausted—he felt. By the time the girl returned to press the pink bag and his change into his hand, he was able to stand without embarrassment. He thanked her.

"Come again," she said.

He started to leave, and then looked at the burned-up girl's map and saw the pictures of the pig, cow, and fish, and realized that it was going to be an ordeal to explain to a butcher what he needed, so he called to the salesgirl.

"Excuse me. Could you do me a favor, please?"

On a fresh piece of pink stationery with red and silver hearts on it, she wrote in English: *4 quarts, cow, pig, or fish blood*. It would be much easier dealing with a new butcher with an order slip to hand them. He thanked her again, bowed, and left the store.

It was no small irony that when he finally found a butcher who could sell him blood, it was a Mexican in the Mission who had to have Okata's one-item shopping list translated into Spanish. Of course, he had blood. What self-respecting Mexican butcher didn't save the blood for Spanish blood sausage? Okata didn't understand any of that. He only understood that after walking half the City carrying jeans, sneakers, and a pink bag of underwear, he finally had a gallon of fresh blood for his burned-up *gaijin* girl. After he left the shop the butcher went to the phone and dialed the number on the card the police inspector had left for him.

Okata went against his normal discipline and took the F car instead of walking. He rode the antique streetcar all the way down Market Street, past the Ferry Building, and a few blocks up the Embarcadero, where he got off and took a moment looking at the extraordinary black sailing ship that was docked at Pier Nine, before dragging his gallon of pig's blood home.

He was sitting beside the futon with a big grin and a tea cup full of pig's blood when she awoke.

"Hello," he said, with a great grin.

"Hello," said the burned-up girl, her fangs showing when she smiled. Her hair had grown through the day, and now hung down to her chest, but it was dry and crispy.

Okata handed her the cup and steadied her hand while she gulped the blood. When she finished he gave her a paper napkin and refilled the tea cup, then sat down and drank tea from his own cup while she sipped the blood. He watched the color move over her skin like there was a pink light moving there, and she began to fill out, the flesh coming up on her bones as if she was being inflated.

"Did you eat?" she said. She made the motion of chopsticks scooping rice and pointed to him. No, he hadn't eaten. He'd forgotten to eat.

"No," he said. "Sorry."

"You need to eat. Eat." She made the motion and he nodded.

While she drank her third cup of blood he retrieved a rice ball from his little refrigerator and nibbled it. She smiled at him and toasted his tea cup with her cup of blood.

"There you go. Mazel tov!"

"Mazel tov!" said Okata.

They toasted and he ate and she drank blood, and he watched as her smile became full and her eyes bright. He showed her what he had found for her at the Levi's store and the Nike store, and at Victoria's Secret, although he looked away and tried to hide a little-boy grin when he showed her the red satin bra and panties. She praised him and held the clothes up to her body, then laughed when they looked too big and took a big gulp of the blood, spilling it down the sides of her mouth and on the kimono.

And she saw his new shoes, too, and pointed and winked. "Sexy," she said. He felt himself blush and then grinned and did a little dance step, a universal Snoopy dance of ecstasy to show just how comfortable the shoes were. She laughed and ran her hand over them while rolling her eyes.

After he had drank a whole pot of tea and she almost a whole gallon of blood, she sat up on the edge of the futon and threw her thick red hair back over her shoulders. She was no longer a charred skeleton, a burned-up wraith, a desiccated marble crone, but a voluptuous young woman, as pale as snow, as cool as the room, but as vibrant and alive as anyone he had ever seen.

Her kimono fell open when she stretched and he looked away.

"Okata," she said. And he looked at her feet. "It's okay." She closed her robe, then ran her hand over his cheek. Her palm was cool and smooth and he pressed into it.

"I need a shower," she said. "A shower?" She mimed washing, falling rain.

"Yes," he said. He brought her a towel and a bar of soap, then presented the shower, which stood open to the room next to a pedestal sink. The toilet was in a little closet on the other side.

"Thank you," she said. She stood and let the kimono slide off her shoulders, laid it carefully on the futon, then took the towel and soap and walked to the shower, throwing a smile over her shoulder at him as she stepped into the tray.

Okata sat, dropped really, onto the little stool by the futon, and watched as she washed the last bit of ash from her skin, then let the water stream over her until the whole apartment was full of steam, weariness, and wonder.

He picked up his sketch pad from the floor and began to draw.

He watched her move like a spirit in the steam, drying herself and then combing her hair out with her fingers. She came out of the steam, dropped the towel on the floor by his workbench. He looked away as she approached and she knelt and raised his chin with her finger until he had to look at her. Her eyes were as green as a jade plant.

"Okata," she said. "Thank you."

Then she kissed him on the forehead, then on the lips, and ever so gently, she took away his sketch pad, and dropped it to the floor, then pushed him back on the futon and kissed him again as she unbuttoned his shirt.

"Okay," he said.

Being the Chronicles of Abby Normal: The Mopey Monosexuality of an Outcast Cutie Corpse

Much like the guy in Herman Hesse's novel *Steppenwolf* (which everyone knows means, "wolf going up the steps") who runs into the ENTRANCE NOT FOR EVERYBODY sign outside of the Magic Theater, when it comes to romance, I am definitely not on the list. Loneliness is my "plus one." Bitterness is my boo.

Oh, it was sweet waking up at sundown, nearly in the arms of my Dark Lord, snuggled up in our utility shed on the roof. I probably shouldn't have snatched that pigeon out from under the eave and sort of sucked its little throat, but in my defense, breakfast is the most important meal of the day, and I swore off anything with feathers because they are nasty. Still, I think Lord Flood would have forgiven me spitting bloody feathers on his linen trousers if my tail hadn't harshed our search plan.

There, now everyone knows. I have a tail. Which is kinda the reason we had to return to the love lair instead of continuing our search for the Countess. Foo called just before sunup to say that all the rats had died.

So I'm like, "Non sequitur much, Foo? If you miss me, you can just apologize and grovel a little and we'll move on."

And he's like, "No, Abby, you don't understand. There's something in their DNA, they just sort of expire after a week or so of being a vampyre."

And I'm like, "My poor, sad Foo Dog, are you sure that your mantenna isn't just using dead rats to send an S.O.S. for a return to tuna town? Hmmmm?"

And he's all, "No, Abby, you have rat DNA tied in with your vampirism, the same way Chet has human DNA."

And I'm all, "Nuh-uh."

And he's all, "You have to come back here. Abby, I know you have a tail."

And I'm like, "Fucksocks," and I offed my phone.

So when Flood and I come to in the shed on the roof, I'm like, "We may need to check in with Foo."

And Flood is like, "Call him and tell him that there are old vampyres here to clean up. He needs to be ready. We'll be there in a few minutes."

And I'm like, "I'll text him. I'm not speaking to him right now."

So, like, Tommy showed me how you couldn't run too fast, or someone would notice something was up, so you had to sort of go in bursts and I wasn't supposed to jump over cars and whatnot because that shit is a dead giveaway that you are nosferatu. Although I did "rawr" some tourists on the cable car, because they needed it. And if you ask them they will all be, "She was *très* scary, and back in Cowfuck, Nebraska, we know that 'rawr' is totally a thing because we have family values and whatnot."

So after running in bursts for like three blocks I rawred down a cab that was halted by my awesome dark powers and the hundred-dollar bill I was waving, and we rode to the love lair, where Jared let us in.

And Jared was all, "OMG, OMG, OMFG, Abs, the rats are dead!"

And I'm like, "Not news. Awesome vamp robot pirate ship, equals news."

And Jared is like, "For realz?"

And I'm like, "Totes."

And he kind of does a gayboy squee that was a little embarrassing, so I'm all, "Where's Foo?"

And Foo comes out of the bedroom and I go to kiss him and he sort of stops and holds up his little blood vials, like, "Oh, no kisses, Abby, I have breakables." So I backed off.

And he's like, "Abby we need to change you back. Right away."

And I'm like, "No way, Foo. I am finished with your petty human weakness."

And he like waves to all the rat boxes, and all the rats are just lying in the bottom of them. And I'm all, "So?"

And Foo's like, "They just dropped, within hours of

each other. There's some incompatibility with the vampyre virus."

"It's a virus?" goes Tommy.

And Foo's all, "I don't know exactly what it is, but it binds to the host DNA and it carries the DNA to the infected."

And I'm like, "So?"

And that's when Foo blurts out that I have a tail to Flood, and I just want to crawl in a hole and die, except for it being redundant.

Then Jared's like, "Would you guys like something to drink? Some blood or something?"

And I'm like, "No thanks, I had a pigeon."

And Flood is like, "Yes, I'll have some."

And he's about to take a sip from a wineglass that Jared poured, and I see his fangs, which are *très* sexy now that he's not ripping my throat out with them, and he's like, "Oh, Abby, if this turns out to be drugged, tear Steve's arms off."

And I'm like, "'Kay," then to Foo, I'm like, "Rawr. Shut up."

And Foo's like, "It's not drugged."

So we tell Foo and Jared about the ship and the old vampyres and how they are here to clean house, and about what the Kona guy said about second generation vampyres.

And Foo's like, "That's you, Tommy."

And Flood is like, "I know. I have to find Jody. And you and Jared need to get away from this apartment. Go somewhere, stay until you hear it's all clear or the *Raven* leaves."

And Foo is like, "How did you think to go to the dock anyway?"

So we told him about Madame Natasha and the sunken ship in the north end of the City and whatnot, and he's all rolling his eyes, because he doesn't believe in magic, despite the fact that he's rolling his eyes at two vampyres.

And he's like, "Did you try the Sunken Ship?"

And we're like, "Whaaaa?"

And he's like, "It's a bar down on Jackson Street. It was built on top of one of the Gold Rush ships that was abandoned there. You can still see the ribs of the ship in the basement."

And Flood's like, "The Sunken Ship? That's what it's called?"

And I'm like, "Kind of obvious."

And Flood's like, "We need to go there."

And Foo's all, "No, I have to change you both back. You could drop any minute."

So I go, "As if. We have to find the Countess."

And Tommy's all, "After. All that after."

So Foo goes, "Well, then take these." And he gives Flood and me each a thing that looks like an aluminum flashlight with a blue glass erection.

And I'm all, "Uh, we can see in the dark, and heat, and we have someone on retainer who can see into the future, so, thanks, but . . ."

"They're UV lasers," goes Foo, in the middle of my dismissal. "They use them to fuse UV sensitive polymers in vacuum chambers."

And Tommy looks at me like, "What?" And I look at him like, "No fucking idea."

So Foo runs on like, "They would just burn me or Jared if you held it on us, like a high-intensity sunlamp. But you'd have to hold it there for about five seconds."

So Flood looks at me like, "What?" And I look at him like, "I got nothing."

So Foo takes Tommy's flashlight from him and he goes, "Like this." And he points the flashlight at one of the dead rat boxes and it busts out with this intense blue beam and *whoosh* instant rat charcoal.

So Flood and I are like, "Oh."

"You can't just leave them on like the UV jackets. They work with a capacitor that builds a charge and lets go with a two-second burst, but you can probably cut a vamp in half in that time. I made them for Rivera and Cavuto."

And Tommy goes, "Well don't give one to them, for fuck's sake, they're hunting me and Jody."

"And me," I go.

"And me," goes Jared. And we look at him. And he goes, "Not because I'm a vampyre. Because that big cop hates me." Then he looked embarrassed and he goes, "Hey, you guys, your eyes are bleeding."

And I look at Tommy and I'm all, "WTF?"

And Foo's like, "You guys should probably wear sunglasses with UV filtering if you're going to use those, or, you know, they could hurt your eyes."

So Flood's like, "Good to know."

And Foo's like, "You should know that they can't go to mist if they're hurt or under exposure to any significant UV. I tested it with the rats. Which means you can't either."

And we're all, "Uh-huh."

And he's like, "What will you do?"

And Flood is like, "We're going to the Sunken Ship and see if we can find Jody, and then I guess we're going to see if we can get on a pirate ship. What about you?"

"I have to break the lab down first, but I know some guys in my program at Berkeley that have an extra room. I can stay there."

And Flood is like, "Take Jared with you. Elijah saw him. Anyone Elijah knows or who knew about him is in danger."

And Jared is all, "Nooooo, Berkeley is way too butch."

So I 'splain to Tommy, "Jared is afraid of butch lesbians. They were invented in Berkeley."

And Foo is like looking at Jared, and looking at me, and looking at Flood, and looking at his dead rats, and he's all, "Can't you at least leave Abby here and let me change her back?"

And Flood looks at me and I'm all, "Bitch, please, I have a light sabre." And I grabbed Foo and kissed him hard, but I could feel him pulling away.

And he's like, "Abby, after this is over—"

And I'm like, finger on his lips, "Shh, shh, shh, Foo. Do

not awkwardize the moment with sniveling. I've been preparing my whole life for this."

And I have.

So we jammed.

And outside Flood is like, "You okay?"

And I'm all, "Yeah. Do you think I'm a freak because I have a tail?"

And he's all, "No, not because of that."

Which was awesome for him to say.

So we did the low-profile walk to Walgreens, where we bought three pairs of sunglasses and a disposable cell phone for Tommy and I got some Gummi bears, which I am dipping in blood and eating now—biting off their little bear heads. Then we go over to the financial district and we find the bar called the Sunken Ship on Jackson Street in the old section, and there's a big picture of a sailing ship, and THE SUNKEN SHIP is carved in big letters, and we're not two blocks from the roof where we spent the night, and I'm all, "Oops."

And Flood is like, "Now what?"

And I'm like, "Don't you have fake ID?" I was kind of fucking with him for pretending to be five hundred years old when we first met, when he's only nineteen.

And he's like, "No, do you?"

"Yeah. Like six of them. I'll go in and look around."

And he's like, "Okay."

So I start to go inside, where all these suits and citizens are, and I hear, "Hey," a girl's voice. Quiet, but like she knows we can hear.

And it's the Countess, palming a door shut on this below-street apartment. And she's in like black jeans carrying a pair of Nikes, but her hair is all glorious, and in like an instant she's up over the rail, not even touching the stairs, and in Tommy's arms. And it was beautiful, and sad, and I felt my heart break, but then it was like leaping for joy, because I really do love the Countess, and I love Tommy, but they love each other, and well—fucksocks.

So I'm like, "Cold-faced killers on the clock, bitches, we don't have time for your bonery right now."

And the Countess like lets Tommy go and gives me a big hug and she's like, "So, girl-e-girl, the dead thing, it works for you."

And I'm like, "Duh."

And she looks at Flood and she's, "I'm not sure about the tropical thing though."

And he's like, "Abby sprayed pigeon blood on my pants."

And she's like, "No, that part's good."

And he's like, "She has a tail."

And I'm like, "Traitor!"

Then she looks all sad, and she's like, "Tommy, we need to talk."

And he's like, "No, we need to move."

So, while we walk toward the water we explain about the old vamps and the clean up, and the *Raven* and whatnot.

'Kayso, now we're on the roof of the Bay Club, which is a really nice gym across the street from the dock, and we are staking out the *Raven,* and from up here we can see into the cockpit, which is like the size of a whole apartment. And they're there. The three of them and Kona, the blond Rasta guy. Two women and a guy. And they're looking all fly in their black bodysuits and black trench coats and all. But the tall blond guy has something on the table, a long case, and he takes something out and starts putting it together.

I'm all, "What's he got?"

"It's a rifle," goes the Countess.

WTF? WTF? WTF? I go, "A gun?"

And Tommy goes, "What's with the gun?"

And I'm like, "Yeah, guns are for shit on vampyres. Uh, us." I still totally don't want to get shot.

And Jody's like, "They're not going after vampyres."

And Tommy's like, "Abby, would you stop typing. Please?"

And I'm like, "Rawr!"

And Jody's like, "He's leaving the ship."

And I'm all, "WTF?"

And Jody's all, "We have to follow."

'Kayso, gotta jet. L8erz.

Meeting at the Palace

RIVERA

They traded in the Ford at the city motor pool for one that had a Plexiglas divider between the front and rear seats. Cavuto's knees were pressed against the glove compartment, since the seat didn't adjust, but it was worth the trade-off. It turned out the organic dog biscuits that Rivera had bought gave Marvin gas. He now had his own little glass partition in which to exhaust, and the inspectors drank their coffee relatively free of doggy stench.

"I don't sleep well during the day," Cavuto said.

"Roger that," said Rivera. "I feel like I've been up for a week." He dialed his messages, then looked at his partner. "Fifteen unplayed messages? Are we out of the service area or something?"

"You turned it off when we were zeroing in on that litter of dangerous kittens."

Rivera tried to drink his coffee while handling the phone and ended up pulling the car over to the curb. "They're all from the Emperor. Something about a ship down at Pier Nine being full of old vampires."

"No," said Cavuto. "There are no more vampires until I've had two full cups of coffee and a healthy piss. That's my personal rule."

Cavuto keyed the radio and checked into dispatch. They did most of their communications by cell phone these days, but there were still rules. If you were a rolling unit, dispatch needed to know where you were.

"Rivera and Cavuto," said the dispatcher. "I have you guys tagged to call if there are any cases of cats attacking humans, is that right?"

"Roger, dispatch."

"Well, live the dream, Inspector, we have report of a giant cat attacking a man at Baker and Beach. We have a unit on the scene reporting nothing."

Cavuto looked at Rivera. "That's the Palace of Fine Arts. The Marina is new territory."

"There might not be anything now. The uniforms don't know to look for clothes with dust and I don't want them to. Tell them we're on the way."

"Dispatch, we are responding. Tell unit on scene that we'll take care of it. Part of an ongoing investigation of a 5150 making false reports." Cavuto grinned and looked at his partner.

"Nice improvisation."

"Yeah, but I think this cat might be out of the bag, Rivera."

"I hope not."

They rolled up to the great faux stone classical dome, the only building left from the World Exposition of 1911, when San Francisco was trying to show the world that it had recovered from the earthquake of '06. The uniform unit was on the far side of the reflection pool, standing by their squad car. Cavuto waved them on. "We got this, guys. Thanks."

What there wasn't, was a huge shaved vampire cat attacking a guy.

"You think it's a hoax?" asked Cavuto.

"Pretty outrageous coincidence if it is."

Cavuto got out of the car and let Marvin out, who waited for his leash to be attached, then dragged Cavuto over to a tree by the pond to have a wee. Swans who had settled under the trees for the night stirred and gave Marvin dirty looks.

"Nothing here," said Cavuto. "Marvin's not doing his signal thing."

Rivera's phone chirped and he looked at the screen. "It's Allison Green, the creepy little Goth girl."

"If she called this in I will put her in Juvi overnight."

"Rivera," Rivera said into the phone.

"Turn your sun jackets on right now," she said. "Right fucking now, both of you."

Rivera looked at Cavuto. "Turn on the LEDs on your coat, Nick."

"What?"

"Do it. She's not fucking with us." Rivera hit the switch on the cuff of his sun jacket and the LEDs came on blindingly bright. A few blocks away they heard a man scream. Marvin barked.

"Oh, *très bon,* cop. Byez," Abby said. The line went dead.

"The fuck was that about?" said Cavuto.

ROLF

Rolf was actually looking forward to shooting someone. After hundreds of years, you get bored with killing, with hunting. The three of them had gone through cycles of stealthy killing of the unwanted, to outright slaughter of whole villages, to long periods where there was no killing at all. But it had been fifty years since he'd actually had to shoot someone. The change of pace was nice.

Of course, it was messy, bodies, waste of good blood, but better that than having policemen running around telling people about them. No matter what kind of debaucheries they had indulged in over the years, and there had been many kinds—these too went in cycles—the one rule they held fast to was "stay hidden." And to stay hidden, you couldn't permit yourself to get so bored that you didn't care about living. Well, surviving.

Maybe it was just the two cops from last night. Elijah, in a rare moment of lucidity finally admitted that there were only two policemen that he knew of, and because they had

taken money from the sale of the old vampire's art collection, they did not want the secret known. Clearly though,
they were beyond their depth with the cats.

He and Bella had made short work of the smaller cats.
They used rapid-fire pellet guns, nearly silent, that fired
pellets containing a liquid that destroyed vampire flesh on
contact—a heinous, herbal mixture that someone in China
had discovered hundreds of years ago. A weak UV light on
the front of the weapons held the animals in solid form long
enough for the pellets to impact. The pellets would injure a
human vampire, but they were devastating to a feline. The
Chinese had somehow tuned it to the cats. They had used
the mixture to contain every outbreak since its discovery.
Rolf remembered firing it from crossbows.

Rolf keyed his cell phone, then called the emergency
number and reported a man being attacked by a giant cat.
Then he set up the bipod on his rifle, zeroed the twenty-
power scope in on one of the swans under a eucalyptus
tree, and lay down to wait.

Seven minutes later the police cruiser arrived. They
were both fresh-faced young men with bright pink life auras. From his rooftop, four blocks away, Rolf could just
make out the squawking of their radios. They knew nothing. They panned their flashlights under the bushes surrounding the pond, and he watched them shake their heads
to one another.

Seventeen minutes after the call, the brown unmarked
car pulled up and Rolf relaxed into his shooting posture.

These were the two from the night before. The big red dog. The dog looked his way, briefly, then dragged the big cop down to a tree by the pond.

He put the crosshairs on the thinner cop's face. But no, a headshot was arrogant. He had to make two shots, very quickly, so he would go for the center of their bodies. Shoot the thin cop first, then pan to the big one. A bigger target. Even if his first shot didn't kill him, it would drop him.

He waited, waited for them to get clear of the car and the cover. The thin cop was walking toward the other one, then stopped to take a phone call. Rolf put the crosshairs over his heart and began to squeeze the trigger.

Then the entire side of his head seemed to explode with pain and he screamed and grabbed at the flames that were shooting out of his empty eye socket.

TOMMY

"Are we doing this right?" Tommy asked. They were several blocks behind Rolf, who was moving so smoothly and easily through the Marina district that Tommy would have thought he lived there and was out for his evening jog. Except that no one in the Marina would be wearing a black duster. It would either be cashmere or Gore-Tex, business or fitness. The Marina was a rich, fit neighborhood.

"We're following him," said Abby. "How many ways can you do that?"

Jody was leading them. She held up a hand for them to stop. The blond vampire had stopped at the corner of a four-story apartment building and was scaling it using just the space between the bricks as handholds.

Tommy looked around and spotted a flat-roofed building down the alley. "That one has a fire escape. We'll be above him, we can watch him."

"I don't think watching is going to be enough," Jody said.

"He looks badass," said Abby.

"He's watching those cops over at the Palace."

"He won't just shoot a cop," said Tommy. "Why would he shoot a cop?"

"Plain clothes unit pulling in," Jody said. "It's Rivera and Cavuto."

"And Marvin," Abby said.

"He knows they know," said Tommy.

"We need to go," Jody said. "Abby, you have Rivera's number?"

"Yeah."

"Call him. Give me that laser thing."

"The light from their jackets magnified through the scope will work," Tommy said.

"Let's go." Jody ran to the edge of the roof and stopped.

Abby hopped on her toes. "Spider-Man it, Countess."

"No fucking way," Jody said, looking down just as Tommy ran by her and jumped across the alley to the next building.

They were coming across the roof of a building a block away when they saw the side of the vampire's head ignite and heard him scream. He rolled away from the gun, clawing at his face.

"Too far," Jody said. The final gap between roofs was over a full street, not an alley, and they were a floor lower than the blond vampire. "Down."

Without thinking, Tommy jumped, then said, "What the fuck did I just do?" He landed on the balls of his feet and went down to crouch, catching himself just as he was about to drive his knee into the concrete. He looked up. Jody was still on the roof.

"C'mon, Red, I'm not going up there alone."

"Fuck, fuck, fuck, fuck, fuck," she said, and then landed beside him and rolled.

When he saw she wasn't hurt, he said, "Graceful."

"He's getting up," she said, and she pointed at the next building.

Tommy knew if he thought about it, he'd never do it, so he just started climbing up the corner of the building as fast as he could. He'd done this before. He didn't remember it, but his body did. Climbing the wall like a cat. Jody was right behind him. As he reached the top of the wall he stopped and looked back. "Sunglasses," he whispered so faintly that only someone with vampire hearing would hear.

He wedged his right hand between the bricks, then reached into his shirt pocket, flung open the sunglasses, and put them on. He couldn't climb with the laser in his hand. He'd have to clear the top, then grab the weapon out of his pants pocket.

Jody had her glasses on, too. She nodded for him to go.

He coiled, and sprang to catapult himself over the edge of the wall, but in midair a bright light went off in his head and he felt himself spinning, then a bone-crushing impact on the ground. Something had hit him, probably the rifle butt. He rolled over and looked up the wall.

Jody was still clinging there, six feet below the edge, too far to be hit with the rifle. The blond vampire, his face charred, was turning the rifle, working the bolt. He was going to shoot her in the face.

"Jody!"

He saw her let go with one hand, reach for the small of her back, then there was another blinding light. He'd lost his sunglasses during the fall. Something splatted beside him on the pavement. He could smell burned flesh, and blood.

"You okay?" she said.

He felt a hand on his face. "I'm kinda blind. And I think I have a couple of broken ribs." He blinked the blood tears out of his eyes, then saw something dark, circular on the pavement.

"What's that?"

"That's the top of his skull," Jody said.

Footsteps, then Abby was there. "That was awesome. Gruesome, but awesome. You were amazing, Countess."

"Not feeling all that amazing."

"You probably should drink some blood, Tommy. You're kind of fucked up."

He took the plastic blood pack from her and bit into it, draining almost the whole pint in seconds, feeling his bones and skin knitting together. Then Abby snatched it away from him and started drinking herself.

"I feel like death on toast. I probably shouldn't have eaten that pigeon."

MARVIN

Marvin ruffed three times fast, "Biscuit, biscuit, biscuit." Then, as he pulled Cavuto around the corner and smelled the fourth dead one he ruffed again. "Another biscuit." Then, mission accomplished. He sat.

"Marvin!" Abby said. She dropped the empty blood bag and scratched between his ears, then fed him a Gummi bear.

Rivera came around the corner with his Glock drawn. Jody stood, reached past the gun, and snagged the battery out of the cop's inside pocket. Abby did the same to Cavuto, who leveled a long orange Super Soaker at her.

"Really, Ass Bear?" she said. "Really?" She snatched the squirt gun out of his hand and backhanded it a full block down the street where it shattered.

"I have a gun on you, Missy," said Rivera.

"Biscuit," Marvin ruffed. Clearly there are three dead people here and part of a fourth, and biscuits are in order.

Jody snatched Rivera's Glock out of his hand so quickly he was still in aiming position when she popped the clip out of it. Cavuto started to draw the big Desert Eagle and Abby caught his arm and leaned in close. "Ninja, please, unless you're going to use that to take your own life out of humiliation for the squirt gun, just let it go." She turned and looked at Tommy, who was sitting splayed-legged on the sidewalk, holding his ribs. "This fucking vampy power rocks my deepest dark." Then back to Cavuto. "I'd slap you around a little, but I'm feeling kinda nauseous."

"Yeah," said Cavuto. "I get that. That's how I know you're around."

"So you three are, all, uh, *them,*" said Rivera.

"Not exactly *them,*" Tommy said. "Jody just took the top off the head of one of *them.*" He pointed at the charred brainpan.

"He was about to take you out with a sniper rifle," Abby said. "That's why I called. Thanks for just doing what I said and not being an assbag, by the way."

"You'll find the rest of him along with the rifle on the roof," Jody said.

"That's who called in the vampire cat attack?" Cavuto said.

Tommy nodded. "There are at least three of them. Maybe two, now. Very old. They came in that black yacht that's down at Pier Nine. They are cleaning up the mess Elijah left. They must know you guys are hunting Chet and the vampire cats."

"He must have seen us last night, with the Animals. We thought the cats got Barry."

Tommy climbed to his feet. "Barry's dead?"

"Sorry," Rivera said. "So they know about the Animals, too?"

Tommy said, "The Animals were the ones who took Elijah's art collection and blew up his yacht. Of course, they know about the Animals."

"We've got to get over there," Rivera said. "They'll be hunting the Emperor, too. He's been calling all day about a black ship. I thought it was just more craziness. I don't even know where to start looking for him."

Jody handed Rivera back his gun and the battery to his jacket. "Wire those back up as soon as you get back in your car. They work."

Marvin let go with a barrage of barking, which translated, "I have found some dead people and I am going to make a fuss if I don't get a biscuit and the ear-scratch girl is *dead* and sick."

"Easy, Marvin," Abby said. She steadied herself against the big dog and Cavuto caught her by the arm to keep her from falling. "I really don't feel good." She crumpled to the sidewalk. Tommy caught her in time to keep her head from hitting the concrete. "My tail kind of hurts."

Jody snatched Rivera's gun out of his hand again. "Give Tommy your car keys."

"What! No!"

Jody smacked Rivera's jacket, heard a jingle, then

reached in his pocket and took the keys. Rivera stood there like he was five, being dressed by his mother. Jody threw the keys to Tommy.

"Take her to the loft. Foo will still be there. Maybe he can change her back in time."

"Where are you going?" Tommy said.

"I'm going to the ship. Maybe I can stop one of them there. They're going to come to the loft, so be ready."

"Not so fast, Red," said Cavuto.

"You will shut the fuck up!" Jody said. "You guys are six blocks from the Marina Safeway. The Animals should be at work, or will be there in a few minutes. That's where I went when I wanted to find them, that's where these vampires will go. So shag ass over there and warn them. Wire the batteries back into your jackets on the way there or they'll have you for lunch. Call for another car if you need to, but we just saved your lives and *your* car is ours."

Rivera smiled. "I'm okay with that."

Cavuto said, "You are?"

Tommy picked Abby up and held her with one arm while he reached into her messenger bag, took out her phone, and handed it to Jody. "Call Foo, tell him we're coming."

"I will. Be careful." She kissed him. "Save our minion."

"Got it," Tommy said.

Marvin whimpered at them as they went away, which translated to, "I'm worried about the ear-scratching dead girl with the Gummi bears."

23

Brat in the Paper Aisle

MAKEDA

She stood under the eave of a post office that looked out on the Safeway parking lot, watching the old man with the dogs pounding at the door. Well, that would make seven. She knew she should wait for the others, but what fun was there in that. A lean black guy let the old man and his dogs into the store, then locked the door behind him.

She moved to the side of the building, then along the front behind a long train of shopping carts, where she could look through the windows without being seen herself. They were spread out, each working an aisle to himself. She really should call for the others. Neither would be that far away, but she did so little on her own anymore. She examined the window. Thick Plexiglas, she wasn't going through that. She could kick the door down, of course, but then they would run and there'd be chasing and if any got away Rolf would pout with disapproval for months. Not that she wasn't beyond pouting herself. She once awakened to find Bella and Rolf merged together in mist without her and refused to take solid form for a year except to feed.

That was how they began each night, merged in mist form, still inside their titanium chamber, experiencing every corner of each other's consciousness, every memory, every emotion, every want, every fear—complete knowing, complete intimacy. After an hour or so, they would assume their solid forms, then leave the chamber and feed, or watch a video of a sunrise or sunset. That was it! Mist. She would go into the store by stealth. Except for the one with the dogs, they were all young men, weren't they? She knew she could hold the rapt attention of a young man. She'd take each one, drain him without the others even knowing what happened, then share the experience with Rolf and Bella tomorrow night. It was always fun to bring something new and dangerous to their night.

She wouldn't be able to wear her special suit, or take any of the weapons, but it was just as well. She couldn't leave bodies. Seven. She'd be as full as a tick, ready to pop. She checked that none of them was by the door, hid her weapons under the shopping carts, then lay down and oozed out of the Kevlar bodysuit, across the sidewalk, and under the door.

Rock and roll was blasting out of the PA system, filling the store with a relentless chainsaw rhythm guitar that drowned all other sound. She swirled around the registers, then started to make her way across the aisles. The first two were empty, then in the third, the old man was sitting all by himself on a milk crate. Scented candles were lit up and down either side of the aisle, as if someone had laid out a landing strip. She could sense the others around her, but her perceptions weren't as sharp in mist form and the odor and heat from the candles made it nearly impossible to tell how far away they were. Their heartbeats and breathing were lost in the music, but there was blood in the air. All over in the air. She floated up to the ceiling, where she could see over the tops of the shelf gondolas. There were two of them working on the other side of the store, bobbing in time to the music.

Rolf would have wafted back out the door and called the others, and Bella would have drawn an elaborate plan to stalk them, one at a time, and pick them off when they were alone, but that was exactly why she wasn't going to do either of those things.

As she pulled herself into solid form she felt a horrible wrenching in her chest, like her heart caving in on itself. Not a physical pain, but a sudden absence. One of the others was suddenly not there. Rolf. Just not there. She stood there in front of the old man, naked, shaking, trying to bring herself back to the hunt.

"Don't scream," she said.

THE EMPEROR

He didn't like that the men were locked in the walk-in cooler, and he didn't like that the Animals had tied him up, rubbed liver and steaks all over him, and set him on a milk box, but he had done his duty to his city. He had alerted the only people who would listen to the presence of the black ship, told them what the strange faux-Hawaiian had said about the old vampires coming for them, and he could have some peace of mind in that. They didn't have to duct tape his hands so tightly, and tape his ankles to the milk box. They could have just asked. Ah, youth.

She materialized about twelve feet in front of him, nude, nubile, and athletic, so black she might have been made of polished ironwood, yet the death-pallor made her lips appear lavender. Her hair was trimmed close to her scalp, her eyes appeared to be gold, but he couldn't tell for sure. She shivered for a moment, as if a current was being applied to her body. He watched her muscles tensing and relaxing, rippling under her skin in waves.

Then she stopped shaking and opened her eyes.

"Don't scream," she said. Blood tears formed in the corners of her eyes.

"Oh my, if you aren't lovely," said the Emperor.

She smiled and he saw fangs there, and he suddenly felt as if he might wet himself.

She moved a few steps closer to him. "Are those steaks on your shoulders?" she said.

"Yes. There's liver in my pockets as well."

She cocked her head as if listening. "Where are the others?"

"I don't know," he said.

Her hand shot out and in an instant her fingers were wrapped in his beard and she was pulling his head back, not yanking, but pulling with an irresistible strength, as if he'd been hitched to a power winch. "Where are they?"

He could feel his vertebrae cracking, feel her raking her fangs over his neck. Then the sound of a high-pressure gas burst and she wasn't there, and there was a length of heavy nylon line in the space where her face had been.

"Down!" came Lash's voice, as he, Troy Lee, Jeff, and Drew all rolled out of the shelves where they had been hiding behind rows of toilet paper and paper towels.

The vampire woman's head was pinned to a bale of paper towels with the stainless-steel spear from Barry's spear gun. She screeched like a wildcat and pulled herself away and leapt at Drew, who was leveling a Super Soaker. Lash yanked the spear gun and the nylon line whipped her around. Jeff and Troy Lee opened garden sprayers on her from the front, while Drew unloaded the Super Soaker from the back.

She screeched and writhed in the streams, but her flesh was coming off in great slimy chunks, as if she were wax and had been dropped into a foundry furnace. It was all over in ten seconds, and every item for twenty feet in either direction had been knocked off the shelves, the Emperor was on his back, unable to right himself, and the ancient vampire was a puddle of red goo that still bubbled as it broke down.

"What do you know," said Troy Lee. "Grandma's tea worked."

Lash nodded and threw the spear gun to the floor with a clank. "Clint! Clean up on aisle four!"

JODY

Because she never liked going to the gym, Jody decided to stake out the *Raven* from the roof of an office building next door instead of on the Bay Club. The fact that she'd been able to leap from brick balcony to brick balcony until she was on the roof, six floors up, proved what she had always maintained, at least when she was alive: working out is narcissistic bullshit. She almost wished that the girls she'd worked with at the Transamerica Building could see her now—all of them stuffing themselves into Spandex and nylon after work and heading to the Bay Club or 24 Hour Fitness in hope of meeting someone who wasn't a creep and, in the case of the Bay Club members, someone who was rich.

She imagined them saying, "Do you want to come with us? We can get you a guest pass. Mohitos afterward?"

"No thanks," she'd say. "I'm going to go bench-press an Audi a couple of sets, grab the satchel with the three-hundred grand I stashed on a roof up the street, and go back to my loft and fuck my immortal boyfriend until dawn."

Okay, that wasn't really what she was going to do, but she for goddamn sure was not going to the gym and getting all sweaty so she could meet guys. She didn't even want to be on the roof of the gym, knowing that there was unprotected fitness going on below.

She could see the *Raven* across the Embarcadero, and the Rasta kid was doing nautical stuff with different instruments. At least she thought he was doing nautical stuff. He could have just been dicking around with expensive equipment. None of the vampires was there. There were lights coming from a few of the ports below the cockpit, but she didn't see any movement. The sense of immediacy that had driven her here had evaporated somewhat. She thought about calling Tommy, but didn't have any idea what his new cell phone number might be. She used Abby's phone and dialed Foo's number, but it went to voice mail, which she didn't see as a good sign.

If the other two vampires were out of the ship, and she had to wait for them to return, she'd never get a shot at them from this far away. If they didn't come back until dawn, she'd be caught outside at sunrise. There was a warehouse by the pier, perhaps that roof. And she'd set herself a time limit. If they didn't show by a half-hour before sunup, she'd head back to the loft. Even at a slow, human jog she'd make it in plenty of time.

She'd have to sneak down the back of the building, though. You didn't want people to see you jumping two or three stories at a time. She understood why the vampires had to keep their secret, she really did, but not at the expense of them killing her friends.

"Good view?" A woman's voice came from behind her.

Jody rolled and whipped around, pulling Foo's UV laser from the waistband of her jeans. She didn't have on the sunglasses so she pointed the laser at the figure coming across the roof toward her, closed her eyes, turned away, then fired. The laser buzzed out a blue beam that lasted two seconds, then started making a high-pitched whining sound as it recharged its capacitor.

"Oh, very nice," came the voice.

It was definitely a woman, amazing figure, wearing a skin-tight black suit, a black mask, and sunglasses, and carrying some sort of weapon. She looked like a superhero.

Jody was on her feet, in a crouch. The laser thing was still charging, but maybe it would fire a weaker blast, give her time to move.

"Nah, nah, nah." The woman raised her weapon, and fired. A stuttering stream of pellets peppered Jody's arm and she lost hold of the laser. Jody felt as if her arm were on fire. She looked to see ten tiny holes, each smoking, with a clear liquid, not blood running out of it.

The woman whipped off her hood and sunglasses, but kept the weapon trained on Jody. She was stunning, a pale, Mediterranean beauty with waist-length hair like black silk and almost impossibly large eyes. "That light thing is sweet, but you should get one of these," she said. "It's basically just a pellet gun modified to fire chemical pellets, but the chemical, there's the magic."

"It burns like hell," Jody said.

"Yes, it does. And I could cut you in half with this before you could get to me. That's the problem with light weapons, they don't have range and it doesn't take much to stop them. Like this suit, for instance. I mean, this thing has a

UV light on it, but that's just to keep you from turning to mist. Can you do that, fledgling?"

"That's what Elijah called me," Jody said.

"That's what he called all of us in our day."

Jody tried to figure out how to get to the woman. She knew she could move impossibly fast for a human, but this was another vampire, a very old vampire. She had once squared off against Elijah thinking all things were equal among vampires and he'd nearly ended her.

As if she was reading Jody's thoughts the vampire fired her weapon and Jody felt her other arm light up with pain from shoulder to elbow.

"Ouch. Fuck. You bitch!"

"*Bella,* not bitch. And what were you going to do to me, fledgling? Do you have any idea what you've done? We have been together hundreds of years. You ended pieces of history. You took parts of me."

She fired again and Jody's right leg gave way.

"What do you mean, pieces?"

"You don't know what it is to merge with another being then? With a lover? We were lovers, Rolf, Makeda, and me, for hundreds of years, and now they are gone."

"I don't know what you're talking about."

"Both are gone, I could feel it. Funny, I didn't know I was always aware of their presence until they were gone. Not an hour ago. I'm alone now. I should let you live if only because we've lost two. There are fewer than a hundred of us, fledgling, and you might have been one of us."

"I didn't know," Jody said.

"I don't even care anymore. Maybe I'll just kill you and lie down and wait for the sun to come up. I'll never even know what happened."

"Trust me, that's not as painless as you think it is," Jody said.

"Don't!" said Bella. She raised her weapon again but this time, when the little UV light came on, Jody pushed off with her good leg, did a high backflip, and fell six stories to the courtyard below.

She expected to feel bone-crushing pain, hear the crackle of vertebrae, maybe even the crunch of her skull, but instead she felt warm water envelop her. She had landed in the Bay Club's pool, which meant she must have launched herself a good forty feet away from the roof. Her predator mind, the one that had risen to tell her that the City was hers, now kicked in, assessing survival. She was under water, that was good. The pellet weapon wouldn't penetrate the water more than a foot before losing it's effectiveness. Plus, the pool water was flushing out whatever heinous chemical had been burning her. She felt herself healing, even as she hovered at the bottom of the pool. She could stay there indefinitely without breathing if necessary.

The bad news was that Bella was still up there, and as soon as Jody left the water, the good news would end. It was very unlikely she could take the older vampire hand-to-hand, even if she could get past the pellet weapon, but she could run. Even if she was no faster than Bella, she knew this neighborhood. She'd worked here for years, and she wasn't three blocks from Okata's dismal little apartment.

She dug in her jacket pocket and found Abby's phone. It was a weatherized model and the screen was still showing the time. Still four hours until sunup, and that was a guess. She had to cut it extremely close, but if she could bolt away from the *Raven* with just enough time to find shelter herself, but not enough time for Bella, she just might get away. And maybe in the meantime, Rivera and Cavuto would call out a S.W.A.T. team to storm the black ship. Or the Animals would blow it up, like they had Elijah's yacht. Maybe Bella would dive into the water after her, although losing the high ground would take away a distinct advantage. Maybe one of the people in the apartments above would look down and think there was a body in the pool, and she could make her escape when the EMTs came to rescue her.

That's it. She assumed the yoga posture called "down-floating corpse" and waited, listening for any disturbance that might indicate she had company in the pool, and concentrated on her wound healing. Maybe if she healed enough she could go to mist and sneak out that way. She hadn't moved a lot in mist form, nor had she ever changed under water and she wasn't sure she could, but it might be worth a try.

A shadow fell across the bottom of the pool, cast by the mercury lights above, and she flipped over to see Bella moving catlike at the edge of the pool.

Then again, maybe not.

CHET

He'd watched them slaughter all of his fellow vampire cats and instead of running, as would have been his feline instinct, he tracked the killers, which was behavior born entirely of his human side. The three sides of his nature were in constant conflict. Even now, his cat side hated water, and wanted to flee, but his human side felt hate rising and wanted to attack. The vampire side told him to remain hidden, to approach in stealth, as mist, but his cat side told him to pounce, rip her throat out with claw and fang. It occurred to him, as he watched from the roof of the Bay Club as she paced around the pool in her skin-tight black suit, that water or no water, revenge or no revenge, he was going to hump the bejezus out of her before any other action took place. There was part tomcat in all of his natures.

He'd started his pack by mating with any female in heat, then they turned males, and so on. And he continued his undead romp through the alleys and backyards of San Francisco, but as he grew larger, and the human part of him manifested, he was just too big to finish the deed. If he fed on them, they went to dust before he got to hump them, and if humped them, they didn't survive for him to feed on them, and he'd humped a bunch of cats to death before he figured that out. It turned out, size did matter.

But here was the perfect solution. Moving strong and sexy, just the right size—he could lock his jaws on her neck and have at it, then drink her blood or bite her head off as the whim hit him, and all the time that horrible weapon would be pointed away from him.

He went to mist and oozed down the side of the building in a stream that blended with the night fog creeping in off the Bay.

JODY

Jody just happened to be looking up at Bella's watery silhouette against the mercury light when she saw another shape appear behind Bella, leap on her back, and pull her away from the edge of the pool. Jody was not going to sit around checking references, whatever that thing was, it was an ally.

She came out of the water like a rocket, and in two steps she leapt to the top of the twelve-foot security fence and looked back. Something had pulled Bella around and now had her face-down on the pavement and appeared to be humping the bejezus out of her.

Jody knew she shouldn't, but she paused. Big kitty ears, big kitty tail, big kitty sinking his fangs into the back of Bella's neck. Kitty was as big as Bella, maybe a little bigger. Chet. Bad kitty, Jody thought.

Bella shrieked, then launched herself backward with her arms, lifting both of them into the air, where they did a half-backflip and landed on the concrete with Chet's back as the point of impact. He let go with his jaws and Bella spun around and let loose with the pellet weapon. Chet yowled and jerked on the ground. Bella strafed his neck, which dissolved instantly into a mass of goo. He stopped moving.

Jody had seen enough. She leapt off the fence to the sidewalk and took off into the financial district, taking a right at the next corner, then a left, going as fast as her legs would carry her—to hell with someone seeing. She tried to go to mist, but couldn't. Either the fear or her injuries were stopping her. She could hear Bella's footsteps behind her, a block away, now less than a block. What was the range of that pellet weapon anyway?

Left on Broadway, left on Battery, right on Pacific, footsteps on her ass, now left on Sansome, next left, she heard the pellet gun sputter and she felt her right leg go out from under her. She rolled and tried to come up but the gun sputtered again and her left leg was gone. She rolled over onto her back, pushed away, scooting on her butt. The gun spat and her left elbow stopped working.

"Fuck, how much ammo does that thing have?"

"More than I'll need to turn you to soup," Bella said. "Oh look, no swimming pool."

"Shame, I guess you won't get to enjoy another kitty fuck."

The gun spat. Jody's right arm folded behind her with a splash of pain.

Bella ran her nails over her breast. "Didn't happen. This suit will stop light, even small-caliber firearms—"

But evidently not blades, Jody thought.

Because she was a vampire, and things happened more slowly to her predator eyes, she saw the blade come over Bella's shoulder, enter her body at her left trapezius, and zip across her chest and her kitty-dick-proof suit to exit just under her right arm. Bella's head and right arm slid right, her left arm and the rest of her body fell left. She had a rather surprised expression on her face that stayed there, even as her mouth continued to work soundlessly, as if she really, desperately wanted to finish that last sentence.

"Hello," Okata said.

Jody looked past the swordsman to the sign on the corner that read: JACKSON STREET.

A Love Story?

JODY

It wasn't the first time she'd crept out of a guy's apartment in the middle of the night with her shoes in her hand, but it was the first time where the decision had been because she didn't want to kill the guy. He was so little, so frail, so lonely. She had taken people before who had the black ring in their life aura like Okata's, and they had thanked her. It had been mercy, relief, the end of pain, yet she couldn't make herself do it. She'd left him there, not to die alone, although he probably would, and not because he had been so kind to her, saving her, which he had, but because the prints weren't finished. He was a strange little man, a hermit and a swordsman, and he carried some great pain in him, but above all that, he was an artist, and she couldn't bear to stop that. So she'd left.

Now she was back.

He sheathed his sword and tried to lift her to her feet. Her limbs still felt like they were on fire, and she could move only her right arm on her own. She nodded toward Bella's pellet weapon. "Give it to me, Okata." She made a grasping motion.

He leaned her in a sitting position against the wrought-iron railing that surrounded the steps to his apartment, then retrieved the weapon and fit it into her hand. Then he held the barrel firmly and said something stern in Japanese.

"No, I'm not going to off myself," she said, and she smiled.

He let go of the barrel of the gun and she sprayed Bella's corpse with pellets until the gun stopped firing, then she threw the gun over the rail and motioned for Okata to help her into his apartment. Bella's body was nothing more than slimy chunks of meat by the time Okata got her through the door. In the morning, when the sun hit it, there would be only a charred stain on the sidewalk with burned gobs of plastic that had been a Kevlar suit, shoes, and sunglasses.

Okata helped her to the shower, where he rinsed out her wounds, then dried her off and retrieved the last bit of the pig's blood, which he'd kept in the refrigerator.

Jody felt a horrible twinge of guilt. He'd been waiting for her, probably had been outside looking for her when Bella had chased her around the corner.

After she drank the blood, and her legs had healed enough to hold her weight, she went to his workbench and turned on the light. The last print was there. Not finished, but two of the woodblocks had been finished, the black and the red. There she was, in the shower, her red hair streaming behind her in the water, black bits of ash puddling at her feet.

Okata was beside her, looking at the print critically, as if there was something he might have to fix at any second. She bent down and looked back from the angle of the print into his face.

"Hey," she said. "Thank you."

"Okay," he said.

"Sorry," she said.

FOO DOG

Abby lay on the futon in the loft's great room. The empty rat cages were stacked in the corner of the room and Foo had unscrewed one of the plywood panels over the windows to let some light in. He'd been monitoring Abby's vital signs since six in the morning. At least she had vital signs. She hadn't even started with those. At noon, she opened her eyes.

"Foo, you dick, I'm mortal."

"You're okay!" He threw his arms around her.

She pushed him away. "Where's Tommy? Where's the Countess?"

"Tommy's in the bedroom. I don't know where Jody is."

"She didn't call?"

"No."

"Fucksocks! Did you turn Tommy back, too?"

"No. I started making his serum, but he didn't want to do anything until they take care of the other vampire. We need to, though, Abby. He won't live much longer if we don't."

"I know. The pirate Rasta guy on the black ship told us. Other vampire? Only one?"

"Rivera called while you were unconscious. The Animals took one of them down at the Safeway."

"Did you tell him to stay off the black ship?"

"Tommy did."

"What about Chet?"

"I don't know."

"He could be— Hey, where's my tail?"

"It sort of fell off when you turned back to human."

"Did you save it?"

"Well, no. I left it on the coffee table and when the sun came up, well, it sort of burned up."

"You burned up my tail? That was a part of me."

"It was a disgusting part of you."

"You're such a racist, Foo. I'm glad we broke up."

"We did?"

"We were going to, weren't we? Wasn't that what you wanted to talk about? About how I'm way too complex and mysterious for you and you need to return to your traditional science-nerd values and live in the Sunset with your parents, instead of the awesome love lair with your goddess-like vampire girlfriend, who will never do you again, even when you beg, even out of pity, no matter how fly your sexy manga hair is? Isn't that what you were going to say?"

"Not in so many words. I'm going to move to Berkeley. It's hard, Abby—"

"Well, save your breath, *s'il vous plaît,* I'm over you. I will not be further abused by your toady banalities and whatnot."

"Your mom called. She wants you to come home."

"Yeah, that's going to happen. Oh, what's this, monkeys flying out of my tailless butt?"

"She said they sent your report card. You passed Mr. Snavely's biology class."

"I did?"

"She said she almost fainted. Jared said it was your extra-credit project that did it. Why didn't you tell me you took one of the rats to school with you?"

"Well, I didn't think it worked out that well. I mean, the rat was already vamped, so when I took him out of the shoe box, he just looked kind of dead. And Mr. Snavely was all, "'Oh, that's lovely, Allison, a dead rat.'" But it was sunny in biology lab, and all of a sudden my rat just spontaneously combusts, and I'm all, 'Check it, bitches, spontaneous rodent combustion, it's the wave of the future.'"

"Well, because he couldn't figure out how you did it, he passed you."

"I am the dark mistress of Biology One-oh-two. Fear me. Rawr!" she said. Then she kissed him hard, but not as hard as she had when she was a vampire, which was a relief, but then she pushed him away and slapped him.

"Ouch. I didn't think you were a slut."

"I know, that's was our bittersweet break-up kiss. I will go grieve now until Lord Flood awakes and we resume the search for the Countess. I'm starving. Do you want to go get a sammy and a Starbucks? I have like ten grand in my messenger."

T✟E L❖VE LAIᴙ

He awoke at sundown with her face in his mind's eye and panic running up his spine. He bolted out of the bedroom into the great room, where Abby was hanging up the phone.

"That was the Countess," Abby said. "She's okay. She'll be here in a few minutes."

"And you're okay? You're alive. You have heat." He could see the heat coming off her and the healthy life aura around her.

"Yeah, thanks. Foo destroyed my tail." She turned and looked to the kitchen. "The traitorous racist heartbreaking fucktard!"

"Little harsh," Tommy said. "He saved your life."

"Heartbroken. Grieving. Inconsolable. Tail's gone. Going to have to get totally repierced and tattooed."

"But you showered and your eye makeup isn't all racoony anymore."

"Thanks. I like the blood splatters on your pants."

"Hi," said Foo Dog from the kitchen, where he was filling a syringe with what looked like blood. "I have your serum ready, whenever you're ready."

"I'm not ready."

"You have to, you know."

The doorbell buzzed. Tommy keyed the intercom.

"It's me," Jody said.

He buzzed her in and she was at the top of the steps in an instant, then kissing him. He pushed her back and looked at her clothes, shredded at the elbows and knees, stained with blood.

"What happened to you? Where were you?"

"One of the old vampires? She ambushed me on a roof across from the black ship. That weapon they have did this. It's horrible. We can't let them get near us with that thing."

"How did you get away?"

"I was hiding at the bottom of a pool, trying to figure out what to do, when Chet jumped her. I got out of there while Chet was dry-humping her."

"Yeah. Go Chet!" said Abby.

"Abby!" Jody ran to Abby and hugged her, kissed her on the forehead. "I was so worried about you. You're alive. Really alive."

"Yeah. Foo changed me back. I want to be nosferatu again."

They all turned to face Foo, who was still in the kitchen. "Can't do it, Abs. You won't survive a second time. I tried it on the rats. You're only human."

"Doomed," Abby said.

"Jody," Tommy said, "what about the vampire who attacked you?"

"Gone. Destroyed. Someone rescued me just before she killed me. So there's only one left, right?"

"They're all gone," Tommy said. "Rivera called. The Animals got the other one. There's only Elijah on the black ship."

Jody put her hand to his face. "Tommy, we have to talk."

"I know," he said.

Foo Dog said, "Jody, I have no way of knowing when Tommy might, uh, expire. He could go faster than Abby was going."

"Come with me." Jody took Tommy's hand and led him into the bedroom. "I've got to show you something. You two, do not come into this room, do you hear me?"

TOMMY AND JODY

"We can't make crazy monkey love now, Jody. They'll hear us, and we usually end up breaking all the furniture."

"You learned how to go to mist, when you were with Chet. You said you learned?"

"Yeah, that's how I got these clothes. They're stupid, aren't they?"

"Tommy, the vampire, the old one, her name was Bella, she told me something. Kiss me. Kiss me and go to mist. Don't think about it, don't stop, just melt into the kiss."

She kissed him and felt him as he faded from solid, and followed him exactly, until they were a single entity, sharing every secret, every fear, every victory, everything, the very essence of who they were, wrapping around each other, winding through each other as each lived the other's history, as every experience they had, they had together, with comfort and joy, with abandon and passion, without words or boundaries, and as often happens to two in love, time lost all meaning, and they might have stayed there, like that, forever.

When they finally fell out of it they were naked, on the bed, giggling like insane children.

"Wow," Tommy said first.

"Yeah," she said.

"So, Okata saved you?"

"Yeah, he needed to save someone. He had always needed to save someone."

"I know. I'm okay with it, you know?"

"Yeah, I know," she said.

"I can't do it, Jody. It's amazing, and I adore you, but I can't do it."

"I know," she said, because she did. "This is me now, Tommy. I like this, I like the night, I like the power. I like not being afraid. I was never anything until I was this. I love being this."

"I know," he said. He knew that she had always been cute, but not beautiful. Always a little dissatisfied with who she was, worried about what men, or her mother, or any-one thought of her. But she was beautiful now. Strong. She was exactly what she wanted to be.

He said, "I need the words, Jody. It's who I am."

"I know."

"I'm not a vampire. I'm a writer. I came here to be a writer. I want to use gelatinous in a sentence. And not just once, but over and over. On the roof, under the moon, in an elevator, on the washing machine, and when I'm exhausted, I want to lay in my own gelatinous sweat and use gelatinous in a sentence until I pass out."

Jody said, "I don't think gelatinous means what you think it means."

"It doesn't matter. It's what I need to do. I need to write something. I need to write my little Holocaust girl story."

"I thought it was a little girl growing up in the segregated South."

"Yeah, whatever. It's important."

"You know I know this already, right?"

"I know, but that's what I'm saying, I need the words. I love you, but I need the words."

"I know," she said. "Let's go let Foo change you back into a word guy."

"And you're going to go away?"

"I have to."

"I know," he said. "You know, I think that merging might have ruined me."

"Why?"

"Because you're lying there completely naked and I don't want to sex you up."

"Really?"

"Let me think about it. No, false alarm, I'm okay."

"C'mere, writer boy. Let's break some furniture."

THE RAVEN

"Praise Jah's sweet love for given us a fired-haired snowy biscuit," Kona said. "Welcome, me sweet deadie sistah. Welcome aboard."

"Mistress," Jody said. "Sweet deadie mistress."

"Troot, mistress. Welcome aboard."

The ship was a wonder of technology and luxury. Kona had lent Foo Dog his security bracelet and Foo had gone aboard and reset the security so the ship didn't kill anyone who set foot on board, then he and Kona had walked her through the ship showing her the thousand different ways it had been set to kill a person. It was an elegant, redundant death trap.

"You'll want to turn the systems back on," Foo had said. "There's a reason they had this kind of security."

Jody said good-bye and led him off the ship. Now that she had one of his UV lasers in one hand and a number of vacuum blood vials in the other she followed the ersatz Rastaman down to the deepest chamber of the ship, where Foo had not gone. They approached a wide, white, waterproof hatch with a small porthole and a heavy stainless-steel wheel securing it.

Kona hit a light switch. "That make just a wee UV, mistress. Make dat dogheart bastid turn solid so he can't sneak out."

Jody looked in the port and a face hit it with a snarl, leaving bloody spit on the thick glass.

"Well, hello, pumpkin. How have you been?"

The vampire snarled. It was Elijah, the old vampire who had turned her, turned them all, really, if the legend was true. But he looked like a wild animal now, naked, his fangs bared, snarling at the tiny window.

"Can he hear me?" Jody asked.

"Oh yeah, he hear. You got to tell him to go to the back of da room, ma. I'n'I can lock him back there with the second door. Like an airlock. Dat's how we feed dat old buggah."

"Go to the back of the room, Elijah. I have something I need you to do."

The vampire snarled at her.

"Okey dokey," she said, and she put on her sunglasses, placed Foo's laser against the glass, and promptly blasted Elijah's right ear into ash.

He roared at her.

"Oh, I know that had to hurt. Hear that high whining sound, Elijah. That's the laser recharging. Takes about a minute. When it's done I'm going to burn off your willie unless you get your ancient ass to the back of the cell." She smiled.

"Shoots, brah, she a cold heart bitch don't you know. You outta-shoulda do what she say, yeah?"

The old vampire backed through the inside door, snarling, and Kona worked the switch, sealing it. Then he opened the heavy outer hatch.

Jody placed the vacuum vials in the chamber, then said, "Okay, Elijah, I need you to fill these with that sweet, first-generation vampire blood."

They sealed the outer hatch, and Elijah snarled and resisted, but after having his other ear burned off, relented. Twenty minutes later Jody was holding the four vials of Elijah's blood and Elijah was lapping two quarts of tuna blood out of a stainless-steel bowl.

"He be all right," Kona said. "Dem ear heal up in minutes and he be back in the mystic fo' weeks."

"And how long to get the rest of the art supplies onto the *Raven*?" she asked.

"It's all on board, mistress."

"Then cast off, Cap'n."

"Aye, aye, mistress."

Jody turned to Okata, who had stood silently, his eyes wide, watching the whole scene.

"These are for you," she said, holding out the vials. "I'll help you. I hope you like night scenes. You're going to have a lot of prints to make. But you'll have time."

"Okay," said the swordsman, with a smile.

Being the Chronicles of Abby Normal, Failed Nosferatu, Heartbroken Day Dweller, and Deposed Backup Mistress of the Greater Bay Area Darkness

My heady powers of the night are gone, my manga-haired love monkey with a most fly ride is gone, even my tail is gone—worst of all, the Countess is gone. We watched her sail off just before dawn, the Rastafarian imbecile piloting the *Raven* out past Alcatraz as we stood there on the dock.

Then Rivera and Cavuto came blazing up in their shit-brown cop-mobile and jumped out of the car, all "We have totally watched a number of cop shows and now know how to look urgent."

And Cavuto is all, "Don't even move, missy." And he's holding a Super Soaker again. This time, a yellow one.

And Rivera is all creeping up the other side of the dock, as if we don't see him, even though the dock is only like fifteen feet wide and there's no cover and it's almost dawn.

And Tommy's like, "You guys, I should probably explain."

But before he can say anything else, I jump up and I'm all, "Rawr," at them, coming down with total monster claw hands and scary face.

And they fire up their sun jackets and totally open up on Tommy and me with the Super Soakers, until we are wet and laughing so hard that we're falling down on each other. And Marvin jumps out of the car window and runs over to us all doggie "whaaaa?" face, because he doesn't see a lot of laughing in the cadaver dog business.

And Rivera looks at Cavuto, then turns off his sun jacket, and Cavuto turns off his, then holds his squirt gun like it's just turned into a giant yellow turd. And he's all, "Well, fuck."

And I'm all, "Oh ass bear, you make me wet," which totally made us giggle some more, and Marvin ran over and started licking my face, which made me laugh even more, until finally Rivera pulled out his handcuffs and we stopped laughing.

So we explained about the old vamps being dead and how they had gotten rid of all the kitty vamps and Chet, and how everyone else had been changed back like us, and it was all good so they just needed to chill the fuck out.

And Rivera's all, "What about the black ship?"

And we're like, "It was owned by this eccentric bazillionaire, and the vamps had taken it over, but now that they were dead he was going home."

And Rivera was all, "But the Emperor said—"

And I'm all, "Bitch, please. The Emperor of San Francisco, protector of Alcatraz, Sausalito, and Treasure Island, you mean?" Snarking hard.

And Rivera is all, "Okay, good point."

And then the Animals all pull up in two cars, and they jump out all loaded up with squirt guns and garden sprayers, and the Emperor and his dogs jump out, and they are all ready to kick ass, when Rivera stopped them and 'splained and they went off to get high and the Emperor walked off down the waterfront, watching the *Raven* sail out to the Golden Gate.

'Kayso, now the sun is up and Rivera and Cavuto realize that we are totally not vamps, so they take Marvin and climb in their shit-brown mobile and drive off.

So Tommy and I are just standing there, at the edge of the dock, and we can just barely see the *Raven* out by the Golden Gate Bridge, her sails up now, all silver in the sun.

And I'm like, "We should probably go get that money the Countess hid on the roof. It's like three hundred thousand dollars." The Countess told us where it was before she left. She said she wouldn't need it.

And he's like, "Yeah. It might be a little harder to get up there now that we don't have super powers."

And I'm like, "She said there's a fire escape most of the way."

And he's all, " 'Kay." And he's just staring at the ship.

So I'm like, "So I know you're not nosferatu anymore, but I could still be your minion, if you needed one."

And he's like, "I'm kind of broken-hearted over here."

And I'm like, "Me, too."

And he's all, "Besides, I think you've sort of advanced beyond the level of minion."

So I'm like, "I could be your girlfriend."

And he's all, "I thought you loved Foo."

And I'm like, "I kind of do."

So then he's like, "I thought you loved Jody."

And I'm all, "I do. I'm polyamorous."

And he's like, "Now you want to fuck parrots?!"

And I was about to go off on him, but I saw he was grinning, so I just elbowed him in the ribs, like, *you dick,* as we watched the ship disappear into the fog outside the bridge.

And he's like, "When do you think the *Raven* will be back?"

And I go, all scary voice, "Nevermore."

Then he looks at me, with a big smile, and he takes my hand. And I totally wanted to kiss him, with plenty of despair and tongue and whatnot. But then I would have had to slap him, so he didn't think that I was a slut, since I'd only been dumped like hours before. But then I thought, he might slap me for the same reason, so instead of a kiss I decided to do a small celebratory booty dance of forbidden passion, which made him grin like a big doof.

So we sort of stood there, holding hands, looking at

where the ship used to be, realizing that the future was fucking ginormously huge. Like the abyss, only, you know, with better lighting.

And I'm all, "So what now, cornflakes?"

Then he's all, "I think I'll write a book."